CHIUN DID NOT
BELIEVE HIS EYES.

Chiun watched as brutally, like a python squeezing his prey, the Dutchman tightened his choke hold on Remo. Remo's face darkened with congesting blood. Remo's arms flailed, his mouth gulping air like a beached fish.

"Remo! Do not let him defeat you!" Chiun cried. He started for them, but a line of granite blocks exploded into a thousand pieces and forced Chiun to retreat.

"I am invincible," the Dutchman shouted at the top of his lungs, as he disdainfully held Remo's limp form by the scruff of the neck. "There is no greater Master of Sinanju than me. Do you hear me, Chiun? I am supreme! Supreme!"

Chiun could hear him. And Chiun could not deny his words. For Chiun knew all too well the source of the almighty strength of this foulest of fiends in fairest of human forms—and knew just as well that there was no way to stop it. . . .

#73

The Destroyer

LINE OF SUCCESSION

Created By

WARREN MURPHY & RICHARD SAPIR

A SIGNET BOOK

NEW AMERICAN LIBRARY

PUBLISHER'S NOTE

This book is a work of fiction. Names, characters, places, and incidents either are the product of the author's imagination or are used fictitiously, and any resemblance to actual persons, living or dead, events, or locales is entirely coincidental.

Copyright © 1988 by Richard Sapir and Warren Murphy

SIGNET TRADEMARK REG. U.S. PAT. OFF. AND FOREIGN COUNTRIES REGISTERED TRADEMARK—MARCA REGISTRADA HECHO EN DRESDAN, TN., U.S.A.

SIGNET, SIGNET CLASSIC, MENTOR, ONYX, PLUME, MERIDIAN and NAL BOOKS are published by NAL PENGUIN INC., 1633 Broadway, New York, New York 10019

First Printing, July, 1988

1 2 3 4 5 6 7 8 9

PRINTED IN THE UNITED STATES OF AMERICA

For James E. Malone and the memory of the Yellow Ghost—one for the old days.

Old Pullyang was the first to see the strange purple birds.

Pullyang squatted in the dirt, smoking a long-stemmed pipe and letting the last warming rays of the day soak into his elderly bones. Smoking kept him awake, for he was the caretaker of the village of Sinanju, the birthplace of the sun source of the martial arts, which was also known as Sinanju. And being the guardian of the sleepy little town on the West Korea Bay meant unrelieved boredom.

No one came to Sinanju who was not of Sinanju. Sinanju had no enemies, no natural resources, no desirable real estate. It did have a treasure, but few knew of it. Those who knew dared not seek it. The reputation of the Masters of Sinanju, a line of assassins that went back some three thousand years, was a greater deterrent to thieves than an armored division.

Thus, old Pullyang squatted in the sun, smoking to keep awake and patiently awaiting the return of the Master of Sinanju, knowing that he had nothing to fear except nodding off. If he nodded off, the other villagers would note the day and the hour and inform the Master of Sinanju upon his return. Then Pullyang would surely be punished and one of them would be appointed in his place. The post of caretaker of the treasure house was much coveted in Sinanju for it allowed one to indulge in the chief village trait, which was a kind of studied laziness, without fear of scorn or punishment.

Pullyang watched intently as the sun set over the surging waters of the bay, falling between the twin rock formations on the beach that were known as the Horns of Welcome. The ocean turned red. This was Pullyang's favorite time of day. It meant that mealtime approached.

Just as the solar disk touched the water, Pullyang's pipe
went out.

Old Pullyang muttered imprecations under his breath because relighting the pipe meant a good deal of work. The
stem was over four feet long. First he would have to reel in
the bowl. Then he would have to stand up and walk over to
one of the cooking fires for a smoking ember. That was the
difficult part.

Old Pullyang never got to the difficult part. After he had
peered intently at his pipe bowl, he happened to look up.

He saw the birds.

There were two of them. They flew over the village in a
languorous circle. At first Pullyang thought they were very
near. Their wingspans seemed huge. But on closer inspec-
tion, he realized that they were very, very high up.

That bothered old Pullyang even more. The birds were so
high above that they were black against the sky, yet they
still seemed large.

Old Pullyang thought the large birds might be herons.
They had long-billed heads and very long necks like herons.
Their floating wings resembled heron wings. But they were
too big for herons. It was a puzzlement.

Clambering to his feet, he called down to the other villagers. He called them as a group, adding the words "lazy
ones" because it made him feel good after squatting all day
to call the others lazy.

"Look!" he called, pointing to the sky. His long-
stemmed pipe quivered in his hand.

The villagers stopped their preparations for the evening
meal and looked up.

They all saw the lazily circling birds, black and indistinct
because they were so high.

"What are they?" someone asked fearfully.

But Pullyang, who was the village elder after the Master
of Sinanju, did not know.

"It is an omen," he proclaimed loudly.

"Of what?" asked Mah-Li, who was the betrothed of the
next Master. She was very young, with lustrous black hair
framing an innocent face.

"Of evil," said old Pullyang sagely, who knew being
ignorant was not the same as admitting it.

The villagers gathered about the treasure house of Sinanju, which was built of fine woods on a low hill in the center of the village, because it represented safety. All of them watched the ominous birds. The sun's glowing rim slipped into the water, making it seem to bleed. It appeared as if the birds were dipping lower too.

"They are coming down," said Mah-Li, her eyes wide.

"Yes," said Pullyang. He could see their color now. It was purplish-pink, like the internal organs of the pigs they slaughtered for food.

"They have no feathers," whispered Mah-Li.

It was true. The birds were featherless. They had wings like bats—leathery purple wings that flapped and folded nervously as they circled lower, their hatchet faces twisting so that their side-mounted eyes could look down.

Their eyes were bright green, like lizard eyes. They were definitely not herons.

The children were the first to break and run. Naturally, the mothers ran after them, screaming. The men were next. There was a frantic exodus to the path that wound beyond the rocks to higher ground, away from the village.

Old Pullyang turned to Mah-Li.

"Go, child," he quavered.

"You come too," Mah-Li urged, pulling on his skeletal arm.

Pullyang struggled free, dropping his pipe.

"No! No!" he spat. "Go! Away from here!"

Mah-Li looked up at the purple birds, and she backed away.

"Please!" she cried.

Stubbornly Pullyang turned his back to her.

Mah-Li turned and ran after the others.

Old Pullyang was left alone. He shrank back under the curving edges of the treasure-house roof, where he hoped the circling birds could not see him.

The birds swooped over the Horns of Welcome. Pullyang saw that their huge wings were bright and shiny like the plastic toys that were sometimes brought to the village from the cities. And then they settled, one on each horn, folding their wings close to their hairless bodies like creatures in mourning. They were three men high.

Old Pullyang huddled on the ground. He was alone and the baleful green eyes of the birds-that-were-not-birds were fixed squarely on him. The birds did not move. They simply stared. The sun disappeared under the ocean, its dying rays backlighting the purple birds.

Old Pullyang was determined not to leave his post. It was his duty. He would not shirk it. He would remain. No tattletale villager would ever say to the Master of Sinanju that Pullyang, the caretaker, had forsaken his sacred responsibility.

Night fell. The two birds became two shadows with eyes. The eyes did not wink in those bony hatchet faces. They stared at Pullyang as if they had all eternity in which to stare.

Pullyang set his teeth together to keep them from chattering. Let them stare. They could stare for all time. Pullyang would not flee. He wished he had gone for that smoking ember, though. His pipe would have tasted very good right now. More than anything, he wished his pipe had never gone out. Perhaps if it had not, Pullyang would not have looked into the sky and seen the circling birds in the first place. Superstitiously, he believed they had come to earth because he had seen them. He was convinced of this. It was the way they stared at him with their unwinking serpent eyes.

Pullyang huddled before the door of the treasure house, a determined old man, and squeezed his eyes shut.

When the moon came up, throwing the beach into relief, Pullyang could not resist checking to see if the purple birds still roosted in the moonlight.

He saw that the moon had thrown long shadows across the rocky beach. The Horns of Welcome made those shadows. Then Pullyang noticed that the birds, perched on top of the Horns, cast no shadows.

With a screech of fright, Pullyang ran—away from the treasure house, away from his responsibility, and most of all, away from his fear. He ran up the inland path after the others.

Pullyang did not look back. He did not want the evil purple birds to follow him.

The moonlight transformed the village of Sinanju into a landscape of stark peace. Into this peace strode a man.

He was a white man with a too-handsome face that was

just beginning to take on the angular planes of maturity. Sea breezes tossed his long blond hair. He wore a two-piece garment of purple silk, a yellow sash belted around his middle. Serpents retreated from the path of his sandaled feet, as if in fear.

He did not gaze in the direction of the Horns of Welcome as he sauntered cool and catlike up from the rocks and through the fragrant steam from the deserted cooking pots in the village square. He went directly to the door of the treasure house, called the House of the Masters.

The door was locked. Not with a padlock or by a key, but by a cunning arrangement of wooden bolts concealed within the teak of the door. Reaching up, the man pressed two tiny panels simultaneously. They clicked, and a hidden locking mechanism slid from its receiver. Kneeling, he then removed a long panel that ran the width of the door. It revealed a wooden dowel in a recess. With great care he extracted the dowel.

When he got to his feet, a firm push opened the door. A wave of must and candlewax rolled out to greet him. Wiping his sandals at the threshold, he stepped inside. No one must know he had been here.

The white man looked around the room. Moonlight, coming through the open door, cast irregular shadows, causing the stacked gold ingots inside to gleam and striking fire off the open jars of cut jewels.

The white man disturbed none of these things. He desired no treasure. Not all the money in the world would have mattered to him. It was too late for money, for anything. He walked into an inner room where there was no available light, disdaining the unlit tapers on the floor. He needed them even less than he desired the wealth of Sinanju.

In this central room lacquered trunks lay about in profusion. He fell to his knees beside them, swiftly lifting each lid.

The scrolls were in the fourth trunk.

Carefully he lifted one out, undoing its gold ribbon. The parchment unrolled stiffly. He read the ideographs at the head of the roll. It was an old one, describing Mesopotamia thousands of years ago. He wanted the more recent scrolls.

Squatting on the bare mahogany floor, the white man with

the uncut yellow hair carefully opened scroll after scroll, reading and retying the ribbons until finally he found the ones he sought.

He read them slowly, knowing that he had all night. The purple birds would keep the villagers away.

After he had read the scrolls through, he took paper and pen from his yellow sash and, referring to the scrolls often, wrote a letter. Then he copied the text of the first letter exactly, but changed the salutation.

With great care he retied the scrolls and restored them to the lacquered trunk.

He stood up. His eyes were bright, like blue neon. He had succeeded. No one would know he had been here. Not even the Master of Sinanju.

In his hands he held the letters containing the secrets of the present Master of Sinanju. All that remained was to mail them. And sign them. He had not signed them yet.

Struck by a sudden inspiration, the man with the yellow hair pressed the letters to a wall and wrote one word at the bottom of each.

The word was "Tulip".

He reset the door mechanism on his way out.

And then he disappeared down the shore road, past the Horns of Welcome, which awaited the rising of the sun, naked and forbidding. The snakes did not reemerge from their holes until long after he had gone.

2

His name was Remo and he was trying to catch the fly with a set of chopsticks.

Remo sat in the middle of the room in which he had lived for nearly a year. He sat completely still, because he knew that the fly would not come near him if he moved. He had not moved in more than an hour. The trouble was, neither had the fly. It clung to the windowpane. Remo wondered if it was asleep. Did flies sleep?

The room had bare beige walls, a television and video-recorder setup on the floor, and a sleeping mat in one corner. Remo sat on a sitting mat, which was thinner and made of reed. A small eating taboret stood before him and on it rested a bowl bearing the remains of Remo's most recent meal, duck in orange sauce. Remo had deliberately left it there to attract the fly, but the fly didn't seem interested.

Remo could have gotten up and moved to the window faster than the fly could react to him. Before the fly's multifaceted eyes could register his presence, Remo could easily swat him. But Remo did not want to kill the fly. He wanted to catch it alive between the wooden chopsticks which he held in one hand.

Eventually the fly stirred, spun on its multiple legs, and after brushing its wings clean, lifted into the air.

Remo smiled. Now he would get his chance.

The fly was fat, black, and flew silently. It looped around Remo and settled on the rim of the bowl filled with duck remains.

Remo allowed the fly enough time to get comfortable. He carefully separated the chopsticks with his fingers.

The door suddenly opened and the fly jumped. Remo's hand was already in motion. The chopsticks clicked shut.

"I did it!" Remo said, bringing the chopsticks to his face.

"What is it that you have done?" asked Chiun, reigning Master of Sinanju. He stood on the threshold to Remo's room. He was a birdlike Korean in a canary-yellow suit with bell-shaped sleeves, very old, but with very young hazel eyes watching curiously from a face which might have been molded from Egyptian papyrus. What little hair he had collected in white tufts above his ears or trailed from his chin.

Remo looked closer. The chopsticks grasped air. He frowned. "Nothing," he said unhappily. The fly was circling the ceiling.

"So it appeared to these aged eyes," said Chiun.

"Could you please close the door, Little Father?"

"Why?"

"I don't want the fly to escape."

"Of course, my son," said Chiun amiably, complying with Remo's request. The Master of Sinanju stood quietly, his head cocked to one side as Remo tracked the fly with his deep-set eyes, careful not to move unnecessarily. The chopsticks hung poised in the air.

The fly looped, dipped, and circled Remo curiously.

"The poor fly," said Chiun.

"Shhh!" hissed Remo.

"Alas for the fly. It is hungry."

"Hush!" said Remo.

"If you would not sit so still," continued Chiun, "the fly would be able to distinguish you from the other garbage. Heh, heh. Then it could eat its fill. Heh, heh, heh."

Remo shot Chiun a withering look. Chiun ignored him. Instead, the Master of Sinanju dug into a pocket of his suit and pulled out a handful of cashews. He ate one, chewing it as thoroughly as if it were a tough morsel of steak, and sampled another.

Remo watched the fly as it spiraled down toward the bowl.

The Master of Sinanju balanced a cashew on the index finger on one long-nailed hand. He raised the hand slightly, squinting at the fly with a single bright eye.

When the fly was almost to the bowl's wooden rim, the Master of Sinanju sent the cashew flying with a flick of his thumb.

Simultaneously, Remo's hand flashed out.

"Got it!" Remo shouted, standing up. "Look, Little Father."

The Master of Sinanju hurried to Remo's side.

"Let me see, Remo!" he said. "Oooh, how clever you are."

"Thank you," Remo said, holding the chopsticks so that he wouldn't crush the object in their grasp. "Not many people could catch a fly on the wing like that, huh?"

"Not many," agreed Chiun, smiling benignly. "And you are not one of them."

"What's that supposed to mean?"

"Look closer, O blind one."

Remo looked closer. Caught between the eating implements was a hard brown wingless object. Remo dropped it into his palm.

"What is it?" he asked, puzzled.

"Search me," said Chiun, nibbling on a handful of cashews. "Want one?" he asked politely, offering Remo his open palm.

Remo realized that he held one of Chiun's cashews. He dropped it. "Why'd you have to do that, Chiun?" He demanded angrily. "I almost had him that time."

"O piteous disappointment. O miserable failure," mocked the Master of Sinanju. "Shall I leave the room so that you may end your wretched life from the shame?"

"Knock it off," said Remo, settling back onto the mat.

The Master of Sinanju walked over to the window. He came back to Remo's side, executed a deep bow, and offered an upraised palm.

"What's this?" Remo asked sourly.

"The object of your desire. O disappointed one," Chiun said blandly. In his wrinkled palm the fly lay immobile.

"Forget it," Remo said dejectedly. "I don't want it anymore. It's dead."

"It is not," said Chiun. "It is merely stunned. I do not kill flies."

"Unless you're paid," Remo said.

"In advance," Chiun agreed with a smile. "You will not accept this humble present?"

"No," said Remo.

"A minute ago you were most anxious to capture this insect."

"I wanted to do it myself," Remo said testily.

"Then do it yourself," said Chiun, throwing the fly into the air. It took wing and, somewhat unsteadily, orbited the room. "See if I care."

"Okay," Remo said, coming to life. "Just sit quietly and let me handle this."

"While you are handling it, as you say, talk to me, my son."

"About what?" asked Remo out of the side of his mouth. He had returned to his lotus position and sat still as a stone.

"I have invested countless years of my life training a white man in the magnificent art of Sinanju, and I walk into this room to find my pupil engaged in nonsense."

"It's not nonsense. It's a test of skill, catching a fly with chopsticks. The idea is not to hurt him, you know."

"Do tell," Chiun said in a mock-American accent.

"I got the idea from a film I rented."

"What film?" asked the Master of Sinanju, genuinely curious.

"This one," mumbled Remo, surreptitiously touching a remote control unit beside his leg. Across the room, the TV set winked on. Remo pressed another switch and the video recorder on top of the set started to play.

Frowning, the Master of Sinanju watched a scene from the middle of a film. It showed a sweaty teenage boy waxing a car.

"Smith told me about it," Remo said. "He said it reminded him of you and me."

"How so?" asked Chiun.

"It's about an Italian kid from Newark who meets this old Japanese guy. The old guy teaches him karate."

Chiun spit on the floor. "Karate was stolen from us. It is not Sinanju."

"I didn't say it was. But count the similarities. I'm from Newark."

"Your mother's fault, whoever she was."

"Remo is an Italian name. I might be Italian like the kid in the picture."

"Your last name is Williams. That is not Italian."

"No, but Remo is. I don't know who my parents were, but having an Italian first name must mean something."

"It means that your parents could not think of an appropriate name for you," said Chiun.

Remo frowned. "I wish you wouldn't insult my parents so much," he said. "They might be good people. We don't know."

"Better not to know. The disappointment is less painful."

"Can I finish telling you the story? Now this kid moves to California, where he meets the old Japanese guy, who's a lot like you."

"Show me this old man," demanded Chiun.

Remo, seeing that the fly had returned to the window, came out of his immobile pose and lifted the remote control. He fast-forwarded the tape until a famous Oriental actor appeared on the screen.

"See?" he said, pointing. "There he is. I told you he kinda looks like you."

When Chiun looked at Remo disdainfully, Remo added, "A little. Around the eyes."

"His eyes look Japanese," Chiun sniffed. "If my eyes resembled his eyes I would pluck them out of my head and crush them beneath my feet."

Remo sighed. "Anyway, he teaches this kid karate and the kid goes on to win a big karate tournament."

"How is that like us? We do not play games. We are assassins. I have trained you in the art of Sinanju, from which all the lesser fighting arts have been stolen, to be an assassin. I have turned your body into one of the finest instruments of human power imaginable. Normally I would have done as much for your mind, but you are white and my time on earth is not without limit."

"Thanks a lot," said Remo.

"You are quite welcome. I am glad now that I made the decision not to concentrate on your mind, for it is obviously confused. I ask you to explain your bizarre behavior and you have told me a lame story about this film. I am still waiting for a proper explanation."

"I was getting there."

"I am over eighty years along in life. Do not take too long."

"One of the things he tried to teach the kid to do is catch a fly with chopsticks. It's supposed to be the mark of a great karate master. The Japanese guy can't do it, even though he's been trying all his life, but the kid does it after a few lessons.''

"Goody for him.''

"I thought I'd try it," said Remo.

"It is as I thought," said the Master of Sinanju sadly.

"What is?''

"You are regressing.''

"I am not.''

"Denial is the first symptom of regression," Chiun pronounced seriously. "Let me explain this to you, Remo.''

"Whisper it,'' Remo said, suddenly lifting the chopsticks like antennae. "Here comes the fly again.''

"The thieves who stole karate from the House of Sinanju were Korean. From the lazy south, of course. They copied the movements, the little kicks and chopping blows of the hand. They were like children pretending to be adults. But because they copied magnificence, as inept as they were, they achieved a certain mediocrity. They could fight, break boards with their hands, and because they were all mediocre and knew it, they insisted on wearing belts of different colors so that some could pretend to be less mediocre than others of their ilk. In truth, they were all inferior to Sinanju. And they knew that, as well.''

"I know that story," Remo said, watching the fly.

"Then you should know that catching flies with chopsticks goes back to the early days of karate.''

"That I didn't know.''

"Of course not. If you had, you would not now be shaming me by copying the mediocre karate dancers.''

"I think it's a pretty fair test of skill. I just want to see if I can do it. What's your problem?''

"The karate dancers tried to copy Sinanju in other ways too,'' Chiun went on as the stubborn fly lingered over the wooden bowl. "They, too, attempted to hire themselves out to kings and emperors as bodyguards. Many karate dancers found that breaking sticks was not the same thing as breaking bones. In their folly, the karate dancers almost became extinct.''

"Shhh!'' said Remo.

The fly suddenly veered from the bowl toward Remo.

Remo's hand shot out. The chopsticks closed. This time they did not click.

Remo looked. Between the tongs, the fly struggled, its tiny legs working.

"Look," Remo said, grinning.

"Go ahead," said Chiun blandly.

"Go ahead and what?"

"The next step. Surely the film revealed the next step."

"They must have cut that part out," said Remo.

"I will help you," said Chiun happily, edging closer to Remo. "Lift the fly to your face. Keep your eyes carefully upon it so that it does not get away."

Remo did as he was told. The fly buzzed its wings just inches in front of his high-cheekboned face.

"Are you ready?" asked Chiun.

"Yes," said Remo.

"Now open your mouth. Wide."

Remo opened his mouth. His brows knit in perplexity.

Chiun took Remo's hand in his and guided the chopsticks closer. As he did so, he continued his story. "The karate dancers who survived gave up trying to be assassins and repaired to their villages, where they searched for other methods of sustaining themselves. But alas, they were poor fishermen and indifferent farmers."

"You mean . . . ?" Remo asked.

Chiun nodded happily.

Remo shut his mouth abruptly.

Chiun grinned. "Why do you think they used chopsticks? It saved them so much time."

A pained expression on his face, Remo released the fly and let the chopsticks clatter into his bowl. He pushed the bowl away in disgust.

"You always do this to me," he complained.

"Is this my thanks for being the bearer of messages?"

"What does Smitty want now?"

"Nothing that I know of," answered Chiun. "This message is from Sinanju."

Remo leapt to his feet. His expression became one of surprised joy. "From Mah-Li?"

"Who else would waste ink on a fly-chaser such as you?" asked Chiun, producing an envelope from one voluminous sleeve.

Remo snatched it like a hungry man offered bread.

Chiun's parchment face wrinkled in disapproval. "Do not be so eager," he sniffed. "She merely asks the same tiresome question put forth in her last twenty letters. Honestly, Remo, how could you think of marrying such a nag?"

"You read my mail?" Remo asked, shocked.

The Master of Sinanju shrugged casually. "It was damaged in transit. The flap was loose and the contents fell out."

Remo examined the flap. "It's sealed now."

"Of course. If I had not sealed it with my parched old tongue, the letter might have fallen out again and become lost."

Remo ignored Chiun's answer and sliced one end of the envelope open with the sweep of a sharp fingernail. He read the letter eagerly.

"She says everything is fine in Sinanju," Remo said.

"Tell me something I do not know."

"She wants to know when we're coming home."

"Tell her you do not know."

"Cut it out, Chiun. We've only got another few weeks before our contract with Smith is over. We're free after that."

"What is the rush to return?" said Chiun. "I have been thinking. How long has it been since we've had a vacation? Perhaps we could tour this wonderful land of America before we leave its shores forever. By train. The airplanes are no longer reliable."

"Neither are the trains," said Remo. "And the rush to return is for my wedding. Mah-Li and I should have been married three months ago. The engagement period was supposed to be only nine months. I've been stuck in America now for almost a year, thanks to you."

"Stuck?" squeaked Chiun, shocked. "How can you say you have been stuck when your every waking hour has been spent in the awesome presence of Chiun, reigning Master of Sinanju?"

"I'm bored," said Remo. "Smith hasn't had any assignments for you lately. And I've been cooling my heels in this room so long I'm reduced to catching flies for entertainment."

"You could get a job," suggested Chiun. "It is not un-heard-of for persons such as yourself to find honest work."

"No way," said Remo. "We'll be out of here before I can read my way through the classified section."

"Correction," said Chiun. "I will be out of here. When my year of service is completed—assuming Emperor Smith and I do not come to a new understanding—Smith will offer me return passage to Sinanju as a final payment for the service I have rendered him. Because you do not work for him in an official capacity, that boon will not be extended to yourself."

"You wouldn't leave me stranded in America, would you, Little Father?" Remo asked quietly.

"Of course not. I would allow you to accompany me."

"Then it's settled. I'll write Mah-Li to expect us on the first of the month."

"Be sure to leave the year blank," said Chiun blandly. "For we are not returning directly to Sinanju."

Remo's expression became stony.

"I am considering going on a world tour," Chiun said loftily.

"You've seen more of the world than a spy satellite. So have I, for that matter. Screw the world. And the tour of it."

"Oh, this is not a mere tour of the world," said Chiun. "This is a world tour, like the ones famous people do."

"World tour, tour of the world," Remo said, throwing up his hands. "What's the difference?"

"The difference is that I will be treated like a star in every capital. I will stay in the finest hotels. I will be feted by heads of state as befits my exalted position in the affairs of the world. And of course I will give a benefit concert in every major city. I am thinking of calling it the Sinanju World Tour."

"You can't sing," Remo pointed out.

"Nor will I."

"You don't do stand-up comedy either."

"I was hoping you would perform that function," said Chiun. "I will require a warmed-over act."

"That's warm-up. Warm-up act."

"A distinction without a difference."

"Then what, pray tell, will you do at these concerts?"

"Why, what I do best."

"Heckle me?"

"No, insolent one. I will show the world the wonders of Sinanju. For a price, of course."

"I thought you said these would be benefit concerts."

"They will be," said Chiun. "They are for the benefit of the starving villagers of Sinanju, who are so poor that sometimes they have to drown their infants in the cold bay because they have no food. Did you ever hear of an Ethiopian doing that? No, yet people give them millions."

Remo folded his bare arms. "The picture is becoming clear. But wouldn't performing feats of Sinanju onstage bring us down to the level of the karate dancers?"

"Remo! I am shocked. I do not propose to waste Sinanju doing stupid magic tricks. No, I will first contact the local governments and offer to eliminate their most dangerous criminals and political enemies—at a reduced rate. They will bring these wretches to the exhibition halls, where I will dispose of them before a live audience, who will naturally pay for the privilege of watching perfection at work."

"I'm not sure many people would be interested in watching you kill people onstage."

"Nonsense. Executing criminals was a highly popular entertainment in Roman times. In fact, that is where I will launch the Sinanju World Tour. In Rome."

"You could clean up, at that," Remo said thoughtfully.

"Oh, the live audience is nothing. They will be there merely to provide applause. The real money is in the TV rights. I will sell rights to the concerts to the networks of countries on the formal tour, which will naturally create interest in further tours."

"This could go on for years," Remo said with a sigh.

"By the time we return to Sinanju, we will be wealthy men and will have created new markets for our illustrious descendants. Think of their gratitude, Remo."

"You think of their gratitude. I'm thinking that if I don't return to Sinanju soon, I won't have any descendants."

"Just like you to think of sex when your mind should be on matters of lasting importance," Chiun scolded.

"I'm not thinking of sex. I'm thinking of Mah-Li. You just don't want me to settle down. You think if we go back to Sinanju, the villagers will fall all over me like they did last time and ignore you because I promised to support the village after you retire."

"You lie. My villagers love me. They worship the very path I walk upon."

"As long as the path is paved with gold, yes."

The Master of Sinanju stamped an angry sandal, but said nothing. His cheeks puffed out in repressed fury.

"And I'm not playing second banana to you in any freaking world tour," Remo added. "That's final."

"I will let you be my personal manager, then," Chiun said testily. "But it is my final offer."

"Pass," said Remo.

Chiun opened his mouth to answer but was interrupted by a knock at the door.

"Enter," said the Master of Sinanju grandly.

"This is my room, remember?" Remo pointed out.

Dr. Harold W. Smith entered the room looking as pale as the gray three-piece suit hanging off his spare frame. He was a symphony in pallor. His sparse hair nearly matched his white shirt, and behind rimless glasses his frantic eyes were color coordinated with his suit. He tightened his Dartmouth tie until the knot threatened to strangle him.

"Hail, Emperor Smith, Keeper of the Constitution and defender of the secret organization called CURE, about which we are in blissful ignorance," Chiun said in a loud voice.

"Shhh!" hissed Smith, his pinched face paling even more. "Not so loud. And what are you two doing together?"

"Singing your praises," said Chiun.

"Having a family argument," said Remo.

"You're not supposed to be seen together while you are residing here at Folcroft Sanitarium. I deliberately gave you separate quarters for that reason. Master of Sinanju, I will have to ask you to return to your room. It is critical that the Folcroft personnel continue to believe you to be a patient here."

"It will be done," said Chiun, bowing. But he did not move from his place in the middle of the room.

Smith turned to Remo Williams.

"Remo, we have a problem. A grave problem," he blurted.

"Don't talk to me. Talk to him," protested Remo, point-ing to the Master of Sinanju. "He works for you. I don't."

"This has nothing to do with CURE operations," said Smith, wiping his shiny upper lip with a gray handkerchief. "The grass needs cutting and the hedges are extremely rag-ged."

"Why talk to me? You have a gardening staff."

"Our agreement was that I provide this room for your use and you would be on the Folcroft employee records as the head gardener. Surely you remember."

"Oh, right. It's just that this is the first time you've asked me to do anything."

"You will have to forgive my son," said Chiun gravely. "He is frightened by work. Just before you entered, he turned down an excellent job opportunity involving fame, travel, and a modest salary."

"Modest, huh?" Remo shot back.

"I pay according to worth. In your case, I was willing to pay more because we may be distantly related, but you have turned me down, so it is of no use to discuss it further. But Emperor Smith has always been generous to you. Perhaps you should listen to his fine offer."

"This is an emergency, Remo."

"Oh? Has the crabgrass gotten into the computers again?"

"I've just received notice that the Vice-President is com-ing here tomorrow. Somehow, Folcroft has been selected as a stop in his campaign for the presidency. He's slated to make an important speech at nine A.M. All the networks will be here."

"Can't you wave him off?" asked Remo. "Call the Pres-ident?"

"I tried. The President thinks that if he pulls any strings, it will just draw attention to Folcroft. I have to agree with him. If we just batten down the hatches and ride out the storm, we should be all right. The Vice-President has no inkling that Folcroft Sanitarium is the cover for CURE."

"So what's the problem?"

"I told you. The grass and the shrubbery. They're a mess. The regular gardening crew has gone home for the day and there won't be enough time for them to spruce up the grounds. They want them fixed up."

"I was never good with gardening tools," Remo said. "I have a brown thumb or something."

"Never mind the tools. After dark, when the advance men are gone and we're on skeleton staff, can't you do something, um . . . special?"

Remo looked at his fingernails. They were clipped short, but through years of diet and special exercises they had hardened until they were as sharp as the finest surgical scalpels.

"Oh, I suppose," Remo said airily. "For a price."

"What?" Smith asked cautiously.

"When Chiun's year is up, I get to accompany him on the submarine ride back to Sinanju."

"Consider it a wedding present," said Smith, who had planned all along to make sure that Remo returned to North Korea with the Master of Sinanju. Twenty years of his life spent dealing with the two of them was more than his share.

"You were right, Little Father," Remo said, grinning at Chiun. "Smith is a generous guy."

"Too generous," said Chiun, turning to leave.

"Just a minute, please, Master of Sinanju," Smith called. "Yes?"

"I'm afraid I will have to ask you to surrender your American Express Gold Card."

The Master of Sinanju's aged hand flashed to a pocket of his suit. "My wonder card? The one you gave me when I reentered your service? The card which I show to merchants whenever I purchase their wares, which so impresses them that they do not ask me for payment?"

"It's not my doing," said Smith. "The company is recalling it. As cosignatory, they've asked me to make good on all unpaid bills and tender the card to them."

"Bills?"

"Yes, the payment requests they send each month. Didn't you receive them?"

"Since I returned to your shores, I have been plagued by much junk mail," admitted Chiun. "Offers of inferior cards which are not gold, and useless magazine subscriptions. I throw them all out, of course. Isn't that what Americans routinely do with junk mail?"

"Junk mail, yes. Bills, no. You are expected to pay for all credit-card purchases."

"No one told me this," Chiun said firmly.

"I thought you understood. I told you when I got you the card that you were responsible for it. It was not part of our contract, but a way of advancing you spending money until you got settled here. I'm sorry if you misunderstood." Smith held out his hand. "Now, the card, please."

Slowly, almost tearfully, the Master of Sinanju plucked the gold-colored plastic card from his person and surrendered it.

Smith broke the card in half.

"Aiiie!" wailed the Master of Sinanju. "You desecrated it. It was one of a kind."

"Nonsense," said Smith flatly. "Most Americans have them."

"Then I want one too. Another card."

"You'll have to take that up with American Express. But I think you'll have a problem. Your credit history is a disaster."

"I tried to explain it to him," Remo told Smith. "But he wouldn't listen to me."

"Go tend to the emperor's needs," snapped the Master of Sinanju, stalking from the room. "Oh, woe is me, for I have trained an assassin and ended up with a weed killer."

Smith looked at the VCR, which was still running. "Did you enjoy the movie?" he asked.

3

Dr. Harold W. Smith was in a panic.

"I'm sorry," he said. "It's simply impossible. I will be tied up with urgent business all day."

"What can be so urgent about running a sanitarium?" asked Harmon Cashman. As the advance man for the Vice-President, he was used to dealing with flustered officials. But this lemon-faced bureaucrat, Smith, acted as if the sky was falling.

Smith busied himself trying to get the childproof cap off a bottle of aspirin. He was sitting behind the big oak desk in his dingy office in the south wing of Folcroft Sanitarium. Behind him, the waters of Long Island Sound danced quietly. The cap would not come off and a sheen of sweat broke over Smith's balding forehead.

"Take it easy, Smith," Cashman said soothingly. "Here, let me help you with that." He gently took the aspirin bottle from Smith's shaking hands and worked the cap confidently. As he did so, he kept talking.

"By the way, that was an excellent job your people did on the grounds. The place looks as sharp as an old-fashioned straight-razor shave."

"Thank you," said Dr. Smith, clenching his hands together. He was practically wringing them. "But what you ask is out of the question."

"Look, the speech won't last more than a half-hour. Your part won't take two minutes. It's customary when a presidential candidate gives a speech before an institution like this one to have its highest official formally introduce him."

"I get nervous at public functions. I get tongue-tied. I tense up. I'll ruin the entire proceeding, I just know I will."

Harmon Cashman was inclined to agree with Smith. The man was a wreck. He thought of trying the "but-this-man-

may-be-our-next-President'' approach, but decided against
it. Smith might have a heart attack and that would really
screw up the day's schedule. The Vice-President's motorcade was already en route.

Cashman considered furiously. He twisted the safety cap
until its plastic edges scraped his fingertips raw. "What is
this stuff?"

"Children's aspirin," said Smith distractedly. "My stomach is too sensitive for adult dosages."

Cashman recognized a drawing of a famous cartoon char-
acter on the label. "A child-proof cap on a bottle of kids'
aspirin? Isn't that kind of defeating the purpose?"

"Could you please hurry? My headache is getting
worse."

"If it's the pounder you say it is, these won't make much
of a dent."

Smith suddenly snatched the bottle from Cashman's hand
and cracked it against the edge of the desk. It broke open.
Pink and orange tablets scattered everywhere. He gulped
down four tablets, chasing them with a glass of mineral
water.

Harmon Cashman looked at Smith a long time. This guy
needed a long vacation, he decided. Probably in a padded
cell.

"All right," Cashman said resignedly. "Maybe we can
get the mayor to do the honors. I'll have to give him a call.
What's the name of this town, anyway?"

"Rye. New York."

"I know the state. I'm not that overworked. Let me use
your phone."

"No, not that one!" Smith screamed, frantically throwing himself across a red telephone in one corner of the desk.
Smith swept it into a top desk drawer. "It's broken," he
explained weakly.

"Yeah, wouldn't want to electrocute myself dialing a broken phone," Cashman said slowly, accepting the receiver
of a standard office phone. As he dialed, he told Smith,
"The Vice-President's not going to be happy, you know. He
requested that he be introduced by you personally."

Smith scooped up another aspirin and swallowed it dry.
He coughed for five minutes without stopping as Harmon
Cashman, one finger in his free ear, asked the mayor of Rye

to perform a civic duty that anyone would have given a year's salary to perform. Except Dr. Harold W. Smith.

The Vice-President's motorcade arrived a crisp two minutes before the speech was to begin. Over the sprawling grounds of Folcroft Sanitarium, security helicopters orbited noisily. The Secret Service had already been through the grounds and the big L-shaped brick building that constituted the Folcroft complex—but was also the nerve center of America's deepest security secret, CURE.

Smith sat nervously on a folding chair. He had purposely chosen a seat in the back behind two very tall men, so the television cameras would not record his face. He had tried to avoid sitting with the other VIPs on the hastily erected platform, but Harmon Cashman refused to hear of it.

Smith's watch read only 8:54 A.M. and he had already decided that it was the worst day of his life. Folcroft Sanitarium, which had been converted into CURE's operational headquarters in the early sixties, had never been exposed to public attention like this. Smith had run it quietly and efficiently for more than two decades so that no undue attention was attached to it. He had conducted his private life just as self-effacingly. And now this had come out of the blue.

Smith tried to tell himself that it was a brief storm that would soon pass. CURE had been compromised more than once in its long history, and this was after all, merely a scheduling fluke of a politician who might soon be Smith's immediate superior. But the numbers of Secret Service men crawling over the complex made him feel somehow violated. He had taken every precaution to avoid any difficulty, including sending Remo and Chiun away for the day.

But Smith had already slipped up once—forgetting to hide the dialless red telephone which was his direct link to the White House. Fortunately, no one would ever suspect its true function. The only other tangible evidence of CURE operations—his desktop computer terminal—sank into his desk at a touch of a hidden stud. It accessed a worldwide network of data links through computers hidden behind a wall in Folcroft's basement. No casual search would ever find them, either.

Smith tried to relax as the Vice-President's limousine pulled up and the man himself stepped out, buttoning his

coat and trying to keep his thin hair from being blown into
disarray. The Vice-President climbed the platform steps and
the VIPs came to their feet, eager to shake his hand. Smith
remained seated, just in case. Maybe this would not be so
bad.

"Where is Dr. Smith?" a voice asked. Smith felt his heart
clutch. The inquiring voice was that of the Vice-President
himself.

Harmon Cashman ushered the Vice-President into Smith's
presence. Smith came to his feet awkwardly.

"Here he is, Mr. Vice-President. May I present Dr. Harold W. Smith?"

"Ah," said the Vice-President, grinning crookedly.
"Glad to meet you at last. I've heard a lot about you,
Smith."

"You have?" Smith croaked, shaking the man's hand
limply.

"Harmon tells me you were very nervous about this
visit."

"Er, yes," Smith said. He felt suddenly giddy.

"Not many men would turn their nose up at any opportunity like this, so they tell me. Harmon informs me you
act like a man carrying a guilty secret. But of course that
can't be, now can it? After all, you are the director of this
excellent health facility. Your business is *curing* people."

"Of course not," said Smith, feeling his knees go weak.
And then they ushered the Vice-President to a seat, where
he was surrounded by Secret Service agents carrying walkie-talkies.

Smith sank back into his chair shakily. His bitter face was
whiter than his shirt. The Vice-President's words had hit too
close to home. Of course, they were a jest. But even so,
Smith was angry at himself for having been so flustered as
to draw attention to his reluctance to be a part of the ceremony. Still, if all went smoothly, there would be no permanent harm done.

When the Vice-President was seated, the audience took
their seats. Rows of folding chairs had been assembled on
the Folcroft lawn. A few members of Folcroft's staff had
been allowed to join the handpicked crowd of supporters.
Smith noticed his secretary, Mrs. Mikulka, seated in the
back, beaming with pride. The mayor strode to the podium,

adjusted the microphone, and gave a short speech introducing the Vice-President, ending it with a welcoming sweep of his hand and the words. "And now, the next President of the United States!"

The Vice-President came to his feet and rebuttoned his coat as he walked up to the podium.

"Thank you for the warm reception," he said, trying to still the loud applause with a quelling motion of his hand as, off to the side, his campaign staff gave the secret signals to keep the applause high and loud. The network news crews obligingly recorded what appeared to be a spontaneous outburst of enthusiasm.

"Thank you," the Vice-President repeated. Finally he gave his own signal and his campaign staff passed along the finger-code message for the audience to subside. And they did.

"Well, I haven't had a reception like that since the Iowa caucuses," the Vice-President joked. The audience chuckled in approval.

"I'm here today," the Vice-President went on, "to reaffirm a pledge I made way, way back when this campaign started. Now, it's no secret that there's been a lot of criticism of the current administration—of which I have been an active participant, of course—regarding covert activities. Some people believe that the current administration has been committed to covert action, to extralegal pursuit of its policy aims, and, in general, to operating outside of constitutional authority."

Dr. Harold Smith felt his mouth suddenly go dry.

"Now, I wanna tell you that that won't happen in my administration."

The crowd applauded supportively.

"I was not a part of any of that stuff under the current President, a man I very much admire, and I'm not gonna stand for it when I sit in that Oval Office down in Washington. No way. It won't happen. That's a promise."

He's just politicking, Harold Smith told himself, his heart racing. This is campaign rhetoric. It means nothing.

"Now, I won't tell you that buried in the CIA or the Defense Intelligence Agency or elsewhere in the intelligence community there might not have been rogue operations in the past. Some may still exist as holdovers from previous administrations. Well, when I get there, I'm gonna root 'em out. Yes, sir.''

This is cheerleading, Smith told himself. Nothing more. But he felt a chill that wasn't carried by the late-fall breeze.

''For all I know, there are extralegal, extraconstitutional organizations in existence at this very moment, implementing policy and conducting operations,'' the Vice-President continued, jabbing a finger at the audience emphatically. ''I want those folks to know that their days are numbered. When I get in there, I'm gonna clean house.''

The audience applauded wildly. Smith sank lower in his seat. His headache was coming back with a vengeance.

The Vice-President looked around the crowd. He beamed. He drank in the approval of the audience. His lifted hand could not quiet them. He glanced back at the seated VIP's and grinned boyishly, as if to say: what can I do? They love me.

But when his eyes locked with those of Dr. Harold W. Smith, he winked knowingly.

Smith, seated at one end of the back row, turned around and, under cover of the thunderous applause, vomited over the back of the podium.

When he was done, he twisted back into his seat and wiped his mouth free of food flecks.

The Vice-President knew. His wink was a clear warning. Somehow, he had learned about CURE. And he intended to close it down. It was all over.

Harold Smith sat stony and unhearing as the Vice-President's speech droned on for another twenty minutes. After the last ripple of applause had faded, the Vice-President was hustled back to his limousine by the Secret Service and whisked out the stone gates of Folcroft Sanitarium.

Like a man who had been condemned to death, Smith stumbled back to his office. He did not hear the hard clapping of wood chairs being folded and stacked, or the cheerful chatter of his secretary as she followed him back to the office. He did not feel the wind on his cheek or the sun on his stooped shoulders. He did not hear or feel anything because he knew that his life was over.

4

Michael "The Prince" Princippi had come a long way in his quest for the Democratic presidential nomination.

When he had first broached the possibility of running for the highest office in the land, they laughed at him. Even his chief supporters voiced serious reservations.

"You're a sitting governor," they said. "If you lose, you'll never get reelected in this state. They'll call you an opportunist who's using the office as a stepping-stone to national office."

"I'll take that chance," he told them.

"No one knows you. Nationally, you're a nonentity."

"So was Jimmy Carter, and look what he did in seventy-six."

"Yeah, and look what happened to him in eighty. Today the guy couldn't get nominated to run a bake sale."

"I'm not Jimmy Carter. I'm Michael Princippi, the Prince of Politics. Even my enemies call me that."

One by one, he had shot down their misgivings, their weak arguments, their timid objections, until he knew in his heart he was presidential timber. But his supporters remained unconvinced.

"You don't look presidential," they finally said.

"What do you mean, presidential?" he had asked. "I'm a two-term governor of a major industrial state. I've been in politics all of my adult life."

They had shuffled their feet and looked down at the carpet. Finally one of them had blurted out the objection that was on all their minds.

"You're too short," he said.

"Too ethnic," another one added.

"You're not the type," a third offered.

"What is the type, then?" he had asked, wondering if he

33

should throw them out of the house. Then he remembered it wasn't his house, but that of a financial backer who had given them the use of it for this strategy meeting. The governor's own house was too small for his family, never mind staff meetings.

"John F. Kennedy," they chorused.

"Look at the rest of the Democratic pack," one of them explained. "You can barely tell them apart. They all have the same haircut, the same hearty face. They copy his mannerisms, his speaking style. Hell, half their speeches are rewrites of the 'Ask Not What Your Country Can Do,' chestnut. You'll never be able to pull it off. We think you should forget it, Prince."

But he didn't forget it. The man his cronies called the Prince of Politics knew that the very reason his supporters didn't think he stood a chance at getting the nomination was going to catapult him into the White House. In a crowded field of tall, rangy Kennedy clones, he was a short, intense man with a slightly hooked nose and dark bushy eyebrows. In a sea of sandy-haired candidates, he was the only brunet. In debate after debate, as the cameras panned the seated debaters, he stood out, distinct and separate.

This strategy had worked for Michael Princippi in one of the most heavily Irish states in the Union. Among the Connollys and the Donnellys, the Carringtons and the Harringtons, the O'Rourkes and MacIntyres, Michael Princippi stood out like a raisin in a bowl of snow peas.

It was even more effective on national television. In debate after debate, Michael Princippi had held his own in his quiet confident manner. The pollsters swiftly singled him out as a dark horse, a long shot, an outsider in a race where every other candidate primped and studied for hours to blend in with the pack. And one after the other, the other would-be candidates had dropped out until the Democratic convention, in one of the swiftest counts in recent history, had gone with him on the first ballot.

The latest polls had Michael Princippi slightly ahead of the Republican nominee, with just days to go until the nation went to the polls. That slight margin was meaningless, he knew. And so he campaigned as if his very political future was at stake. Because it was.

At a campaign stop in Tennessee, he took time out of his

busy schedule to watch his rival, the Vice-President, give a speech. He switched on the hotel-room television and, dismissing his key aides, settled onto the unmade bed to watch.

The speech was broadcast live from the grounds of an institution in New York State.

The speech was a bore. The Vice-President gave it his best preppy shot, but it was the standard "I'm going-to-clean-up-the-dark-corners" speech Michael Principi had given when he was first elected governor. But as the speech went on, the Vice-President grew more intense, his voice filling with conviction. It made Michael Principi stop and think about a letter he had received over the weekend. A very strange letter.

When the speech had ended, the network anchorman came on with an instant wrap-up that was half as long as the speech itself and not nearly as clear. The anchorman signed off with the redundant reminder that he was "Reporting live from the grounds of Folcroft Sanitatrium, in Rye, New York."

For some reason, the name Folcroft sounded familiar to Michael Principi, but he couldn't place it. Then he remembered. The letter.

Principi bounced off the bed and shut off the TV on his way to his briefcase.

He pulled the letter from a pocket of the briefcase and shook it from its envelope as he settled into a chair. He had assumed it was a crank letter, but it was so crammed with facts and details that he held on to it. Just in case.

The letter was addressed to him personally, the envelope marked personal and confidential. It had been postmarked in Seoul, South Korea. Michael Principi skimmed the letter again, looking for the name.

Yes, there it was. Folcroft Sanitarium. His eyes jumped back to the beginning and he read the letter quickly. When he was done, he read it all over again more slowly.

The letter purported to reveal the existence of a highly secret governmental agency that operated from the cover of Folcroft Sanitarium and was run by Dr. Harold W. Smith. The organization was known as CURE. Its letters signified nothing, said the letter. It was no acronym, but a statement of intent. Set up to cure America of its internal ills, under Dr. Smith CURE had become a rogue operation, no longer responsible to presidential or constitutional restrictions. With access to the computer files of every government agency and major corporation in America, CURE was the ultimate Big Brother.

More damning than the privacy issues at stake, the letter writer went on, CURE had hired as its enforcement agents the aged head of a house of professional assassins, whose name was Chiun. He was the Master of Sinanju, a ruthless, vicious professional killer. The letter went on to relate that this Chiun had trained a supposedly dead American police officer, one Remo Williams, in the deadly art of Sinanju. Together, under Dr. Smith's direction, the pair had been the unofficial instruments of domestic policy for several administrations, often resorting to assassination and terror. The letter concluded with the hope that Michael Princippi might use this information to further his quest for the presidency.

The letter was signed, simply, "Tulip."

Michael Princippi folded the letter thoughtfully and replaced it in its envelope. It was on his mind that maybe he was not the only one to receive such a letter from the mysterious Tulip. Perhaps the Vice-President had gotten one too. That would certainly explain why a speech about covert operations was given at an odd place like Folcroft Sanitarium.

Michael Princippi decided to look into the specific details the letter claimed would prove that CURE existed.

After that he would have his writers prepare a speech in which Michael Princippi, too, promised America that when he assumed office the American intelligence community would be purged of all extralegal operations. Scratch that, he thought quickly. He would ask the writers to put it another way—one which would show both the Vice-President and the head of CURE that Michael Princippi was on top of intelligence matters too.

Dr. Harold W. Smith waited until the Vice-President's entourage had left the Folcroft grounds before he called the President.

To pass the time, he locked his office door on his gushing secretary—who couldn't get over the fact that Folcroft had hosted the Vice-President of the United States—and brought up the concealed computer terminal from its desktop recess.

Smith scanned the digest feeds of possible CURE-related news events. There were the usual gangland murders, updates on ongoing federal investigations, national-security bulletins, and CIA "burn notices." Nothing of immediate importance. Today nothing would have seemed important. But somehow the flashing green blocks of data smoothed Harold W. Smith's unquiet soul. Seated behind a computer screen, he was in his element.

When he was done, Smith removed the red telephone from the desk drawer and picked up the receiver. He cleared his throat as, without any other action on his part, an identical phone somewhere in the White House began ringing.

"Hello?" said the cheery voice of the President of the United States. "I hope this isn't an emergency. I'm really enjoying my last few weeks in office. Do you know that I've had three offers this week to play myself in a movie? My advisers say it would demean the office if I accepted them, but I don't know. I'm going to have a lot of time on my hands and, darn it, I'd like to get in front of the cameras again. What do you think?"

Without skipping a beat, Smith plunged into what he had to say. "Mr. President, we've been compromised."

"The Soviets?" The President's voice shook.

"No."

"The Chinese?"

"No, Mr. President. It is not a foreign matter. I have reason to believe that your Vice-President has learned about CURE."

"Well, I didn't tell him," the President insisted.

"Thank you for volunteering that, Mr. President. I needed to hear it directly from you, just to keep the record straight. That settled, he does know. He just gave a speech on the ground of my cover institution in which he all but acknowledged it openly."

"Well, what's so bad about that? When he's elected, he'll be your boss. At least it won't be a shock to him like it was to me. Why, I remember when the last President broke the news to me, I—"

"Yes, Mr. President," Smith cut in. "That's not the point. Listen carefully. First, somehow the information got out. That means a leak somewhere. Second, the Vice-

President's speech contained a not-very-veiled threat to shut down my operation."

"Hmmm," said the President. "Could be just talk. You know, get the voters stirred up."

"No, sir. I'm sure the Vice-President arranged for this speech specifically to send me a message."

"Well, as you know, once I leave office, I will have no influence upon the Vice-President, but I'll talk to him if that's what you want."

"No, Mr. President, that is not what I want. It will be the decision of the next President, once he assumes office, to decide whether or not to sanction future CURE operations. As you know, we exist at the discretion of the current officeholder. I am prepared to be terminated, if it comes to that."

"Well-spoken. So what's the problem?"

"As I said, if the Vice-President knows about CURE, and you did not tell him, he obtained his information from another source. Which means that someone outside of the loop knows. For security reasons, the person in question must be eliminated, or CURE must go. One or the other. That is the decision I am asking you to make, Mr. President."

"Well, now, I don't know about this," said the President carefully. "Can I sleep on it?"

"Do you wish me to investigate the leak on this end before you come to your decision?"

"Why don't you do that, Smith," the President said amiably. "Yes, go to it. Let me know what happens."

"Yes, Mr. President," said Harold W. Smith, and hung up. He frowned. The President had not seemed concerned. True, it was his own Vice-President who had learned the truth, but that was not Smith's principal problem. It was the source of the Vice-President's information. For all Smith knew, CURE could be an open secret in the executive branch. And he couldn't very well order the liquidation of the President's entire cabinet and advisers to preserve CURE.

Instead, Smith knew he should be prepared to execute his ultimate responsibility as CURE's director—the destruction of operations and his own suicide.

5

He crossed the Green Line on foot.

He carried no weapon. It was suicide to cross the Green Line unarmed. The Syrians often looked the other way, even though they had nominal control over the city. The Lebanese Army was virtually invisible. Even the native militias—of which there were several—did not cross the Green Line with impunity.

But he would. He had business in the western part of the city. And because he was not in a hurry, he walked, his white sandals making no sound on the streets littered with crushed glass. No wind stirred his blond mane of hair. The purple silk of his garments stood out, the only splash of color in a city that had once been the jewel of the Middle East but was now a scorched and shattered ruin.

Tonight Beirut was quiet, as if dead. In a way, it was.

He crossed the Green Line where it paralleled the Rue de Damas. Here the Green Line was truly green. It was a sunken strip of perpetually muddy ground fed by a broken water main. Ferns grew profusely. He stepped through them, and although he was quiet, the fat rats scrambled out of his way, their beady eyes bright with a too-human fear.

He found the Rue Hamrah easily. He walked between the cracked facades of its high-rise buildings. The remains of firebombed cars sat rusting on their wheels like permanent fixtures. He felt eyes upon him. No doubt they were peering through the bullet holes that pocked the few buildings which hadn't been reduced to twisted tangles of concrete and reinforced wire. He felt a subliminal pressure against his back that warned him the barrels of automatic weapons were pointed at him.

Even at night, they would see that he was white. He wondered if they would decide to kill him, or possibly take him hostage. He was not worried. He had asked for this meeting. They would at least hear him out. And if they decided to harm him, they would learn that not all people who happened to be born in America were frightened by the Hezbollah.

In the middle of the street, he stopped. The air smelled dead. The stench of gunpowder was a permanent understink. He moderated his breathing rhythms to keep his lungs clear.

They came in pairs, clutching their rifles, their faces wrapped in colorful *kaffiyehs* so that only the dirty patches of skin around their eyes showed. A few stood with rocket-propelled grenade launchers slung carelessly across their shoulders. That was simply to impress him, he knew. They dared not use them at close quarters.

When he was ringed by seven of their number, he asked a question in their native tongue.

"Which one of you is Jalid?"

A man stepped forward. His face was wrapped in a green checkered *kaffiyeh*. "You are Tulip?"

"Of course."

"I did not expect you to come in your pajamas." And Jalid laughed.

The blond man smiled back at him, a cool insolent smile. If this warlord only knew the power he faced, he would tremble in his scuffed boots.

"*Maalesh,*" Jalid said. "Never mind. You wish to ransom hostages? We have many fine hostages. American, French, German. Or perhaps we will take you hostage instead. If we do not like you."

They were bandits, nothing more. The world thought the Hezbollah were fanatical Moslems loyal only to the rulers of Iran. He knew different. Their ties to Iran were real, but their absolute loyalty was to money. For the right price, they would release their hostages and Iran's rulers be damned. There were always more hostages to be taken, anyway.

They understood only one thing other than money. That was raw power. When they had kidnapped Russian diplomats during the civil war, the Soviets sent in their own agents, kidnapped members of the Hezbollah, and sent them back to the Hezbollah warlords, a finger and an ear at a time, until the Soviet diplomats were unconditionally released. That was the kind of power they understood.

He would show them.

"I wish to hire your skill, Jalid."

Jalid did not ask: For what? He did not care. Instead he asked, "How much will you pay?"

"Something very valuable."

"I like your words. Talk on."

"It is more valuable than gold."

"How much more?"

"It is more precious than the finest rubies you could ever imagine."

"Tell me more."

"It is more precious to you than your mother's very life."

"My mother was a thief. A good thief." Jalid's eyes crinkled, indicating that he smiled behind his *kaffiyeh*.

"It is your life."

Jalid's eyes uncrinkled. *"Bnik kak!"* he swore. "I think you will die here, *ya khara.*"

The blond man turned his electric-blue eyes upon the man beside Jalid, whose fine rifle indicated that he was second in command.

"Aarrhh!" the man howled suddenly. The others looked at him, their eyes not straying far from the unarmed white man.

"Bahjat! What is it?"

"I am on fire!" Bahjat howled, his rifle clattering to the cratered pavement. "Help me. My arms are burning!"

The others looked. They saw no fire. But then vague blue flames, like a faintly luminous gas, ran down their comrade's arms. His arms browned delicately, then blackened. Bahjat screeched and twisted onto the ground, trying to put the flames out. They would not go out. The others fell to his assistance, but when the first man touched him, he jumped back, staring stupidly at his hands.

Spiders spilled out of his palms as if from a hole in a dead tree. They were large and hairy, with eight reddish eyes each. They scrambled up his arms and swarmed over his face.

"Help me, help me!"

But no help came. The others were busy, each with their own nightmare. One man felt his tongue swell in his mouth, forcing his jaws apart until the hinge muscle strained beyond endurance. He could not breathe. The pain was excruciating. In despair he fell on a dropped grenade launcher and, bringing the warhead to his face, triggered it with the toe of his boot. The explosion obliterated him from the chest up and killed others who were nearby.

Another man thought his legs had become pythons. He slashed off their heads and laughed triumphantly even as he fell to the street, blood pumping from the stumps of his ankles until there was no fluid left in his entire body.

Jalid saw it all. He saw, too, as if in a dream, an old enemy facing him. It was a man he had killed over a gambling dispute years ago. The man was dead. But here he was again, coming at him with his knife held low for a quick disemboweling thrust.

Jalid shot the man to pieces with his rifle. Standing over the man's quivering body, he laughed triumphantly. But the figure shimmered, revealing a face obscured by a twisted *kaffiyeh*. Jalid undid the *kaffiyeh* and beheld the face of his younger brother, Fawaz. He sank to his knees beside the boy, tears starting from both eyes.

"I'm sorry, Fawaz, my brother. I'm sorry," he repeated dully.

"Stand up, Jalid," said the white man with the electric-blue eyes. "You and I are alone now."

Jalid came to his feet. He saw the blond man standing there, his hands loose and empty at his sides, unarmed. He exuded an insolent confidence that humbled Jalid, whose belt bristled with knives and pistols and whose cruelty had ruled this part of Ras Beirut ever since the Israelis had retreated across the Awali River.

Jalid raised his hands in defeat.

"You did this," he said resignedly.

The blond man nodded quietly. Then he asked a quiet question.

"You have other men than these?"

"Almost as many as I have bullets," Jalid said.

"An empty boast. But however many men you have, let us gather together three of the best. They, and you, will accompany me. I have work for you. And I will pay you with more than your chicken-boned life."

"What kind of work?"

"Killing work. The only kind you are fit for. You will like the work, for it will enable you to kill Americans. You will return to Beirut a hero to your Hezbollahi brothers, Jalid."

"Where will we kill these Americans?" asked Jalid. "There are none left in Lebanon."

"In America, of course."

Jalid was frightened. He and three of his best men, dressed in Western business suits and without weapons, sat together on the flight to New York City. They whispered fearful words in their native tongue to one another, hanging over the seat headrest to talk to those in the other seats and warily eyeing the stewardess, who was just as warily eyeing them back.

"Sit still," said the blond man who called himself Tulip. "You are attracting attention to yourselves."

The blond man sat alone in the seat behind them. Jalid called back to him in Lebanese.

"My Moslem brothers and I are fearful."

"Did I not get you through the Beirut airport safely? And did you not walk unchallenged through the airport in Madrid when we changed planes?"

"Yes. But American customs will be different."

"No, they will just be American."

"All my life, I am a brave man," said Jalid.

"I do not choose women to do my work for me. Be not a woman, Jalid."

"I have grown up in a city torn by war. I first fired a machine gun when I was nine. Before I was ten I had killed three men. That was many years ago now. There is little I fear."

"Good. You will need your courage."

"One thing I do fear is America," Jalid went on. "I have had nightmares of being taken captive and brought to America for trial. These nightmares have never gone away. And now I am letting you take me to America. How do I know that this is not an American trick to put me and my brothers on trial before the world?"

"Because if I was an American agent," the man called Tulip replied, "I would also bring back with me the American hostages your people are holding prisoner. Tell that to your brothers.''

Jalid nodded his understanding and he and his friends huddled again. The stewardess decided, because they were in the back of the plane and away from the other passengers, to neglect to ask them if they wanted something to drink.

At Kennedy Airport they were escorted to a holding area, where they were given preprinted pamphlets describing customs procedures. When the time came for them to pass through the turnstiles, the customs agents asked them for their passports. This was the moment Jalid had feared. They had none.

But the man called Tulip handed the customs official a collection of green customs passes. The customs official glanced at them briefly and then handed them back, careful to give each man his correct passport.

Jalid opened his passport, intensely curious to see the picture the customs guard had used to verify his identity. He had no idea a photo of himself even existed.

Jalid saw instantly that one did not. The photo in the picture was of a woman.

''Look,'' whispered Sayid in his ear, showing his passport photo. It was of an old man at least forty years older than Sayid, who was nineteen. The other passports were also clearly the property of other people. The man called Tulip had made no attempt to doctor them at all.

When the customs officials went through their luggage, the others relaxed. Not Jalid. Although Tulip had specifically forbidden them to carry in weapons, Jalid could not resist placing a dagger in the lining of his suitcase. The customs guards saw the evidence of tampering and stripped the lining. The knife gleamed under the cold airport lights.

''What is this?'' the airport guard asked harshly.

The man called Tulip stepped in, smiling. ''Allow me,'' he said. And with a movement so quick that the human eye could not register it, he was holding the long dagger, bending the blade double.

''It's only a toy,'' Tulip said. ''Rubber painted silver. These men are touring magicians. They could not resist a little practical joke. Please forgive them.''

The customs guard did not see the humor, but he replaced

the dagger and returned their luggage without further comment.

Jalid took his suitcase and carried it with a blank, uncomprehending expression on his face.

"That dagger was of fine steel," he said thinly.

"It still is, fool. The guard saw what I wished. All of you did."

"How did you do that?" Jalid wanted to know.

"With my mind."

"With your mind you conquered my best men back in Beirut?"

"With my mind I can conquer the world, just as I have conquered you," explained Tulip.

At the Parkside-Regent Hotel overlooking Central Park, the man called Tulip brought out stacks of weapons. Fine handguns, modern Uzis and Kalashnikov assault rifles, other close-in fighting weapons, and boxes of ammunition. Jalid and his men fell upon them eagerly. With weapons in their hands, they felt like men again.

"I am going to leave you after today," said Tulip, uncrating a case of hand grenades with one hand. "There is spending money in the ammunition boxes. The rental on this room is paid up for the next three months. From this moment on, there will be no communication between us until your mission is completed."

"What is our mission?" asked Jalid, spilling bullets and money onto the sofa.

"You are to assassinate the U.S. Vice-President and the Democratic nominee for the American presidency, whose name is Governor Michael Principi."

Jalid's men exchanged wide-eyed glances.

"The President too?" Jalid asked.

"I don't care. Kill whoever else you want—after you have carried out my orders. Here are photos and the current itinerary of the two targets. You can follow any schedule changes through newspapers and by watching television."

"What about our money?"

The man called Tulip set a leather briefcase on the coffee table and unlocked it for all to see. In neat packages were stacks of American money. Each stack had a thousand-dollar bill on the top. Jalid picked up a stack at random and riffled through it. It was a stack of thousand-dollar bills. So were the rest. Jalid checked every single one of them, showing the bills to each of his men as he did so.

"I will place this briefcase in the hotel safe," promised the man called Tulip. "When your mission is completed, I will return, give you the briefcase, and help you escape America for your homeland, such as it is."

"How do we know you will do this?"

"You may accompany me to the hotel's security safe. I will instruct the hotel manager not to release this briefcase to any of us unless at least two of us are present, myself and you—or one of your men if you do not survive."

"I will survive. I have spent my entire life surviving."

"I know how that is," said Tulip in a flat voice.

"But how do we know you will not abandon us, briefcase and everything?"

"You have met me. You know my face. You can describe it to the American authorities and with my description possibly plea-bargain your way out of any legal difficulty you encounter."

That made sense to Jalid and his comrades.

"Done," Jalid said, satisfied. He felt suddenly confident. How hard could it be to kill two political leaders in a soft country like America, where successful assassinations were often carried out by fools and idiots? He was a trained soldier. The money was as good as spent, Jalid thought as he followed the handsome man with the long blond hair down to see the hotel manager.

On the way, they passed a mother towing a little boy down the hallway. Jalid noticed the boy suddenly cower. He thought the boy was frightened by him, but the boy's wide eyes were fixed on Tulip's impassive face.

"Did you torment that boy with your mind?" he asked.

"No," said Tulip. "Children are sensitive. That boy simply recognized death when it walked by him."

6

The Master of Sinanju paused at the door to Remo's room and listened intently. The sound of breathing came shallow and regular through the wood. Good, his pupil was asleep. It was the perfect opportunity to have that important talk Emperor Smith had been avoiding.

Dressed in his ceremonial robe, Chiun took the steps, because he did not like or trust elevators, and knocked sharply at Harold Smith's office door.

It was night, and Smith was still in his office. "Come in," he said hoarsely.

Stepping in, the Master of Sinanju saw a Harold Smith who was more haggard of face than he had been in a long time.

"Hail, Emperor Smith. It is fortunate that you are still holding forth at Fortress Folcroft, the true seat of your power, for the Master of Sinanju has an important matter to discuss with you."

Smith waved an irritable hand. "I'm sorry, Master Chiun, but I'm afraid it is beyond even my abilities to reinstate your American Express card."

"A mere trifle," said Chiun. "I have come to renegotiate the contract between your house and mine."

"I'm afraid that may be premature in this instance."

"Premature?" asked Chiun. "Our current contract has mere days left before it expires. Do you not wish a smooth transition from our current terms to the new ones?"

"Actually, I should have said moot, not premature."

"Excellent." Chiun beamed happily. "Let us make it a point that all our future negotiations are moot. They will be more fruitful that way."

"You don't understand," Smith said wearily. "By this time next month there may not be an operation. The American Vice-President has apparently discovered the truth about CURE and is hinting that he will close it down.''

"Whisper the command and I will deal with him as the traitor he obviously is,'' Chiun said resolutely.

"No, no,'' said Smith hastily. "It is the President's option to terminate CURE when he assumes office. I go through this every time the administration changes. The President tells his successor about the operation and the new President makes the decision whether or not to retain our services.''

"Ah, then I will fly to the President of Vice's quarters and assist him in his decision-making. I guarantee that he will make whatever decision you desire, O wise one.'' Chiun bowed.

Smith sank back into his chair. He had long ago given up trying to explain the democratic process to Chiun, who still harbored the secret desire that Smith would one day unleash him on the executive branch, the better to install Harold Smith the First, rightful Emperor of America, in the Oval Office.

"No,'' said Smith. "The decision is the Vice-President's. If he is elected.''

"If?'' Chiun stroked his wispy beard concernedly.

"There is a chance that he won't be. The Democratic nominee might be elected instead.''

"And what does this other person think?'' Chiun inquired.

"He does not know about CURE. We'll have to await the election results before we know anything.''

"Then let us see that this possibly openminded person achieves the eagle throne,'' Chiun said brightly.

Smith removed his glasses and rubbed bleary eyes. "That, too, is out of the question,'' he said.

"I could do it without your express command. I could take a vacation, and what I do on my own time is my own business. I have watched the hearings on television. I understand now how your government works. Let me be your Colonel South. You will have complete deniable plausibility.''

"Plausible deniability,'' Smith corrected. "And that is not the way the American government operates. We don't have palace coups or anything of that sort here. Why do you think America has lasted over two hundred years?''

Chiun shrugged politely. He did not say what he thought. That his ancestors had served Egypt and Rome and Persia for longer stretches of time than a mere two centuries. That two centuries was scarcely time enough in which to form a stable government. That obviously it would take much longer for America, where the rulers change every few years, preventing any one man from learning the job well enough to be good at it. To Chiun, America was an upstart nation. Politically it was a mess. Smith's own words proved that. He was saying that the Master of Sinanju might not be able to count on future employment from America simply because its ruler was about to change. Again.

The Master of Sinanju's hazel eyes narrowed in thought. More than anything, he wanted to prevent Remo's return to Sinanju. The last time, he had coerced Remo into staying for the duration of the current contract. The same trick might not work a second time, but Chiun felt he had nothing to lose. Returning to Sinanju and retirement was the same as submitting to an early death. Back in Sinanju, the villagers had shifted their allegiance from Chiun to Remo, ignoring the Master of Sinanju completely. Worse, Remo was poised to marry a woman he had known only days before he had decided to marry her. And although Mah-Li was a good woman, sweet and pure of heart, the marriage threatened Chiun's close relationship with Remo. And Chiun was not ready to accept a subordinate position in Remo's life.

''Is there not a period of transition during the passing of the line of succession?'' asked Chiun after a moment.

''Yes. The new President is elected in November, but does not actually take office until the following January.''

''Then there is a period of three months in which you may have need of our services,'' said Chiun happily.

''Yes,'' Smith admitted slowly. ''But as you know, things have been very quiet over the last year. I hardly think that anything crucial will come up, although one never knows. The truth is, Master of Sinanju, even if we are not ordered to disband, CURE may no longer need an enforcement arm.''

''Nonsense,'' snapped the Master of Sinanju. ''An assassin is as indispensable as breathing. But let us accept your

argument for the moment. If you, as you say, fear the ter-
mination of your office, then there is no loss in renegotiating
now. If you are laid off, Remo and I will go our separate
ways.''

''I'm afraid we can't negotiate Remo's role at this time,''
Smith pointed out. ''The current President believes him to
be dead. Killed during that crisis with the Soviets last year,
remember?''

''We will discuss Remo's role at a later date, then,'' Chiun
said firmly, settling onto the rug.

Smith, knowing that was the signal that negotiations had
formally begun, joined him on the floor, a yellow legal pad
on his lap. He held a number-two pencil poised to record
the terms.

''I propose renewing our contract under its present terms.
No additional payment is required,'' Chiun said loftily, certain that Smith would jump at the chance. Chiun had stuck
him with a substantial increase every year for the last decade.

Smith hesitated. His mouth opened to say yes, but he
snapped it shut before the word escaped.

''Too high,'' Smith said flatly.

''Too . . .'' Chiun began, his face clouding. He re-
strained himself. In the entire history of the House of Sinanju, no Master had ever renewed a contract at terms inferior
to those of the preceding year. But Chiun desperately wanted
this contract renewed, so he kept his anger within him. Next
year—if there was a next year in America—he would more
than make up for this indignity. ''Make a counteroffer,
then,'' Chiun said stiffly.

Smith considered. ''I really think you should make the
next offer,'' he said craftily.

Chiun thought rapidly. He knocked forty percent off the
basic terms, and calculated the loss. It made him cringe,
but he offered that amount to Smith. ''No more, no less,''
he added.

''Another ten-percent reduction might persuade me,''
Smith said unconcernedly.

The Master of Sinanju leapt to his feet in a swirl of kimono skirts. His cheeks puffed out. His fingernails, like a
thousand flashing knives, made dangerous patterns in the
air. Smith recoiled.

Then, getting a grip on himself, the Master of Sinanju gracefully sank back onto the rug like a dandelion seed alighting on a lawn.

When he spoke, his soft voice contained the merest breath of menace, like poisoned honey.

"Done," Chiun said.

"Draw up the contract and I will look it over," said Smith.

Stonily the Master of Sinanju found his feet and executed a brittle bow, and without another word he walked stiff-legged from the office.

Harold Smith returned to his desk and allowed himself a rare smile. Never in all his years as director of CURE had he gotten the better of the Master of Sinanju. Smith was a parsimonious man. But each year he had regularly shipped enough of the taxpayers' money to the tiny fishing village of Sinanju to refloat the collective debts of many third-world countries.

Too bad that it was all probably going to be for nothing, he thought as he brought up the CURE computer terminal for a final news-digest check before going home for the evening.

The first item wiped the remnants of the smile from his dry-as-dust face.

It was a news summary of a speech given by the Democratic presidential candidate, Governor Michael Princippi. The gist of his speech was a pledge to transfuse money into the social-security system from the intelligence budget. Specifically, Princippi promised to go after the countless "black projects" that were built into the federal budget, the nameless accounting fictions that enabled the federal government to channel billions of tax dollars yearly into covert operations and defense projects so sensitive that they could not be named or described for Congress except behind closed doors.

"Let's shine a light into the so-called black budget and see who and what we find," Governor Princippi was quoted as saying.

Smith clutched the edge of his oak desk as if to get a grip on himself. First the Vice-President and now this. It was obvious that this speech was a tit-for-tat response to the Vice-President's call for an end to rogue intelligence operations. It did not mean that Governor Princippi knew about CURE. That would be a worst-case scenario if one ever existed.

But in the final analysis, it might not matter. CURE was funded by black-budget money. Fully half of the black-project money appropriated for the Central Intelligence Agency, the Defense Intelligence Agency, and the National Security Agency, not to mention certain segments of the defense budget, actually wound up under Dr. Harold W. Smith's operational control.

Either way, it looked as if CURE were going to go under with the installation of the next President, no matter who won the election. Assuming the presidential candidates kept their campaign promises.

Smith groaned and reached for the shattered bottle of children's aspirin. If this kept up, he'd have to go back to adult dosages, and hang his ulcer.

7

It had been so hard.

First, in Sinanju. He had summoned the purple birds to scare off the villagers before he entered the village itself. He could have slipped in at night, unseen. But a sleeping guard might have tempted the beast within him. He had let the beast out in Beirut. The beast had decimated Jalid's Hezbollah bandits. That had cooled its lust to kill.

On the flight to America, he had had to restrain himself again. He hadn't believed it was possible to shackle the beast during the long transatlantic flight, but he had. He wondered if he were mastering it at last. He doubted it. But he was older, wiser, and stronger than the last time.

The problem was, so was the beast.

He pulled the rental car off the road when he came to the great piney woods of Maine's Allagash Wilderness. There would be no people in these forsaken woods. No people meant no temptation to kill.

He stepped out of the car and stripped off the American-style clothes that felt so heavy and coarse against his pale white skin.

He was nude only as long as he needed to be to don his purple silk fighting suit. He belted the yellow sash around his waist.

He walked into the forest on his bare feet because he liked the feel of pine needles against his naked soles. As a child, growing up on a Kentucky farm, walking barefoot through the corn meant washing manure off your feet afterward. He carried his white sandals in his hands. That was all he carried. He had no need of possessions. He had nothing. He needed nothing. His life was empty except for the goal which had driven him to Sinanju in the first place.

Even the squirrels fled at his approach. He wondered if

it was a scent or a vibration or an aura that caused all animals and children to recoil from him. He was not ugly. He had a pleasant face. Yet they broke before him, the beaver and the bear alike, like the Red Sea parting before the wrath of God.

There was a tiny brown doe nibbling at the grass. He saw her before she saw him. She was beautiful. Just once, he would like to pet an animal. But the beast within him heard and grew jealous.

The doe looked up, saw him, and exploded into a rain of blood, flesh, and fragments of raw bone.

He wept for the doe, even as the beast within him rejoiced at the scent of fresh blood. He walked on.

The cabin stood in a clearing of scattered pine needles. The spiders had retaken the eaves as they always did each summer. The intact webs across the door told him no one had intruded upon his home since he was last here, so many weeks ago.

He opened the door. He had not bothered to lock it. The furnishings were sparse. There was nothing worth stealing, unless someone was desperate enough to walk off with the old black-and-white television that sat in the middle of the living room floor.

He stepped over to the TV and squatted before it like a votary before a pagan idol. He switched it on, but kept the sound turned down. He did not want anything to intrude upon his thoughts.

The television would be his window to the outside. It would tell him when Jalid first struck. That would be his signal that it was time to rejoin the civilized world. In the interim, it was too dangerous for him to remain in the city, where the beast would hunt the innocent, not because he wished it, but because the beast was greater than his own will to achieve his ends.

He focused on the television screen, but it was late and there were only test patterns on all channels. It did not matter. He settled on one and focused all his attention upon it.

It was the only way he knew to focus himself so that the beast remained shackled.

Above his head, the naked ceiling bulb exploded into hundreds of opaque slivers. He had not touched it, except with his mind.

8

Jalid Kumquatti decided that America was an amazing place.

He had driven his brothers of the Hezbollah all the way from New York City to the city of Philadelphia and he was not stopped once. America, whom the rulers of Iran and Libya and other Middle Eastern countries boasted was a cowering paper tiger whose citizens were not safe even within her own borders, had no roadblocks, no security checkpoints, no tanks in the streets, and no impediments to the free movement of foreign agents.

Although they had passed many police cars and they were obviously foreigners, they were not challenged. Once, outside of Levittown, they blew a tire, and while they were stopped, a state-police car came up behind them, its blue light bar washing their startled faces with illumination.

Jalid almost panicked when the state trooper stepped from his vehicle, but he relaxed slightly when he saw that the gray-uniformed man carried only a tiny .38 revolver in a belt holster. In Beirut the .38 revolver was carried by women and children as they went to market. It was not a man's weapon. No Lebanese took a .38 pistol as a serious threat.

Thus Jalid had hissed to his comrades to relax while they waited to see what the man wanted.

"A little trouble here?" the officer asked politely.

"We are changing the wheel," Jalid said nervously. "We are on our way soon. You will see."

"Better hop to it. I don't want to see any of you rear-ended by a speeder. New to America, are you?"

"Very," said Jalid, whose English was acceptable. He had learned the language in order to write ransom notes and negotiate with Europeans.

"Then you may not realize how dangerous an American

highway is. Why don't I stay here with my lights on so
there's no accident," the trooper suggested with a smile.

"Sure, sure," said Jalid, and he busied himself with the
lug wrench. When he was finished and a new tire was in
place, he and his friends jumped into the car and, waving
out the rear window at the trooper, left the scene at a dec-
orous pace.

"He was very nice," said Sayid after a while.

"America is very nice," said Rafik. "Did you notice that
we have traveled nearly fifty kilometers and no one has shot
at us? In Beirut, one cannot go for cigarettes without taking
one's life in one's hands."

"America is a land of fools and so are you all," spat
Jalid. "Do not forget our mission." But even he was amazed
by America, its vastness, it cleanliness. Once, he had heard,
Lebanon had been like this. A rich fertile happy land. Now
it was being torn apart by animals, and Jalid was one of
them. But he had been born into a land caught up in civil
war, he told himself. His earliest memories were of squalor
punctuated by distant explosions. The first music he had
ever heard was the daily ululations of Lebanese women in
mourning. No, his way was the only one possible now.

But driving through America had shown him what living
a normal life must be like, and instead of making him feel
guilty for his participation in the dismemberment of Lebanon, he felt a wave of hatred for America, which had so
much and deserved it so little. He resolved that he would
shoot dead the next police officer who dared to speak to
him.

They sat around in their hotel room, not in the chairs,
but perched on the chair backs, their feet dirtying the cushions, as they cleaned and oiled their weapons. They looked
like vultures squatting on rocks.

"The Vice-President will be having lunch at what is called
a Lion's Club," Jalid said, reading a newspaper he had
slipped off the lobby newsstand when the counter girl wasn't
looking.

"How will we find this place of lions?" asked Sayid.

"Taxicab. We will go by taxicab, because it will save
time and we do not wish to be late. When the driver brings

us to this Lion's Club, we will kill him.'' Jalid dropped the newspaper and considered his men carefully.

"Sayid, my brother," he said at last, grinning suddenly. "Yes?"

"You will have the great honor this day."

"I?" Sayid smiled back. It was not a smile of pleasure but the kind that concealed fear.

"Yes," said Jalid, coming off the chair back. "I have been thinking. There is much money to be had from this work. It would be too bad if we were all killed trying to collect it."

The others looked at one another. They nodded. Except Sayid. His smile grew broader, but his eyes had a sickly light to them.

"We do not know what militias these Americans use to guard their leaders," said Jalid, scratching his sparse dark beard thoughtfully. "Probably they are not much if they guard them as sloppily as they guard their rich and fat cities. Perhaps one man is all that is necessary to eliminate this Vice-President."

"Alone?" asked Sayid uncomfortably.

"We will be outside, perhaps to come to your rescue if necessary."

"But what if you cannot?"

"It is simple, my brother. We will take hostages, and hold them until you are released."

"But what if I am killed in the course of my duty to the Hezbollah?" insisted Sayid, his smile fixed on his face like a clown's rigid makeup grin.

"Then we will send your share of the money to your aged mother. She would like that, would she not?"

"You will be right outside the building?" asked Sayid after long thought.

"Absolutely," said Jalid, coming over and clapping Sayid on the back. The smile on Sayid's sweat-shiny face broke like a soap bubble.

"It is settled, then," called Jalid, throwing up his hands in celebration. "Sayid will be the one who has the honor of striking first. Come, let us order food from the room service before we are on our way. A well-fed warrior is a strong warrior."

And the others laughed boisterously. All except Sayid, who was suddenly not hungry at all.

The Vice-President did not feel hungry either.

He stared down at his plate. Rubber chicken and dry-kernel corn crowded a foil-wrapped baked potato. The potato was almost obliterated under a mound of sour cream. With a dessert spoon he tasted the sour cream and decided to pass on the rest. He wished just once one of these testimonial dinners would serve something different like moo-shu pork or even barbecued ribs, Texas-style. If it wasn't rubber chicken, it was dry roast beef in greasy gravy. If it wasn't a shriveled potato, it was rice pilaf microwaved dry as sunflower seeds.

The Vice-President nudged the plate away and ordered black coffee, to which he added four heaping teaspoons of sugar to keep his energy level up.

From the podium, someone was speaking. For a moment he could not remember who it was. It had been like this for over a year now. He had lurched from group breakfasts to luncheons to dinners in smoke-filled halls, listening to a procession of politicians and giving speeches that, even though they were written by the best speech writers available, all sounded exactly like the speech before that, which had sounded like the one before that, and on and on, stretching back into the Vice-President's dim past—which on the campaign trail meant that misty period prior to six weeks ago.

The Vice-President sipped his coffee and tried to shut out the drone of the speechmaker, whom he recognized vaguely as the governor of the state. Exactly which state would come to him eventually.

It was all so boring. Except for that speech the other day. Where had that been? Oh, yeah, in New York State. It had been an improvisation in his schedule, that stop. He had ordered it over the objections of his campaign staff, who thought he could at least talk about national health care if he was going to speak in front of an insane asylum, or whatever it was that Folcroft Sanitarium was.

He did not tell them what Folcroft was. He did not tell them about the letter he had received, postmarked Seoul, South Korea, which explained in detail about a secret Amer-

ican agency known as CURE, operating from the cover of
Folcroft Sanitarium.

He saw in the letter, true or not, an opportunity to make
an important speech on covert activities. It was a perfect
way of distancing himself from the problems of the current
administration.

The Vice-President did not know whether or not to believe this Tulip who had signed the letter. But on the chance
it was true, he had asked his people to see to it that Harold
W. Smith himself introduced him to the audience.

Smith's refusal and his flustered behavior at the speech
were as good as proof that CURE did exist. Why, the guy
had actually tossed his cookies during the presentation.
What was someone that nervous doing running a covert operation?

The Vice-President had briefly considered going to the
President and getting the true poop, but decided against it.
Revealing the truth about CURE in a major speech was also
out of the question. He had no proof, and it would look too
much like grandstanding just before the election. Better to
wait until after the election. If he won, he would blow the
whistle on the CURE program. It would be a great start-off
for his administration and would once and for all put to bed
the public perception that he was just a spear carrier for the
current President.

One thing puzzled him, however. Just this morning the
Democratic nominee had made a speech very similar to his
own. He had made it before an American Medical Associ-
ation conference, and although the Vice-President had not
watched the speech, a transcript of it was shown to him and
he noted that Michael Princippi had very specifically used
the word ''cure'' several times during his speech.

His advisers had assured him that the Democratic nominee was merely copycatting his own speech, but the Vice-
President was not so sure. He wondered if the Prince had
also received a letter from Tulip.

And not for the first time he wondered who this Tulip
person was. With a name like that, he sounded like a pansy.
But these days you could never tell.

Someone nudged him and the Vice-President snapped out
of his reverie.

''You're on, Mr. Vice-President. He's introducing you.''

"Oh, right, of course," said the Vice-President, rising from his seat. He unbuttoned his coat on the way to the podium and carefully rebuttoned it as he said a quick thank-you into the microphone. His personal-style manager had told him that he dangled his arms like a scarecrow when he walked and that gave an image of a man with time on his hands, so ever since then he made it a point to button or unbutton his coat whenever he left or arrived someplace—even if it was merely walking from a table to a podium.

The audience applauded enthusiastically. He could hear them but he could not see them. They were an ocean of dim faces overwhelmed by the baleful eyes of the TV spotlights. He would not have known if his own wife was in the audience.

"I haven't had a welcome like this since the Iowa caucuses," said the Vice-President, who believed in working a well-received line to death.

The audience laughed and clapped boisterously. The Vice-President smiled into the exploding flashbulbs. He did not see the commotion at the door.

He heard the string of pop-pop-pops but they were not much louder than the flashbulbs.

The next thing he knew, the Secret Service men were all over him. Two agents pushed him to the floor, smothering him with their bodies. Others, placed in the audience with campaign supporters, reached for the handles of their brief-cases with lightning motions. The cases fell apart, exposing stubby automatic weapons.

The firing was brief and sporadic.

Before the screaming subsided, the Vice-President was lifted to his feet and pushed out the back door like a drunk being thrown out of a motorcycle bar. They hustled him to his waiting limousine and the car left the area, its oil pan scraping sparks off the irregular pavement.

When he found his composure again, the Vice-President wanted to know just one thing.

"What the hell happened back there?"

"Assassin," clipped one of the agents. "But we got him, sir. Don't worry."

"If you got him, why'd you have to push me out of the Rotary Club like that?"

"It was a Lion's Club, sir."

"That's not the point. This is going to look terrible on the seven-o'clock news."

"Your dead body would have looked worse. Sir."

The Vice-President sat back in the leather cushions, feeling the starch go out of his legs.

He grabbed the receiver of the car phone and asked the mobile operator to connect him with the White House.

"When you think we're safe, park this thing and stand outside. What I have to say to the President is for his ears only," the Vice-President said in a husky voice. Nobody shot at presidential candidates. Not without a reason. And the Vice-President thought he knew what that reason was.

9

Dr. Harold W. Smith knew why the President was calling.

He knew it before the dialless red telephone began ringing. Before the first ring, his computer terminal had beeped twice, indicating that urgent CURE-related data were being processed.

The computer had flashed on the screen a digest summary of decoded Secret Service message traffic, the gist of which was that the Vice-President had just escaped a near-assassination.

"Yes, Mr. President?" Smith said into the phone.

"Smith, I have to ask this question of you."

"Sir?"

"The Vice-President was nearly killed not fifteen minutes ago. They failed, whoever they were."

"Yes, I know. The first report just reached me. My understanding is that the situation is secure."

"Is it?" asked the President grimly.

"Sir?"

"Relative to our conversation the other day, you didn't order the Vice-President terminated, did you?"

Harold Smith came out of his chair in surprise, his lemony features gathering in horror. The red telephone fell off the desk and Smith had to catch it in his hands before the cord tore from the receiver and disconnected the line.

"Mr. President, I can assure you that terminating the Vice-President is not something this office would undertake except under the most extreme circumstance. If then."

"You have terminated people who had stumbled across your operation before."

"For the good of America. If CURE were to become known, it would be the same as admitting that the Constitution doesn't work. That America doesn't work. Yes, I have issued some distasteful orders in the past, but always within my operating parameters.''

''The Vice-President's discovery of your operation isn't a threat? He has as much as given you notice that you will be shut down when he's elected.''

''That's his privilege—if he is elected,'' Smith said stiffly. He was still on his feet.

''But if he's not, he becomes a target?''

''We've never faced that problem before,'' said Harold Smith slowly. ''But I think, under the circumstances, we would trust him as we do the former presidents with whom we've worked before.''

''Why don't you tell me about that, while we're on the subject? I'm about to become one of those former presidents, so I might as well know now what to expect.''

''Well, Mr. President, it's very simple. As long as a former chief executive keeps his own counsel, we do not interfere with him.''

''Hasn't it occurred to you, Smith, that this leak might have come from a previous administration?''

''Yes, sir. But I think that possibility is a slim one.''

''But you don't discount it?''

''Actually, I do.''

''You sound rather sure of yourself,'' said the President suspiciously. ''What do you do, spy on them for the rest of their lives?''

''No, Mr. President. But beyond that I cannot say. Security reasons.''

''Very well, let's stay with the Vice-President for the moment. Is there any chance that your special person had anything to do with this?''

Smith started to say, ''No sir,'' but stopped in mid-syllable. He remembered his recent conversation with the Master of Sinanju.

''Just a moment, Mr. President,'' said Smith, and he capped his hand over the receiver because the red telephone did not have a hold button. Into his intercom he said, ''Mrs. Mikulka, would you have someone check on the Alzheimer's patient in room fifty-five, Mr. Chiun. See if he is in his room or elsewhere on the premises.''

When the answer came back, Smith breathed a sigh of

relief. Mr. Chiun was in his room. He returned to the President.

"Sorry, Mr. President. Another important call. To answer your question, our special person does not operate unsanctioned. And he does not use weapons. My information is that the would-be assassin in Philadelphia used an automatic weapon."

"I see your point. But this still leaves us in a bad way. The Vice-President just phoned. He wanted to know if I had ordered him terminated because of that speech he gave the other day. The fellow is so scared he thinks his commander in chief wants him out of the picture."

"I'm sure that's just a nervous reaction. People who narrowly escape death often act irrationally for a brief time afterward."

"I had to tell him I didn't know what he was talking about, which, of course, only made him more suspicious. Smith, I can't have the Vice-President thinking he's a target of his own government."

"Why don't I put my special person on it?" Smith offered. "If there's another attempt on the Vice-President's life, we'll be there to stop it."

"Maybe that will prove to him we're on the side of the angels. Okay, Smith. Go to it. Keep a low profile. If we can pull this off, we might be able to get the Vice-President to see the light."

"Yes, Mr. President. Thank you, sir," said Smith, hanging up.

Smith had no sooner settled into his chair then his secretary informed him that the head gardener wanted to see him.

"Who? Oh, send him in," said Smith, suddenly realizing whom she meant.

Remo Williams walked in, clutching a newspaper.

"Smitty, I think you have a problem," Remo said worriedly.

"Whatever it is, it can wait. I have an assignment for Chiun."

"I was reading the paper," continued Remo. "Where is it now?" He rummaged through the newspaper, dropping sections all over the floor. "Here it is," said Remo, folding one page and laying it on Smith's desk.

"I thought you never read the papers," said Smith.

"I was catching up on the funnies," explained Remo. "I came across this little item."

Smith followed Remo's pointing finger.

"I'm surprised your computers didn't alert you to this one, Smitty," Remo said.

Smith read the headline: "PRINCIPPI PROMISES END TO COVERT OPERATIONS."

"The governor gave that speech the other day," Smith said flatly. But he read the lead paragraph anyway.

"Oh, my God," Smith said slowly.

"Are you thinking what I'm thinking, Smitty?"

"Princippi knows too," Smith breathed.

"That's what I thought," said Remo. "The way he ended his speech with the line about curing the country. It just seemed odd to me. What do you mean, 'too'?" Remo said suddenly.

"The Vice-President knows," said Smith, glassy-eyed. He stared at the ceiling.

"Well, that isn't so terrible, is it? I mean, if anyone had to find out, those guys aren't exactly the worst possibilities."

"It's not who they are," Smith said. "It's where they learned about CURE—assuming that is the case."

"The President?"

"He assures me that he did not. And we know that none of the former presidents could have revealed the truth."

"Yeah," said Remo. "Chiun and I have seen to that. A quiet visit while they're sleeping and a simple pressure on a nerve in their temples. A few whispered words, and instant selective amnesia. They don't remember that CURE exists."

"No, the leak is not from our government, past or present. I feel confident about that much."

"What are you going to do about it? I know it won't matter to me and Chiun. We'll be out of here in another few days, but if CURE is terminated, you go down the tubes with it. Call me sentimental, but I'd hate to see that happen."

"Thank you, Remo. It's very kind of you to say that."

"You know, Smitty," Remo said casually, "I used to hate you."

"I know."

"What you did to me—the frame for a killing I didn't do, the faked electric chair, the grave with my name on it—it was all pretty nasty."

"It was necessary. We needed a man who no longer existed because the organization would not officially exist."

"But it worked out. Look at me. I'm Sinanju now. Over in Korea I have a beautiful girl waiting for me and a house I built with my own hands. Everything is going to be all right. I feel pretty good about it. Oh, there were some rough times, but it's going to work out for me. I want it to work out for you too."

"Thank you, Remo," said Smith sincerely. He was uncomfortable with displays of emotion, but he and Remo had been through many trials together. It felt good to know that Remo no longer held a grudge. "Perhaps, Remo, you can do me a favor."

"What's that?"

"The Vice-President has just escaped an assassination attempt. I'm detailing Chiun to watch over him in case there is another incident. Could you pitch in?"

Remo considered. "Sounds like an easy gig. Okay, Smitty. One last assignment. A freebie."

"Thank you," said Smith. "I can't tell you how much this means to me."

"Just keep the submarine gassed up," said Remo, smiling. And he left the room whistling cheerfully.

10

Security around Blair House was the tightest it had been since 1950, when Puerto Rican nationalists had tried to assassinate President Truman, who had been living there while the White House was undergoing renovation.

After the attempt on his life in Philadelphia, the Vice-President had been flown back to Washington to decompress. His private home was considered impossible to defend, so he had taken up residence at Blair House—where visiting heads of state usually stayed—across the street from the White House. Movable concrete barriers were placed in front of the ornate gray building to discourage car bombs, which were a favorite tactic of Middle Eastern terrorists. Snipers were deployed on the roof, and Secret Service agents patrolled the neighborhood, walkie-talkies in hand.

There had been no concrete identification made of the would-be assassin in Philadelphia. He had died at the scene. But he was believed to be a Middle Easterner, nationality unknown. It was assumed that the man had not acted alone because a taxi was seen leaving the scene. It was later found abandoned, its driver murdered in the back seat. A witness had come forward and described three Middle Eastern nationals who had been seen running from the car, and although a manhunt for persons of that type was immediately initiated, no trace of any accomplice was found. But the tentative identification of the dead attacker as Middle Eastern had galvanized the Secret Service. They were prepared for any terrorist attack on the Vice-President's life short of a tactical nuclear weapon.

They were not prepared for the two men who sauntered down Pennsylvania Avenue as if they owned it and all the land around it as far as the eye could see.

Secret Service Agent Orrin Snell received a routine notification when the two passed a Secret Service checkpoint near the George Washington University Hospital.

"Two subjects coming your way," the checkpoint told him via walkie-talkie.

"Descriptions?" Snell asked.

"Male Caucasian, about five-eleven, weight 155, brown on brown, and wearing a black T-shirt and gray chinos. Accompanied by a short male Oriental, balding, age approximately eighty."

"Describe Oriental's attire."

"Words fail me," said the checkpoint. "You'll know him when you see him. He's dressed like Pinky Lee."

"Like who?"

"Like Pee-Wee Herman."

"Oh," said Snell, understanding perfectly. The pair were just coming into view now. He sized up the Caucasian with a glance. No trouble from that quarter. The guy was obviously unarmed. The Oriental was very short and very old. He wore a red business suit that would have been well-tailored except that the sleeves flared like those of a mandarin's robes. He walked with his hands tucked into the sleeves so that they were unseen. There was plenty of room in those sleeves to conceal a pistol or a grenade.

Agent Snell drew his automatic from its shoulder holster reflexively. He was not taking any chances.

"Do not point that offensive thing at me," said the small Oriental in a squeaky voice.

"Hold on, Little Father. Let me handle this," the Caucasian said.

"Please stand perfectly still," Snell ordered. "I need backup here," he called into the walkie-talkie. Almost before the words were out of his mouth, two other agents came around the corner, pistols at the ready.

"What's the problem, pal?" the Caucasian asked.

"No problem, if you cooperate. I'd like your friend to take his hands out of his sleeves. Slowly."

"Is he crazed?" asked the Oriental of the taller man.

"Just do it. He looks nervous."

The Oriental shrugged and separated his sleeves, revealing what agent Snell at first mistook for a handful of needles. Then he realized he was looking at the longest fingernails he had ever seen in his life.

"Okay," Snell said slowly. "I guess there's no problem." The other agents lowered their weapons.

"Excellent," said the Oriental brightly. "Now perhaps you can render us some assistance. We are seeking the residence of the President of Vice."

The pistols came back up.

"What do you want to know for?" asked Snell.

"We're tourists," said the Caucasian hastily.

"Tourists are not allowed into Blair House," said Snell.

"Our mistake," replied the Caucasian. "We'll be on our way now."

"I'll have to ask for identification before you go," Snell said.

The Caucasian turned his pockets inside out, showing empty linings.

"Must have left mine back in Peoria," he said.

"I am Chiun, Master of Sinanju. I carry no identification because all worthy persons know of me," the Oriental proclaimed.

"You don't have any identification either?" asked Snell.

"If you wish someone to vouch for me, ask your President. He knows me personally."

"He does?" said Snell, for a heart-stopping moment wondering if he had stopped a visiting dignitary.

"Yes," said the Oriental, returning his hands to his sleeves. "I saved his life once."

Behind the two men, one of the other agents mouthed a silent word: crackpots. Snell nodded.

"Why don't you just go on your way?" he said.

"That's what we were doing," said the Caucasian.

Agent Orrin Snell watched them walk away.

"Talk about the odd couple," Snell joked, shaking his head. "Did you hear what he called the little guy—father. Okay, everybody back to your stations."

After his men had returned to their positions, Snell couldn't resist looking down the street after the strange pair.

They were gone. Pennsylvania Avenue was deserted and there was no obvious place the pair could have gone. They were not across the street. He radioed to the next checkpoint.

"I've lost sight of a male Caucasian and an Oriental coming your way. Any contact?"

"Negative," was the reply.

Snell rushed up the Blair House steps and knocked on the ornate door in code.

Another agent poked out his head.

"No problems?" Snell demanded.

"None. What do you have?"

"Nothing. Must be a false alarm. I'll be glad when this scare is over," he said, returning to the street. He took his usual position and wondered where the pair had gone. As long as they hadn't gone into Blair House, then it wasn't his problem, he decided.

Remo paused with his head just under the roof cornice of Blair House.

"Getting old, Little Father?" Remo called down. "You used to be the first one to the top."

The Master of Sinanju climbed around a window until he had reached Remo's level.

"I am not getting old," Chiun snapped. "It is these American clothes. They are not made for scaling."

"Maybe you should go back to kimonos," Remo suggested, grinning.

"Nonsense. I am in service to America. I will dress like an American. Did you see how I got us past that foolish guard without arousing his suspicions?"

"That's not how I remember it, Chiun. And if you don't lower your voice we're not going to get past the guards on the roof."

"There are guards on the roof?"

"Listen. You can hear them breathing."

The Master of Sinanju cocked a delicate ear. He nodded. "They will be easy to handle. One of them breathes like a bellows. A tobacco addict, I am sure."

"Why bother?" said Remo. "Let's go in a window."

"Do you have any special window in mind?" whispered Chiun. "I do not want to find myself in a lady's bedroom by mistake."

Remo grinned. "I'll see what I can do." And like a spider in its web, Remo slipped down the building's side until he found an unlit window. Clinging to the casement, he ran one fingernail around the edge of the pane. The glass squeaked like a nail being pulled from a tree.

Chiun joined him, hanging gingerly so that his fingernails were not chipped by the brick.

"If you would grow your nails to the proper length," he said, "you would not get that mouse-squeak sound."

"I can live with a little noise," said Remo, pressing his palm against the glass to test its resistance.

"No," admonished Chiun. "You could die from a little noise."

"Right," said Remo. "Watch this." And he popped the glass in with a smack of his palm. The hand followed the glass in with eye-blurring speed. When Remo withdrew the hand, he held the glass pane between two fingers, intact.

"After you," said Remo, executing as much of a bow as he could, considering that he clung to the side of a building with one hand and both feet.

The Master of Sinanju slipped into the open frame like colored smoke drawn into an exhaust vent. Remo went in after him.

The room was dark. Remo set the pane on a long table and made for the illuminated outline of a door.

In the hall, the light was mellow. It came from brass wall lamps. The wallpaper was expensive and tasteful—but it was almost as thick as the rug. There was a still air about the hall usually found in museums.

Remo went first. He had no idea where the Vice-President would be quartered and said so.

"Pah!" said Chiun. "It is simple. Look for the largest concentration of guards. Then look for the nearest locked door. Behind it we will find the one we seek."

"What happens if they see us first?"

"A good assassin is never seen first," Chiun said, leading the way.

The entire floor was deserted.

"Up or down?" asked Remo.

"Most rulers equate height with safety," said Chiun.

"Then it's up," said Remo, starting for the stairs.

"But when one's life is in danger, the closer one is to the ground, the quicker one can escape an attack."

Remo stopped in his tracks. "Down?"

"Do not be in a rush. I am trying to think like an American," said Chiun, tugging at his wispy beard. "Now, if I were an American, what would I do it a situation like this?"

"Send out for pizza?"

"Do not jest, Remo. This is serious. I am trying to acclimate myself to this country."

"What's the point? This is our last assignment. After this, we're free and clear."

"That, no doubt, is the reason for your high spirits tonight."

"I feel like the world is my oyster," Remo said.

"Oyster, beware the crab," intoned Chiun, listening.

"What's that supposed to mean?"

"It means we go up. I hear the buzz of voices above. We will find the American President of Vice there."

"Vice-President," Remo corrected.

"Possibly him too."

The Vice-President had fallen asleep in an overstuffed chair beside a four-poster bed, the latest poll results in his lap.

He awoke to a gentle tapping on his shoulder.

"Huh? What?" he said mushily.

"Sorry to wake you up," a cool voice said.

Standing before him were two men—a white man and a little Oriental guy in a red suit and green tie that made him resemble one of Santa's helpers at a prom.

"Who? What?"

"He is not very articulate for a leader," said the Oriental. "Possibly we have the wrong person."

"Smith sent us," the white guy said. "You know who we mean when we say Smith?"

"You're here to kill me," said the Vice-President in horror.

"He knows, all right," the Caucasian muttered.

"No, O possible future ruler," said the Oriental. "We are here to see that no harm comes to you."

"Where are my bodyguards?"

"Sleeping," said the white man. "I didn't want them interrupting. By the way, I'm Remo and this is Chiun. We work for Smith, although that won't be the case if or when you're elected."

"That is still subject to discussion," Chiun interjected hastily.

"No, it's not," Remo said.

"Do not listen to him. He is lovesick for a woman he barely knows."

"I've known Mah-Li for a year now," Remo said. And the two of them leapt into an argument in some singsong language.

The Vice-President started to ease himself out of the chair. The white man, Remo, seeing him move, reached out a hand and touched him on the side of the neck. Openmouthed, the Vice-President froze in position, half in and half out of the chair, while the two argued on, oblivious of his discomfort.

"And that's final," said Remo in English when the argument finally ran its course.

"You wish," retorted Chiun.

Remo turned back to the Vice-President.

"Now, where were we? Oh, yeah. It's like this. Chiun and I don't have any stake in your election or in CURE because we're going back to Korea soon. Smith asked us to protect you before we go. That's why we're here. But I thought I'd put in a good word for Smith while we're here. He's really a nice guy when you get to know him. And he's pretty good with the taxpayers' money. Tight-fisted, you know."

"But generous where it counts," added Chiun.

"We want you to know he's not behind the attack on your life, and to prove it and to prove how effective the operation is, we're going to stay with you until we're sure there won't be another attack on your life. That clear?"

The Vice-President tried to nod. He could not move. His feet tingled and he was sure they were falling asleep.

"Oh, sorry," said Remo, reaching out to massage the throat nerve that sent the Vice-President collapsing into his seat. "How's that?"

"Sinanju?" the Vice-President asked huskily.

"You know about that too?" asked Chiun curiously.

"Yes. It was all in the letter."

"What letter told you about Sinanju?" demanded Chiun.

"The one signed Tulip."

Remo turned to Chiun. "Do you know any Tulip?"

"No. I would not have for a friend one who would call himself that. We will ask Smith. Possibly he knows this Tulip."

"Why don't you both go do that little thing?" the Vice-President suggested. "I would like to get some sleep, if you don't mind."

"Sure," said Remo. "We just wanted you to know we were on the job."

"Fine. Consider it written down in my diary."

"We'll be outside if you need us," said Remo, heading for the door. The Master of Sinanju followed him.

Remo paused in the doorway. "You won't forget what I said about Smith and the operation, will you?"

"Never," promised the Vice-President.

"Great," said Remo, giving the Vice-President an A-okay sign with his fingers.

When the door shut, the Vice-President looked for a telephone. He'd get help down here so fast those two would never know what happened. But he saw no telephone in the bedroom. Frantically he looked everywhere. In the side tables, by the window, even under the bed. Finally he realized there wasn't one.

Doffing his bathrobe, the Vice-President crawled into the bed and tried to sleep. Come morning, the Secret Service shift would be changed. Then those two would see what they were in for. And Smith would too. National security be damned. Dr. Harold W. Smith had overstepped himself this time and the Vice-President was going to see that man clapped in a federal cell if it was his last official act as Vice-President.

11

Secret Service agent Orrin Snell knew how to read the street.

He was trained to zero in on the subtle details that never registered on the ordinary person. The little things that were out of place or not quite right. A man walking with his hand hovering instead of hanging limp meant that that person carried a sidearm and was prepared to use it. A furtive walk meant a man who feared notice or pursuit. A car moving too slowly could mean anything, but one moving too fast could only mean trouble.

Agent Snell could hear trouble coming four blocks away. He knew it even before his walkie-talkie crackled the message.

"Late-model Ford coming at you at a high rate of speed. Two males in the front, no further description."

"Backup!" Snell barked, dropping into a crouch behind the concrete barriers on the curb. He set his walkie-talkie down at his feet and pulled his revolver, holding it double-handed.

The car squealed to a stop, fishtailing. Its doors banged open and two men in dungaree jackets and colorful *kaffiyehs* masking their faces exploded out of either side. They carried Uzis.

Agent Snell called for them to drop their weapons. That was his mistake.

A hand grenade arched up from one of the attackers' hands and landed behind him, bouncing twice before it detonated.

Snell felt nothing at first. Then there was a crushing noise and his top of his head seemed to squeeze in on itself. When he opened his eyes, he was on his back, his head somehow resting against a concrete barrier so that he was looking down at himself.

His legs resembled twin meatball sandwiches in the torn wrappers of his trousers. The right one was doubled under his thigh. he could not move either leg. He groped for his revolver, but it was nowhere to be found.

At that moment his backups arrived from around the corner. They stopped, took in the sight of agent Snell bleeding on the sidewalk, and their faces registered the shock of what they saw.

Snell tried to shout at them. Don't look at me, you idiots. Get the ones who did this. What's the matter with you? No words came.

Then two figures jumped from behind the barriers and cut both agents down.

The two attackers went for Blair House's massive double doors. They applied a plastic charge to the lock, jumped back, and waited for the explosion.

A mushy whoom came and the doors fell in.

The two terrorists followed the doors inside, their *kaffiyehs* protecting them against the smoke and swirling plaster dust.

On the ground, Orrin Snell tried to find his gun. His hand brushed something. Through pain-racked eyes he saw that it was his walkie-talkie. He fumbled it onto his chest.

"Two men . . . Uzis . . . inside front door. Stop them," he muttered painfully.

Static answered him. And there was no sound of returning fire from inside Blair House.

What was the matter with them? Snell thought dazedly. Why weren't the inner guards responding? Were they all asleep?

"Still asleep," said Remo, peeking into the room.

He rejoined Chiun in the hall. The Master of Sinanju sat on an antique chair. A long scroll lay in his lap.

"What's that you're working on?" Remo asked.

"Nothing," said Chiun absently, shifting in his chair so that Remo could not see what he was writing.

"Looks like one of your histories, but I know you left them all back in Sinanju."

"Correct," said Chiun.

"Then what?"

"It is none of your business."

"If it's not a history scroll, then it's gotta be a contract scroll."

"What makes you say that?"

"The ribbon you untied from it. It's blue. Aren't Sinanju contracts tied with blue ribbons?"

"So are the birth announcements of the offspring of Sinanju Masters."

"Then it's a contract," Remo said.

"Do not be so quick to assume," said the Master of Sinanju.

"You'd deny it if it weren't. Look, Chiun, I hope you're not cooking up some new scheme to keep us in America. I'm telling you right now that it won't work."

"Why not? It worked last time."

"Aha! So you admit last time was a trick?"

"You are just catching on now, Remo my son? You are duller of mind than I thought. Perhaps you need more stimulating work to sharpen your skills. Weeding has made you soft-witted."

"I only did that once. So what are you doing—looking over the last contract for loopholes?"

"I am trying, but the traffic noise is very bad."

"Yeah, I heard the tires screeching too. Teenagers, probably."

From the end of the corridor there came the dull whump of a muffled explosion.

"What was that?" asked Remo, stiffening.

The Master of Sinanju was on his feet, rolling the scroll and tying its ribbon with a complicated two-handed motion. He tossed it onto the chair.

"Intruders," he snapped. "Let us welcome them."

It had worked perfectly so far, thought Rafik. He and Ismat had penetrated Blair House with almost no resistance. As he bounded up the stairs, he could not believe how lax the security was. He and Ismat worked through the ground floor, room to room, reckless and ready to shoot. They found no guards on the ground floor and climbed the stairs to the second floor.

They found someone here.

There were two of them. A casually dressed white man

and an older, almost tiny Oriental. Neither seemed to be armed.

"Look, Little Father," the taller one said conversationally. "Visitors."

"Shall I make tea?" asked the Oriental, just as casually.

"Let's see how many lumps of sugar they want, first."

"I will let you ask them, for I am an old man, frail in health, and I do not wish to tax myself walking down this long corridor to converse with them. Besides, you need the exercise and not I."

Rafik decided to take them alive. They would tell where the American leader could be found and save him valuable search time.

"Stand where you are," Rafik ordered, pointing his weapon. In spite of the warning, the American walked toward him, while the Oriental disappeared through a side door.

"I said stop," Rafik repeated.

"Do we shoot him?" asked Ismat.

"No," hissed Rafik. "He is unarmed. We will take him easily."

"How do you folks like your tea?" asked the American. His smile was cruel, almost arrogant in his wide-cheekboned face.

Rafik decided to shoot him once in the leg. That would cool his bravado. And get him talking. He snapped off a low shot.

A long rip appeared in the hall runner between the man's shoes.

"You missed," Ismat hissed.

"I will not miss again."

And he did not, because even though the white American had been at the other end of the hall, suddenly he was in Rafik's face. It was as if Rafik had been looking at him through a camera and accidentally tripped the zoom lens.

Rafik knew he could not miss at this range. He pulled the trigger. And felt himself being turned in place. When he felt the recoil of the Uzi, he was no longer looking at the dead eyes of the white American but into Ismat's shocked face.

"You . . . shot . . . me," Ismat moaned. He fell to the floor, twitching.

"You made me shoot my comrade," Rafik spat at the white.

"There are worse things," the American said casually. In his hand he had Rakik's own Uzi and was methodically field-stripping it. The trouble was, he obviously did not know how to take apart a fine weapon like the Uzi because he removed whole sections without disengaging them properly. The Uzi made strange cracking sounds and then fell in pieces onto the rug.

Rafik knew that he was no match for hands that could dismember a pistol like that. He plucked a grenade from his belt, pulled the pin with his strong teeth, and yelled the words that usually quashed all resistance during airliner hijackings: "If I die, we will all die!"

Rafik had no intention of dying. He had not let go of the safety spoon. The grenade would not explode until he did. He expected the mere threat of the grenade to trick the man into letting him back out of the building to the car.

But before he could edge away, the man's hands clutched his upraised wrist. The other hand twisted his thumb in its socket. The safety spoon fell to the floor.

Rafik tried to let go of the grenade. He could not. His hand was frozen around it. Then the man slapped him down onto the floor. Rafik fell still clutching the grenade under him.

He tried to push himself up, but the man was standing on his back, holding him on the ground. The grenade dug into his stomach.

Then the grenade went off.

Under Remo's feet, the terrorist jumped. When he settled back on the rug, Remo stepped off the body. The man lay limp, but there was a pool of blood seeping from under him. His body had absorbed the force of the explosion.

The Master of Sinanju stepped out into the hall.

"How many lumps?" he asked.

"None. They're not thirsty," said Remo.

"That one is ruining the rug."

"Not my fault. He pulled a grenade. If I'd handled it any other way, the shrapnel would have ruined the hall, not just the rug."

Chiun approached. "Did he say who hired him?"

"No. He didn't have time."

"Then you bungled. Never dispatch a source of information until the source gives up what he knows."

"Yeah, well, if you're so smart, why didn't you handle it? I'm just along for the scenery this time out."

"I was making tea," Chiun said haughtily.

Jalid Kumquatti waited until Rafik and Ismat went in the front door before he came out of hiding in the car's back seat.

The street was empty of life. He vaulted the antiterrorist barriers and went around the back. There were no guards there. He had not expected to find any. They had all been drawn to the street, where his Hezbollahi brothers had eliminated them.

Jalid had waited long enough. When Rafik and Ismat did not return to the car, he knew that either they had run into trouble or the search for the Vice-President had taken longer than expected. He decided the situation needed his fine hand. He wondered if Rafik and Ismat were dead. If they were, it would mean more money for him.

Jalid went in through a window. He wrapped the tail of his *kaffiyeh* around his eyes to protect them from splintering glass and took a running jump. He went in headfirst. He rolled as he hit the floor and landed on his feet. He sprang for the door.

There was a tiny elevator immediately outside the hall. He leapt for it, and luckily the rickety doors opened when he touched the button. He rode the cage to the top and got out. It would be easier to work his way down, searching for his target, than to fight his way to the upper floors and then back down again.

The third door opened on a room full of sleeping men. Jalid knew they were American Secret Service agents because they wore sunglasses and gray suits even in slumber. He lifted his Kalashnikov assault rifle to spray the room, but on second thought realized that that would be a waste of bullets.

The agents were dead. They had to be. Six of them were stacked on a big canopied bed, their hands and feet dangling off the edges. Others lay about on the floor. There was no mark on any of them, which was odd because neither Rafik nor Ismat had carried any kind of gas. Perhaps, he thought as he closed the door, they had garroted the agents one at a time. Perhaps that was what had been keeping them so long.

Then it was only a matter of time before he would find Rafik and Ismat and their target, the Vice-President.

Jalid burst into the next room. Empty. He went on to the one across the hall. It too was empty. Outside the next room there was an antique chair on which rested a roll of parchment tied by a blue ribbon.

Jalid kicked the door in. The lock gave on the first kick. The room was dark. He swiped his big hands along the inside wall until he encountered a light switch.

The burst of illumination showed a very sleepy man suddenly sitting straight up in bed. Jalid recognized the famous boyishly mature face.

"Who? What?" the Vice-President said sleepily.

Jalid smiled. He would get the credit for this kill after all.

Remo heard the crash of glass. Chiun looked at him.

"There are others," Chiun said. "Quickly, we must protect our charge, who is possibly our next employer."

"Let's go."

Remo dashed for the elevator. He pressed the button. Too late. The cage rattled past their floor without stopping.

"Someone's on the elevator," Remo said.

The Master of Sinanju bounded for the stairs, Remo hot on his heels.

"If we fail, this will be your fault," Chiun said.

"Can it, Chiun. We won't fail."

On the top floor they saw that the Vice-President's bedroom door was open and spilling light into the hall.

From within there came the brief burst of automatic-weapon fire.

"Aaeeie!" Chiun wailed. "We are too late!"

A dungaree-clad man bounced backward out of the room. He slammed against the far wall, momentarily stunned.

Recovering, he leaned into the wall and lifted his Kalashnikov to fire into the bedroom.

He never got off a shot.

A man leapt gracefully out of the bedroom, landed before

him, and, spinning on one foot, sent the other shooting out at shoulder level. The terrorist's head snapped one way, then back the other when the kick reversed itself. The Kalashnikov clattered to the floor.

The terrorist stared stupidly for the space of a heartbeat, then an openhanded thrust snapped his neck. He slid down the wall into an inert heap.

The man who had vanquished the terrorist turned to face Remo and Chiun.

They saw that he was tall, with the broad, tanned face of a California surfer. His green eyes laughed. He wore a white *gi*, such as karate fighters wore, with the traditional black belt around his thick middle.

"Who are you supposed to be?" Remo asked.

"Call me Adonis. It is my official code designation. I am here to protect the Vice-President's life."

"And a great job you did of it, too," said the Vice-President, stumbling out of the bedroom in peppermint pajamas. He looked at Remo and Chiun. "Where were you two when all this was going on?"

"Taking care of the two terrorists who came in the front," Remo said defensively.

"Is that a fact? Well, if this fellow here hadn't crashed in through the window, I'd be dead meat now. The killer had me dead to rights." The Vice-President turned to his rescuer.

"I'd like to shake your hand," he said warmly.

The man called Adonis bowed deeply. When he came up, he shook hands heartily. The Vice-President noticed his broad shoulders and bronzed healthy face. He compared them against Remo's skinny physique and Chiun's diminutive stature.

"Now, this is my idea of a real bodyguard," he said.

"Don't forget we helped too," Remo pointed out. "We got the two downstairs."

"Yeah, right," said the Vice-President, turning his back on them. "That was some fancy footwork you did there, son. What was it—karate?"

"No, kung fu."

The Master of Sinanju spat on the floor.

"Stolen from us," he said.

"Maybe so," said the Vice-President. "But it looks like he improved upon the original."

"A fluke," hissed Chiun. "Why, with my finger, I could render this pretty boy a writhing bag of suet. Look at him. He is fat."

"Looks like muscle to me," said the Vice-President. "Who sent you, my friend?"

"I will tell you later, when there is no one to overhear us," Adonis said, nodding in Remo and Chiun's direction. Remo and Chiun exchanged glances.

"Say the word, Little Father, and I'll settle this guy's hash," Remo growled.

The Vice-President said, "You'll do nothing of the kind. This man has been sent here to guard me. He's proven he can do it. You two get lost. I don't need you anymore."

"We are charged with protecting your person," said the Master of Sinanju, drawing himself up proudly.

"You're through, washed up. You're both has-beens. Tell Smith I said that. And tell him there'll be an investigation of this business. I don't think it's a coincidence that you two immobilized my Secret Service protection just before I was attacked. This whole thing smells like a setup to me. Take out my bodyguards with one hand while you let in the assassins with the other."

The Master of Sinanju puffed out his cheeks in anger.

"He has insulted Sinanju!" he cried. "For that I will—"

Remo got in his way. "No, Little Father. Do you want to make things worse?"

"There, see! The little guy wants to kill me!" the Vice-President said triumphantly. "That's proof."

Adonis stepped in front of the Master of Sinanju. "Do not fear. He will not harm a hair on your head as long as I'm here."

"The final insult," said Chiun, practically jumping up and down. "A kung-fu dancer threatens the Master of Sinanju!"

Remo took Chiun by his frail shoulders.

"Calm down, will you?" he pleaded. "Look, let's just go. We're not wanted here."

"You are not needed here, either," Adonis taunted.

"We'll see about you later," said Remo, guiding Chiun to the elevator.

"Be sure to tuck him in. He looks very old," Adonis called mockingly.

Remo had to use all his strength to get the Master of Sinanju into the elevator. He wondered how he was going to explain this to Smith.

"We are disgraced," said the Master of Sinanju.

"Cut it out, Chiun. I don't want to hear it."

They were walking along Pennsylvania Avenue. Remo found a phone booth near the Treasury Building.

"Hold on," Remo said, slipping into the booth.

The Master of Sinanju looked at him critically. "What are you doing?"

"Reporting to Smith."

Chiun snatched the phone out of Remo's hands and severed the cord with a vicious fingernail slice.

"Chiun!" Remo said.

"Are you mad? Report to Smith!"

"What else do you want me to do? We report to Smith. He tells us what we should do next."

"Tell him! Tell him what?"

"Why, what happened, of course."

"The truth! You are mad. In the history of Sinanju, no Master has ever told the complete truth to an emperor. It is unheard-of."

"You want me to lie?"

"No, but in situations such as this, one must be diplomatic."

"You want me to lie," said Remo, looking for another phone. There was one adjoining the first booth.

"I do not want you to lie," said Chiun. "But I think we should not jump into the truth too swiftly, like a foolish man who wades out into a treacherous surf, unaware of currents and drop-offs."

Remo lifted the receiver. Then he remembered that he didn't have a quarter on him. In fact, he had no money at all. He turned to the Master of Sinanju and instantly dismissed the idea of asking him directly for the quarter.

"Tell you what, Little Father," Remo said solicitously. "You make the call."

"I will. But let us get our story straight before we plunge in."

"Tell him whatever you want," said Remo, handing Chiun the receiver.

"I do not know the stupid codes," said Chiun.

"Make you a deal. You put the quarter in the slot and I'll work the security code."

"Done," said the Master of Sinanju, removing a red wallet from an inside pocket and extracting a quarter from it. He dropped the coin in the slot, holding the receiver tight to one ear while Remo punched the buttons.

Remo always hated the codes. He could never remember them, and since he was no longer an official CURE employee, he no longer tried. The last time he had used the code, it had been a continuous one. Remo pressed the one button and held it down. He asked Chiun, "Have you got him yet? He should be coming on about now."

"No," said the Master of Sinanju. "I am instead listening to some woman claiming to tell me the correct time. She is off by two seconds." Chiun hung up.

"What'd you hang up for? That was Smith."

"Has Smith become a woman?"

"No, the telephone signal goes through the phone system's correct-time service. Smith comes on after the weather."

"He should have come on before the woman."

"Let's try again, shall we?"

"Your quarter this time," said Chiun.

"I'll have to owe it to you," sighed Remo.

"And I will have to charge you interest," countered Chiun, dropping another quarter into the slot. Remo leaned on the one button. After a moment Chiun began to chatter anxiously.

"It is not my fault, Emperor Smith. I tried. Even Remo tried. We could not help what happened. I hope you will keep our past record of success in mind at the next contract signing, for when deciding such important matters it is always wise to keep the total service of a Master of Sinanju in mind."

"What are you telling him?" asked Remo, grabbing the phone. "What happened to breaking the news gently?"

"I am beside myself with worry. Never has such a thing happened."

"Right," said Remo. Into the phone he said, "Hello, Smitty?"

Harold Smith's voice was dead and flat like that of a man speaking from the grave.

"Remo, please don't tell me that the Vice-President is dead."

"No, he's not dead," Remo said.

"How badly is he wounded?"

"He's not."

"Then what was Chiun babbling about?" Smith wanted to know, his voice rising.

"I'll make it short," Remo said. "There was another attack. Middle Easterners again. Chiun and I got two of them, but one got past us."

"Around us," Chiun said loudly enough to be heard three blocks away. "He did not get past us."

"He got to the Vice-President before we could. Then someone else got to him. Some muscle-bound kung-fu clown."

"As fierce a warrior as I have ever before seen," yelled Chiun. "Swift he was, and deadly of hand and eye. Also, he cheated. He climbed in through a window instead of using the front door like a civilized bodyguard."

Remo just looked at Chin blankly. Chiun subsided into silence.

"As I was saying," Remo went on, still looking at Chiun's worried face, "this guy beat us to the punch. He took out the last killer. Claimed he's the Vice-President's new bodyguard, but wouldn't say who sent him until we were out of the room."

"I see," said Smith. "I assume you're calling from Blair House to request an identity check on this new element?"

"Not exactly," said Remo. "We're out on the street. The Vice-President kicked us out."

"Kicked—"

"Yeah, he thought this kung-fu surfer was great shakes. He also thinks we took out his Secret Service protection just so the terrorists could get a clear shot at him. I think he blamed you, Smitty."

"Me?" Smith's voice was sick.

"He was yelling about an investigation, charges. Says we're all washed up."

"Think of plausibility," yelled Chiun. "It is not too late. I will be as your Colonel South. I have many neat ideas."

"What are you babbling about?" asked Remo.

"It is not of your concern, unemployed person," Chiun sniffed.

"What was he talking about, Smitty?" asked Remo. "Who's this Colonel South? The blond guy, Adonis?"

"No. Never mind," Smith sighed.

"What do we do now, Smitty? We were kicked out, but we take our orders from you. Do we go back in and mop up this guy, or what?"

"I think under the circumstances if the attackers have been eliminated, we might leave the Vice-President in the hands of this new person. You say he's competent?"

"He was fast, I'll give him that much."

"But he was fat," said Chiun. "He is not like us, Emperor, mean and lean. We are the sizzling bacon of the Constitution."

Remo glared at Chiun again. "I wish you'd make up your mind," he said.

"I am negotiating the treacherous surf," Chiun whispered. "Try it sometime. You will get less brine in your mouth."

"Right, brine," said Remo.

"Anything else?" asked Smith.

"No," said Remo in a distant voice. Then, suddenly. "Yes. Actually, there is. We found out where the Vice-President learned about CURE. He says he got a letter from someone who knew all about the operation. And about Sinanju too."

"Any identification on this letter writer?"

"The Vice-President had no idea. Said the letter was signed 'Tulip.' "

"A letter," Smith said slowly. Through the receiver came the tapping of computer-terminal keys.

"While you're fiddling with your files," Remo said, "how about we come back? We're as useless as sponge boys in a cathouse down here."

"Speak for yourself, sponge boy," Chiun said haughtily.

"No," said Smith. "Wait, I'm calling up the current whereabouts of Michael Principi."

"He's calling up the current whereabouts of Michael Princippi," Remo told Chiun, who was tugging on Remo's belt, demanding to know what was happening.

"Good," said Chiun firmly. In a softer voice he asked, "Who is that?"

"Chiun wants to know who Michael Princippi is," Remo said into the phone.

"I did not!" snapped Chiun. "Of course I know the famous black American singer."

"I think you're thinking of the wrong Michael. Or the wrong Prince. I'm not sure which," said Remo. "But the name sounds familiar somehow."

"Michael Princippi is the Democratic nominee for President," Smith said. "Surely you remember, Remo. You showed me an article concerning him only this afternoon."

"Oh, yeah," said Remo. "I forgot. Why should we care where that guy is?"

"If the Vice-President's source for his information on CURE is this Tulip, it follows that Princippi may have also received a letter from this man. Princippi has returned to his office in his home state. Fly there immediately. Identify yourself as CURE personnel and politely but firmly ask about any letters he might have received from Tulip. Find out all you can, Remo. If there is a letter, confiscate it. Maybe it will tell us something."

"Gotcha," Remo said. "Anything else, Smitty?"

"Good luck. As of now, CURE is hanging by a thread."

Remo hung up.

"What did he say?" Chiun asked plaintively.

"He said CURE is hanging by a thread."

"Then let us be as flashing needles, moving swiftly to strengthen that thread," Chiun said, fluttering his fingernails dangerously.

"I thought we were negotiating a treacherous surf."

"That was earlier," said Chiun. "You should stay current."

"I'd settle for staying sane," said Remo, rolling his eyes to the heavens.

13

Michael Princippi liked to consider himself a common man.

During his two terms as governor, he had disdained the trappings of high office. Every day, he faithfully took the trolley to work. When he did have to drive, he used his wife's 1979 station wagon. His office in the State House was furnished with government issue. His campaign literature emphasized his frugal and levelheaded approach to government and characterized him as the son of simple immigrants who just happened to rise to the highest office in his state, and who felt that the highest office in the land was not above his reach.

Those who knew him well knew that Michael Princippi's "frugality" was a nice way of saying the guy was cheap. He was so levelheaded he put fund-raising audiences to sleep, and while he was indeed the son of simple immigrants, he always forgot to mention that his simple parents arrived in America very, very wealthy.

His advisers tried to convince Governor Princippi that his everyman approach was fine for state politics, but ineffective for someone with his eyes on the Oval Office. It wasn't presidential to drive a junkbox, eat lunch out of a brown bag, or to continue to live on a shabbily genteel street where parking spaces were secured by leaving an empty trashcan out by the curb. But Michael Princippi was stubborn. He did not believe in perks or privileges. He would not budge.

Not even when the federal government had insisted on assigning a Secret Service detail to watch over him after he had captured the Democratic nomination for President.

"No way," he had said.

"It's for your protection, sir."

"I appreciate that. But I have state troopers who guard my office. I stopped taking the trolley. You know it costs me almost double? Gas isn't cheap. But I don't need extra protection. I'm the Prince of Politics. The people love me.''

The Secret Service had been adamant. But so was Governor Michael Principi. He won.

As a consequence, when he walked into his office at 6:27 A.M., he was alone. Not even his secretary was at her reception desk.

Governor Principi dropped behind his desk and picked through his latest position papers. With the polls showing the two presidential aspirants virtually neck-and-neck, it was all going to come down to the big election-eve debate in a few days, and Michael Principi was not going to lose the election because he was not up on the issues.

Governor Principi had no time to react to the knock at his heavy office door. The door opened before he could say ''come in.''

He felt a very brief stab of regret about turning down Secret Service protection, but it went away when he saw that the persons entering were obviously no threat to him.

Standing in the doorway was a tall man and a shorter, older Oriental. The man was obviously unarmed and the Oriental was ancient.

''How did you two get in?'' Michael Principi asked pointedly.

''We walked in,'' the tall man informed him.

''I mean into the State House, not this office. There are guards.''

''Pah!'' said the Oriental. ''You call those guards? They are not guards. They did not notice us entering. We are guards. Also assassins.''

''What!'' Governor Principi's busy eyebrows jumped in surprise.

''He didn't mean it like that. Sit down, Mr. Governor. I'm Remo. This is Chiun. Smith sent us.''

''Smith? Oh, that Smith.''

''Yeah, we're with CURE. You do know about CURE, don't you?''

''Perhaps,'' said Michael Principi guardedly. ''If you are who you say you are, you'll have identification on you.''

Remo and Chiun exchanged glances.

''Actually, no,'' Remo admitted.

"No identification? What kind of an organization does not provide its agents with identification?"

Chiun raised a wise finger. "A secret organization," he said.

"The organization isn't supposed to exist, remember?" Remo said. "Or didn't Tulip mention that part?"

"He might have," Governor Princippi said, rolling a pencil between his fingers. "But how do I know that you are who you say you are?"

"Look," said Remo. "Before this mess, we never walked in and identified ourselves like this. We just sort of slid in and out. I used to carry all sorts of fake ID, but technically I'm retired from CURE."

"I would show you my American Express Gold Card," said Chiun, "but, alas, it was taken from me."

"I see," said Governor Princippi slowly.

"You could call Smith," Remo suggested. "He'll vouch for us."

"And how would I know I was talking to this Smith? I've never met him. I don't know his voice."

"He has a point, Little Father," Remo told the Master of Sinanju.

"There are other ways of identifying oneself," Chiun snapped. "Is that an orange sitting on your desk?" he asked Governor Principi.

"Yes. My breakfast."

"You have heard of Sinanju. The letter told you that much?"

"Possibly."

"Then be so good as to toss the orange to me."

Michael Princippi shrugged. What did he have to lose? He flipped the orange with an underhand toss.

It landed, spinning, on the tip of the Oriental's raised index finger. The Oriental dipped his hand and the orange shifted on its axis. In a twinkling, the orange blurred.

Something flashed across the room and plopped onto the governor's government-issue desk. Michael Princippi looked. It was an orange peel as long as his arm. He picked it up. It hung in one piece, a corkscrew of orange peel.

When he looked up, the orange was still spinning on the Oriental's fingertip. It was without its skin.

"Here," said the one called Chiun.

Michael Princippi caught the tossed orange. He examined it. The translucent inner skin was unbroken.

"Satisfied?" Remo asked.

"A nice trick," Governor Princippi admitted. "But hardly proof of anything."

"Have you any enemies?" asked Chiun politely.

"Every politician has enemies."

"Merely choose one and we will dispatch him as my ancestors once slew the infidels of ancient Persia."

"Slay?"

"Consider it an offering toward future employment, should you assume the throne of this fine nation."

"He doesn't mean that, either," Remo said hastily. "This isn't how you negotiate with rulers in this country, Little Father."

"Hush, Remo. I know how to deal with rulers."

"If there is something specific I can do for you, be good enough to state it plainly," said Governor Princippi. "I am very busy."

"We'd like to see the letter Tulip sent you."

"Out of the question."

"Why?"

"I do not share my personal correspondence with others. Especially people who don't carry identification."

"Then you still have it?" suggested Chiun.

Michael Princippi hesitated. His eyes darted to his open briefcase. "Possibly," he said.

"That is all we need to know," said Chiun. "Come, Remo."

"Wait a minute, Little Father, We're not done here."

"I think you are," said Michael Princippi.

"Listen to the man, your possible future employer," Chiun told Remo as he tugged him toward the door. He paused to speak parting words to the governor. "We are going now. May you have much success in your quest for power, and always remember, a good assassin is the true power behind the throne. And among good assassins the name of Sinanju rises above all the others."

"It's not like it sounds," said Remo, closing the door. "We're really nice people. Smith too. Please keep that in mind, just in case."

"Come, Remo," said Chiun.

Remo closed the door after him.

Out in the corridor, Remo stopped the Master of Sinanju.

"Why'd you yank me out of there like that? Smith wants that letter. You could have at least let me keep talking."

"A waste of time," said the Master of Sinanju. "I know where the letter is."

"You do?"

"I am constantly surprised by your astonishment over my amazing powers," said Chiun.

"Huh?"

"Never mind," said Chiun. "You have just solved that riddle for me. I will explain. Did you notice that man's eyes when I asked him if he still had the letter?"

"Not particularly."

"They sought his briefcase. The letter is in that."

"That doesn't put it in our hands."

"No, but it makes our task easier. We will steal the letter."

"Is that a good idea?" Remo asked.

"Success is always a good idea. We will wait until nightfall. Then we will return and rescue the letter for Smith."

"If you say so, Little Father," said Remo as they walked out the front of the State House. State troopers regarded them curiously. "But what do we do in the meantime?"

"We will find a quiet place to sit," said Chiun, extracting the blue-ribboned parchment scroll from inside his coat. "I have an important matter to attend to."

"Want help?" asked Remo, looking at the scroll with a puzzled expression.

"Yes," said Chiun, spotting an empty bench in front of the building. "You can shoo the pigeons away so that I may concentrate."

"That wasn't exactly what I had in mind."

"How can you tell?" cackled Chiun as he settled onto the bench. "Its emptiness is so vast. Heh, heh. Its emptiness is so vast. Heh heh."

14

Antonio Serrano thought he was big-time.

He ruled Trenton Street. He had ruled it since his fifteenth birthday, last December 17. He hoped to rule it when he turned sixteen. Beyond that, who knew? On Trenton Street, even the rulers did not make it much past sixteen, not without moving from the neighborhood.

Antonio Serrano could have moved. He made over one thousand dollars a week. He drove a green Cadillac convertible that cornered liked a parade float. He had plenty of girls. Good-looking girls with plenty of blue eye shadow and tight skirts they bought at the Eastie Mall. He could have lived anywhere. But Antonio had grown up on this street. He would be lost without this street. This was Eastie Goombah territory and Antonio Serrano was the head of the Eastie Goombahs.

Antonio Serrano started off boosting stereos from cars. He had moved up to the big time, dealing crack. That was where the money was. He sold it himself, on street corners and in the school playgrounds, and if there was trouble he had the Goombahs to back him up. The Goombahs got their cut. They also were the ones who got cut when the crap started flying.

Antonio had gotten cut in the old days when he was new to the Eastie Goombahs. That was a long time ago, back in 1986. Antonio had gotten tired of being a grunt and stepped into the leadership position of the Goombahs when the old leader, Alphonse Tedesco, had his stomach ripped open by a gang of blacks from the South End. Alphonse was history. Hell, he had been an old man, practically. He was nearly nineteen when he died.

There was a time when being an Eastie gang member meant hanging around street corners, hustling protection money from people walking through the neighborhood, and carrying a switch blade or, at best, a zip gun. Antonio Serrano had seen an old movie on TV once, which showed how it had been. It made him laugh. Why, compared to those dinks, he was the modern man and they were Neanderthals. He carried a chrome-plated Colt Python revolver. When he needed more muscle, he dug a semiautomatic Uzi machine pistol out from under the seat cushions of his Caddy.

Still, he wasn't as evolved as he'd like to think. Standing on street corners extorting protection money was one Eastie tradition that Antonio would not allow to die.

Antonio lounged at the corner of Trenton and Marion streets, picking at his orange mesh shirt, a silver crucifix hanging from one ear. He was unhappy. Only old ladies passed him on the street, carrying groceries from Tony's Spa. Old ladies never carried much money and they were too much trouble to rob. Besides, most of them knew him by sight.

He gave some thought to sticking up Tony's Spa, just for kicks, but Tony had been robbed so many times that he was talking about moving to the North Shore, away from inner-city crime. Antonio decided it wasn't worth whatever was in the till to risk losing the only convenience store in the neighborhood and went back to picking at his shirt. For some reason, he felt itchy tonight.

A little black foreign car slid around the corner in Antonio's direction, moving slowly.

Antonio watched it curiously, wondering if he was about to be hit. People were always looking to take his action, small as it was in the billion-dollar drug trade. But the car was too wimpy. No self-respecting wise guy would drive a little foreign jobbie like that. Besides, it had Maine license plates. As far as Antonio knew, there was no such thing as the Mafia up in Maine. Wherever that was. He had heard it was someplace north. Or was he thinking of Canada?

The car rolled to a stop down the street and Antonio reached down the front of his jeans, where he kept his Colt. He thought it was macho to wear it there. Also the barrel bulged up his crotch something fierce. The chicks really dug that.

The man stepping out of the car had the weirdest eyes

Antonio had ever seen. They were blue. Like neon. They fixed on Antonio like he was some kind of bug. The man wore casual clothes.

Antonio pulled out his weapon. The blond man did not flinch or run, or do any of the usual things people did when they stared down the barrel of Antonio's gun. In fact, the man acted as if Antonio was holding a water pistol on him.

"I'll bet that gun is hot," the man said in a quiet, reasonable voice.

"Hey, I paid good money for this piece," Antonio said. "I don't have to steal. I make a grand a week."

"I didn't mean stolen," the man said, moving toward him. "I meant hot. As in red-hot."

Antonio wrinkled his forehead. "Get real, man," he said.

But then the grip felt warm, the way a coffee cup is warm when you first take it in your hands. It grew warmer, the way a coffee cup feels when it's full of piping-hot coffee and you forget to grab it by the handle.

"Ouch!" howled Antonio Serrano. His prize pistol fell into the gutter.

The blue-eyed man got to the gun before he did. He picked it up, broke open the cylinder, and emptied the chambers into his hands. Tucking the Colt under one armpit, he calmly twisted the tips off the bullets and shook out the gray gunpowder like a man using a salt shaker.

"What the fuck is going on?" Antonio Serrano asked when the man offered the useless weapon back.

"Don't be afraid to touch it," the man said. "It won't bite you."

Antonio reached out tentatively. He touched the barrel. It felt cool, like metal is supposed to feel. He yanked the gun back, but without bullets it was useless. Still, it felt good in his hand.

"What's your problem, pal?" Antonio demanded, pointing the Colt out of habit.

"I knew if I cruised this neighborhood long enough I would find someone like you."

"Congratulations. I don't give fucking autographs."

"You run with a gang?"

"I lead the gang," Antonio boasted. "The Eastie Goombahs. You musta heard of us. Even the cops are scared of us."

"Even the cops," repeated the blue-eyed man. "Did I mention my name?"

"Screw your name."

"Tulip. Call me Tulip. I like the way you carry yourself."

"Hey, keep that faggy stuff to yourself."

"Don't be crude. I'd like to hire you."

"I'm self-employed, jack."

"So I gathered. A thousand dollars a week, isn't that what you said?"

"Yeah."

"That would make fifty-two thousand dollars a year, assuming you don't take vacations."

"I wouldn't know a fucking vacation if it sat on my face."

"No doubt," said Tulip. "How would you like to make, say, twice your yearly income—one hundred thousand dollars—for a few days' work?"

"Twice fifty-two thousand dollars is one hundred and four thousand dollars. You trying to cheat me? Or maybe you think because I never got past sixth grade, I'm stupid or something."

"No, I don't think you're stupid or something," said the man who called himself Tulip.

"Because you don't pull down the bucks I do unless you can count. Counting's important. Once I had my multiplication fucking tables down, I was set for life. That was my education. I got the rest on the streets."

"I want you to kill two men for me."

Antonio looked interested. "Yeah, who?"

"The Vice-President of the United States is one of them."

"Pass. I heard the Iranians or somebody like that are already working on it."

"They failed. I have a suitcase full of money that they would have claimed had they succeeded."

In spite of himself, Antonio Serrano was impressed. This guy was talking about dusting the Vice-President of the fucking United States. Antonio Serrano had never even left the state.

"You serious, man?"

"What do you think?" asked Tulip.

"You mentioned another guy."

"Governor Michael Princippi."

"Isn't he running for President too?"

"Yes, are you interested?"

"I don't know, man. Drugs are my line. Breaking heads, too. I killed guys before, sure. But only over turf or bucks."

"Work for me. You will make money. What is the difference between killing for territory or killing directly for money?"

"I don't know. Killing for money doesn't have much of a purpose. I gotta have more. Yeah, I gotta have purpose."

Tulip looked around. "This is your turf?"

"Me and the Goombahs own it."

"I doubt that," said Tulip.

"Well, we don't own it exactly. We control it, though. Nobody comes here unless we let him."

"I'm here," said Tulip, smiling thinly.

"All I gotta do is whistle and the Goombahs'll be all over you like bugs on a barbecue."

"I'll take your word for it. Why do you fight for this street?"

Antonio Serrano thought. He shrugged. "For power, prestige, and . . ."

"Money?"

"That's what it all comes down to, sure. I'll give you that."

"Work for me and the money will be bigger and quicker."

"Nah, that's like Mafia stuff, man. If I wanted to join the Mafia, I'd have done that a long time ago. Not me. No way. You think I'm going to work my ass off and turn over half my score to some old Italian guy? That's stupid. I'm not stupid."

"Try it. I will give you one hundred and four thousand dollars for the governor. If it works out, I'm prepared to offer double that amount for the Vice-President."

"I don't know," Antonio Serrano said slowly.

"You don't have to kill anyone yourself. You have men. Send them. Pay them whatever you wish out of the money I offer and keep the rest."

Antonio considered. Whenever he thought, his bushy eyebrows grew together into one long eyebrow. He scratched it absently.

"I don't know. I don't think my guys can handle this kind

of action by themselves. I might have to go with them. You know, to keep them on target. They're not smart like me.''

"It will be easy. The governor does not like guards. He has no Secret Service protection. What have you got to lose, my friend?''

"How do I know you'll give me the money afterward?''

"I have the money in my car. I will show it to you. Then we will go to a bus terminal and put it in a locker. We will mail the locker key to your home address immediately after.''

"Hey, then all I gotta do is wait for the mail. What do I need to kill anybody for?''

"You will not do that.''

"Why not?'' Antonio asked.

"Because after you give me your address, I will know where you live,'' said Tulip.

"I could move.''

"Not you. No one making your kind of money would live here because he liked it. This street is all you know. You were born here and you will die here. Besides, wherever you hid, I would find you.'' And to drive the point home, Tulip jammed his finger into the muzzle of Antonio's pointing pistol. The barrel split along its entire length.

"You got something there,'' admitted Antonio Serrano, examining his ruined Colt.

"It is a deal, then?''

"The governor, sure I can do the governor. He probably doesn't even pack a piece.''

"Fine. Let me show you the money and we will go to the bus station. After that, you will have forty-eight hours to complete this job.''

"One other thing,'' said Antonio Serrano as they walked to Tulip's car.

"Yes?''

"The governor. After I kill him, is it okay with you if I lift his wallet too?''

15

The Eastie Goombahs listened to their leader's unusual proposition. When he had finished explaining his plan to assassinate the governor of the state, they considered their role for all of five seconds, nearly twice their normal attention span.

"No way!" said Carmine Musto, who saw himself as the next head Goombah, and decided that today was as good a day as any to take over. After all, he was nearly fifteen himself.

"You other guys?" asked Antonio Serrano, surveying the semicircle of his followers. He stood in the middle of his living room. The Eastie Goombahs, all of thirteen strong, lounged on his genuine zebraskin furniture, passing a roach from hand to hand.

"What's in it for us?" asked another.

"Prestige," said Antonio Serrano.

"What's that?"

"It's the same as recognition, only different," someone told him.

"Whacking the governor will make us big," said Antonio.

"Will it make us rich?" asked Carmine, who breathed through his mouth because his nostrils were hypersensitized from snorting coke all day. His eyes had that too-bright sheen that makes an addict look alert.

"Believe it."

"How?"

"Trust me. I got a plan. But we gotta pull this off first," promised Antonio cagily. He didn't want the others to know about the money that Tulip pussy had offered him.

"Who's paying you for this?" asked Carmine.

"Whatcha mean?" asked Antonio with an injured look.

He avoided Carmine's beady eyes. The dickhead, he thought. He's getting too smart.

"I mean," said Carmine coolly, "you ain't come up with this brainstorm yourself. Someone's paying you, right? How much?"

"Yeah, how much?" the others chorused.

"Fifty thousand," lied Antonio. "I was planning on splitting with you jerks."

"Fifty!" snorted Carmine. "Shit, man, you been took good. Wise guys get six figures."

"Okay, I got six figures," Antonio admitted, because being caught in a lie was normal, but looking stupid was dangerous. "One hundred thousand he's paying me."

"Oh, wow," Carmine mocked. "One hundred thousand. Split thirteen ways that's maybe two month's pay for most of us—chump change. You want us to hit the frigging governor for chump change?"

"Anybody who doesn't want a piece of this can walk. Right now," said Antonio hotly. "Go on, get outta my crib."

Carmine Musto got to his feet resolutely. "I'm booking. Who's with me?"

A few feet shuffled aimlessly.

"Come on," said Carmine. "Let's get with it."

"The more guys walk," said Antonio, "the more money that's left for the rest of us."

"Chump change." Carmine sneered.

"What's the split?" asked a younger member.

Antonio frowned. He was in a corner. If he came in too low, he'd end up doing a solo. But if he came in too high, he'd be taking big risks for chump change, just like Carmine said.

What decided him was the wary looks on the faces of the Eastie Goombahs.

"One hundred grand split equally," he said reluctantly.

Carmine Musto spit on the tigerskin rug on his way out. "Catch you later, dickhead," he said. Most of the others followed him. Four were left, including himself.

"Twenty-five grand apiece," said Antonio broadly, trying to make the best of a bad situation. It was a good thing he had kept his mouth shut about that extra four thousand— not to mention the governor's wallet.

The plan, as Antonio had explained it to his followers, was simple. They'd drive over to the governor's house, which was on the other side of the city, and bust in shooting. It would be easy. It was true the money was short, as far as this kind of work went, but it would be quick work and there would be more of it. The Eastie Goombahs were going to be famous.

The first hitch in the plan revealed itself to Antonio Serrano when he led his men out onto the street. His green Caddy wasn't there.

"Carmine," said Antonio. "That ratass stole my wheels."

"We can steal another car," one of the others ventured.

"From where? This is our neighborhood. We don't shit where we eat, haven't I told you guys that a million times?"

"What, then?"

"We take the subway. It goes out to the governor's neighborhood."

Their Uzis and pistols in gym bags, Antonio Serrano led the Eastie Goombahs to the subway, and they rode into town. They changed to the surface trolley and settled down for the ride.

The trolley took the Eastie Goombahs through a world they barely knew existed. Only a few miles from their dirty environment there was a place of clean streets and elm-drapped parks. The people on the trolleys dressed neat and looked confident. There were none of the graffiti that marred their own neighborhood subway stops.

"This is weird," said Johnny Fortunato, the youngest Goombah. "Look how clean everything is."

"Shut up," said Antonio. But the kid was right. It was nice out here in the governor's neighborhood. Even the air smelled nice, like they had giant Air Wicks hidden out of sight. Antonio decided that when he made it big, really big, he'd move out here to a nice house. Maybe the place next to the governor's house. Then he remembered. After tonight, the governor would be dead.

Hell, maybe he'd buy the governor's house. Or better yet, figure out a way to steal it. Was it possible to steal a house? Antonio didn't know. But he would look into it.

* * *

"Here he comes, Little Father," Remo said.

"Good," said the Master of Sinanju, rolling up the scroll he had been working on. They were seated in the back of a Lincoln Continental parked in the garage under the State House.

"He's got the briefcase with him," Remo said. "What's your plan?"

"We take it from him."

"Yeah, right. I got that much figured out. I'm asking how."

As they watched, the governor sauntered over to a car that, hours before, when they had searched the garage looking for the governor's vehicle, Remo had instantly dismissed as a candidate.

"He's getting into that beat-up station wagon," Remo said, peering up from the back seat of the Lincoln.

"I thought you said that it would be this car."

"I figured it was. It's the biggest, most expensive one in the whole freaking lot. It's got state plates and everything."

The Master of Sinanju folded his arms angrily. "My great plan is ruined, thanks to your ignorance."

"Tell me about it on the way," said Remo, jumping into the front seat. He slid behind the wheel, broke the ignition off the steering post, and quickly hot-wired the car. The engine roared into life.

"You have done your part," said Chiun, climbing over the headrest. "Now I will drive."

"Nothing doing," said Remo, sending the car wheeling after the governor's station wagon. "I don't have a death wish."

"You are just jealous of my driving skill," said the Master of Sinanju, settling into the passenger side.

"I admit it. You're a brilliant driver. You can make a car do stunts it was never engineered for. Except for minor stuff like staying on the road and stopping for lights and pedestrians. Now, will you settle down? I have to concentrate if I'm going to stay with this guy."

"It is too late. My plan is ruined."

"Maybe if you'd tell me about it, I can salvage something," Remo suggested.

"Very well. But only because recovering that letter is important to Emperor Smith. My plan was simple, but do not confuse its simplicity with ease of execution. It was brilliant but complicated.''

"Just get to it, huh?''

"Unappreciative philistine! I had us hide in the back of this conveyance—which you swore belonged to the governor of this province—so that when he got into the front seat he would, as so many of his type do, throw the briefcase into the back seat.''

"Yeah?''

"Directly into our hands,'' said Chiun triumphantly.

"Okay,'' Remo said slowly.

"Yes!'' said Chiun.

"I got that part. What's the rest?''

"What rest? That was it. Once we had the briefcase, we would be in possession of the letter.''

"Yeah,'' said Remo, stopping for a red light. "But we would have been stuck in the back seat while the governor drove home—or whatever he was doing.''

"So? Once he arrived, we would only have had to wait until he left his vehicle, leaving us with the briefcase.''

"But, Little Father, don't you think that when he reached into the back seat he would have noticed us huddling on the floorboards?''

"Of course not. We are Sinanju. We are trained not to be seen. We are the fog that steals through the woods, the shadow that is cast by no body. Of course he would not have seen us.''

"He would have seen us, Little Father. He would have to be blind not to.''

"He probably is. Only a blind man would own a decrepit vehicle such as that man drives.''

"Maybe.''

"And you are only arguing with me to cover up your ruining of my brilliantly complicated plan.''

"I am not arguing,'' said Remo. The light changed. Remo pulled behind the governor's station wagon as they left the city and found themselves wending through tree-lined residential streets. "And how was I to know he drove a junkbox?''

"You should have known. You were born American. I am still new to these shores.''

"Two decades in America is not new," Remo pointed out.

"Another decade and I will not be new. Why are we stopping here?"

"I think the governor is home," said Remo.

The Master of Sinanju looked up and down the street. Clapboard triple-decker houses crowded tiny lawns covered by riotous autumn leaves.

"Where is his castle?" demanded Chiun.

Remo watched the governor step from his car and up a flagstone walk. He disappeared into a gabled Victorian home.

"That must be it."

"The governor of a whole province," squeaked Chiun. "And he lives there? No, Remo, that cannot be. This man wields the power of life and death over his subjects. He would not live among them like a commoner. No, this must be the dwelling of one of his many concubines. Yes, it is a concubine's house. I am certain of this."

"Well, whatever it is, Little Father," Remo said slowly, "he's inside with the briefcase and we're out here. What are we going to do?"

"We must have that letter," Chiun decided. "We will wait. When the lights go out, we will steal within, cat-footed as ghosts, and—"

"Don't you mean cat-footed as cats?"

"No, ghosts. Cats make noises. We will make none. We are Sinanju."

"Yeah, right," said Remo, who didn't like the idea of waiting for another couple of hours or whatever for the governor to drop off. "We are the wind in the trees."

"The unseen wind," corrected Chiun.

"Yeah, unseen. Wake me up when the lights go out."

Remo dozed off instantly. Chiun's tapping finger seemed to touch his shoulder only seconds later. Remo came awake, every sense alert.

"How long was I out?" he asked, looking around.

"I am not certain. Six, possibly seven minutes."

"Minutes!"

"The governor is obviously a tired man," said Chiun, pointing. Remo saw that the house had gone dark.

"Okay, let's go."

They got out of the car, closed the doors quietly, and approached the house. Remo found a back door that looked like an old servants' entrance and probably led into the kitchen.

Remo set himself against the door and placed one palm over the outside of the lock. He pressed, and kept on pressing. Remo could have shattered the lock with a sharp blow, but he needed to avoid the sound of snapping metal or splintering wood. So he simply exerted a quiet, relentless pressure.

The lock surrendered like a rotted tooth pulled from its socket.

Remo stepped in, his eyes adjusting to the webby darkness of a kitchen that had last been tiled when Eisenhower was in office.

"Let's hope the governor doesn't sleep with his briefcase under his pillow," Remo whispered.

Chiun followed Remo into a frumpy parlor decorated in Danish Modern. Yellowing dollies decorated every flat surface.

"Nothing," said Chiun, looking around. "Fie upon it."

Remo searched the other rooms without success.

"It's gotta be upstairs," he decided. "I don't like this."

"We will be the wind," said Chiun encouragingly.

"We will be in trouble if the governor catches us. He'll howl all the way up to the White House."

"So?" said Chiun. "The President will receive his complaint with thanks and protestations of innocence and then he will order Smith to terminate this troublemaking governor."

"No way," said Remo. "There'll be a scandal. Heads will roll. The President's, Smith's, and probably ours."

"Be extra cautious, Remo," Chiun said. "We do not wish to awaken this important personage."

"Right," said Remo, starting to climb a curving staircase.

The governor's bedroom door was closed. Inside, Remo heard the quiet breathing of two persons deep in sleep, the governor and his wife. Remo and Chiun exchanged knowing glances in the darkness. They split up and checked the other rooms.

When they rendezvoused outside the governor's bedroom, Remo shook his head and Chiun showed empty hands.

Remo shrugged, and signaled Chiun to wait outside. Chiun mouthed two words silently: the wind.

Remo rolled his eyes after he turned his back on the Master of Sinanju and eased the bedroom door ajar. He slipped in. The briefcase was a blob in the darkness. It stood on a nightstand beside the governor's sleeping head.

Remo took it in his hand. He paused in mid-step, wondering if he should take it downstairs and open it there, or take a chance and open it here. He decided that opening it downstairs was just as risky as opening it here. It was important that Governor Principi not suspect that his briefcase had been rifled, although when he later found the letter was missing, he was certain to suspect the truth because Remo had shown interest in it earlier in the day.

Remo set the briefcase down on the floor. It was one of the combination-lock types, requiring that three sets of numbers line up.

Remo was about to start on the combination when he realized that the governor probably didn't bother to lock his briefcase in the privacy of his own home. Which could mean that the combination was already set to the correct number sequence.

Remo tried the unlocking latch. It flipped up.

Grinning in the darkness, Remo went through the briefcase. He found an envelope. Inside was a letter. He saw the signature "Tulip" at the bottom and silently congratulated himself.

Shutting the briefcase, Remo restored it to the nightstand exactly as it had been. He had no sooner let go of the handle than, down on the first floor, there came the heart-stopping sound of automatic-weapons fire.

The governor shot bolt upright in bed and, with Remo frozen not five inches away from his face, went for the bedside lamp.

16

Antonio Serrano and his Eastie Goombahs had gotten off at the trolley stop nearest the governor's house and walked the streets until they found it. Even though neither Antonio nor any of his Goombahs had ever been in this suburb, the governor's house was easy to locate. It had been shown on television often during the campaign as proof that the governor had not lost his common touch, because he was still living in the modest brick home he purchased when he was first married.

"Hey, look," Antonio said. "This is a break."

"What is it?" asked Johnny Fortunato.

They were in the side yard, where they extracted their weapons from nylon gym bags.

"The fool left the kitchen door open. We can just walk right in."

"Then let's go."

They went in.

"Shit!" cursed Antonio, tripping over a wooden chair. He almost overturned a round kitchen table in the process.

"Shhhh," someone said. "You wanna wake him up?"

"Anybody bring a flashlight?" gasped Antonio, clutching his injured knee.

No one had. "Okay, be more careful now," said Antonio, limping into the next room.

"You're the one who tripped," Johnny complained.

"Shhh!"

Antonio bumped into more furniture. This time it was some kind of soft chair. He was glad for that because his knee wouldn't take another hit. He wished he had brought a flashlight.

A faint breath of air swept past him, like the backwash

of a thrown baseball. The hair on his forearms lifted in warning.

"Hey, did you guys feel that?"

"Feel what? What about you, Johnny? Johnny?"

"Oh, shit, I think Johnny booked."

In the darkness, Antonio turned back. A shadow stood before him. A very short shadow. That had to be Johnny, the shortest one in the group.

"No, he's right beside me," said Antonio. "I see him."

But then the one they thought was Johnny raised his hands and there was something wrong about them. Even in the darkness Antonio saw that they were abnormally long, like claws. Vampire claws.

"Johnny?" whispered Antonio.

The claws swept down, and another shadow—a larger one—fell to the floor. The thump was soft, but the vibration in the floor was very, very solid.

"Shit, you're not Johnny," Antonio hissed, and raised his Uzi. "But you're dead, sucker!"

The governor's bedroom light snapped on.

And snapped off again. Remo smashed it against a wall. There was no time for subtlety. He had to get out of the house with the letter before the governor recognized him.

"What is it? What is it, dear?" a woman's thin voice called.

"Call the police," said Governor Princippi, jumping out of bed. "There's someone in the room."

Remo shot out of the door and, after closing it behind him, mangled a door hinge with his fingers. That would slow him down, Remo thought.

Chiun wasn't on the landing, but Remo hadn't expected him to be. The sound of gunfire below meant that someone else had broken in. No one could have entered the first floor without the Master of Sinanju's keen hearing picking it up.

Remo skipped the stairs. He jumped from the second-floor landing to the parlor in a floating leap.

"Chiun, you okay?"

Above, he could hear the governor repeatedly smashing a shoulder into the jammed bedroom door.

Remo spotted the Master of Sinanju in the middle of a clot of armed individuals. He did not respond to Remo's call. He was slipping between the gunmen, teasing them into wasting their bullets. Remo saw him tap one on the back, and when the man whirled, legs apart and hands up in a two-handed pistol grip, the Master of Sinanju ducked between his legs and came up behind him, where he tapped again. The man, frantic, was firing blindly.

"Chiun, cut out the horseplay!" Remo hissed. "We've got to get out of here. I got the letter. Let's go."

"Hush!" Chiun hissed back. "The wind does not speak its name."

"Then let me help you," said Remo, moving in on one of the gunmen.

Then the upstairs bedroom door slammed open. The governor came pounding down the stairs, flashing a jerky ray of light in all directions.

"Oh, great," groaned Remo.

"Who's there?" the governor demanded, snapping on a light at the bottom of the stairs.

There was nothing Remo could do but make the best of a bad situation. As light flooded the parlor, Remo stuffed the letter under his T-shirt. Maybe he could get away with that much, if nothing else.

The light hit Antonio Serrano's eyes like needles. He blinked stupidly, sweeping the room with his Uzi.

Through spots of light he made out the figure of the governor, in an old flannel bathrobe, pointing a flashlight at a faggy-looking guy at the bottom of the stairs. Antonio had a clean shot at both men. He decided the faggy-looking guy would be an easy kill. So he aimed for the governor and squeezed the trigger.

The Uzi burped a short burst, no more than three rounds. They buried themselves in the rug at Antonio's feet. One of them mangled his little toe.

Antonio, still trying to blink the spots out of his eyes, couldn't understand it. He had dropped the gun. He had only begun to pull the trigger and—dumb shit that he was—dropped the gun. That had never happened to him before. Ripping out a curse under his breath, he reached down to pick up his Uzi.

But a strange thing happened. He could not pick up the gun. It was as if his fingers had lost all feeling. And the spots in his eyes wouldn't go away. In fact, the room was going dimmer all the time.

Then Antonio saw why he was unable to pick up his weapon. He *was* grasping it. He saw very clearly, just before everything got truly weird, that his hand was wrapped around the butt of the Uzi. But when he straightened up, the gun stayed on the floor, still tightly clasped. Antonio saw that his lifted wrist ended very suddenly, very cleanly. The hand might have been taken off by a bone saw, it was so neatly done. The blood fountained in spurts, and as Antonio felt his heart beating faster, the blood spurted faster. Funny how that worked.

When Antonio turned to show the other Goombahs how his wrist was spurting, he saw a man shrouded in black staring at him, a long sword raised parallel to his shoulders. He did not see the stroke. He saw the room tumbling around him and in his last moment of conscious thought he saw himself standing, a raw cross section of meat where his neck ended. Funny how he was still standing up even though he had no head. . . .

Remo turned from the governor. The kid with the Uzi was about to fire. Remo moved in on him. Suddenly a figure swathed in black jumped out from behind a dividing screen. The swordsman swept down with his blade, severing the kid's gun hand. The sword swung back upward, then took off the kid's head. Swick swack, just like that. The headless body of the kid stood like a ruined statue for several heartbeats, then crumpled into a bag of dead flesh. The head landed in the crook of one dead arm, so that it looked as if the kid had died carrying his head under one arm. The sight would have been comical had it not been so ghoulish.

"Who are you supposed to be?" Remo asked of the man in black.

"I could ask the same of you," the man said coolly. His face was hidden, except for a swatch around the eyes, by the traditional black hood of the ninja warriors of Japan.

"I'm asking it of both of you," said Governor Princippi, stepping off the stairs. He looked closer. "Oh," he said, recognizing Remo. "What are you doing here?"

"Uh, we heard about an attempt on your life," Remo

said, trying to keep a straight face. "Looks like we got here just in time."

"Is that right?" the governor asked the man in ninja black. "Are you with this man?"

"I never saw this person in my life," replied the ninja.

"I meant Chiun," said Remo. "Little Father, where are you?"

"Right here," said the Master of Sinanju, stepping out of the bathroom. The toilet flushed, and Remo saw a pair of legs sticking up from the bowl. The toilet overflowed, but the legs did not even quiver.

"I know who you are," the governor said. "But who is this man?" He pointed to the ninja.

The ninja bowed low, sheathing his sword. "I am sent here as a personal representative of the President of the United States, entrusted with the protection of your life. I have been concealed in the darkness since you returned home."

"A lie!" said Chiun. "Remo and I arrived first. There was no one here when we entered."

"I stood immobile in this very room. No human eye could perceive me, dressed in black. I am like the shadow of vengeance, awaiting your enemies, governor."

"Tell him why you wear the black scarf over your features," spat Chiun with disdain.

"I have enemies who would seek me out if my face were ever revealed."

"That is not why!" screamed Chiun. "All ninjas go masked because their stealthy arts were stolen from Sinanju. They hide their faces to conceal the shame of what they are—thieves. So it is written in the histories of Sinanju."

"I know nothing of histories," said the ninja. "I live by my wits and my sword."

"If that is the case," Chiun sniffed, "expect a short life."

"You saved my life," said the governor, brushing past Remo. He stuck out a grateful hand. "I owe you."

The ninja shook the governor's hand. "It was my duty, which I am proud to perform."

"You realize that I cannot take you on faith alone. Do you have anything to identify yourself by?"

"Oh, come on. That's not how it works," said Remo.

"Of course," said the ninja, reaching into a hidden pocket. He tendered a black card with writing etched in gold ink.

The governor read the writing. It said:

"TO WHOM IT MAY CONCERN: THE BEARER OF THIS CARD IS A HIGH OPERATIVE IN A SECRET UNITED STATES INTELLIGENCE AGENCY. PLEASE ACCORD HIM EVERY COURTESY."

The card bore the signature of the President of the United States of America.

Governor Princippi looked up. "I'm satisfied," he said.

"But I'm not," said Remo, snatching the card and reading it. "This is ridiculous," he shouted.

"It is worse than ridiculous," said Chiun, taking it from Remo's hand. "This thief gets a magnificent card from the President and Smith denies me a common Gold Card."

"That's not what I meant," said Remo. "Nobody give out cards like these."

"Not to ninjas," added Chiun, slipping the card into a coat pocket. Later he would show it to Smith and demand one of his own.

"The ninjas were the Japanese Secret Service at one time, weren't they?" the governor asked curiously.

"Indeed," said the ninja. "I am a Master of Ninjutsu, which is Japanese for 'art of stealth.'"

"He means 'art of stealing,'" sputtered Chiun. "You should check your cupboards and briefcases after he leaves. Ninjas have sticky fingers."

"Do you mind?" said the governor. "We're having a conversation here." To the ninja he said, "You did an excellent job here."

"Don't tell me you buy his story," Remo protested. "Look at him. He looks ridiculous. And somebody should tell him that the sword went out of style after the Civil War."

"Look at you," said the ninja. "Is that your undershirt?"

"Hey, I dress like this so I can blend in with ordinary people."

"I dress in black so that I may blend in with the shadows. These killers did not see me in the dark. Nor did you."

"Sounds right to me," said the governor. "I used to listen to *The Shadow* on radio. Wasn't that how he did it?"

"What do you do when it snows, pal?" Remo asked smugly.

"I wear white," said the ninja.

"You should wear brown. It's getting knee-deep in here."

"True servants of the emperor do not hide their faces," added Chiun.

"Why not?" said Governor Princippi. "It worked for the Lone Ranger. No doubt this man requires secrecy to protect his private life."

Remo turned to the governor. "There's nothing on that card that says this guy belongs to it—or it to him. He could have stolen it, for all we know."

"I can almost guarantee it," inserted Chiun.

"The card looks authentic to me," said the governor. "And this man saved my life. And I'd still like to know what you two are doing here?"

"I told you. We came to protect you from assassins."

"This other person did that. And someone was in my bedroom a few moments ago. And I don't think it was any of these teenage hoodlums," said the governor, gesturing to the bodies strewn about the parlor. Noticing the headless form of the late Antonio Serrano, he grew a little green along the edge of the jaw. He turned away.

Remo shook his head. "Look, just think about it a minute. This guy waltzes in here, won't show his face, won't tell you his name, flashes a card that says he's from the President but which doesn't bear any name or picture or fingerprint, and you accept him for what he says he is?"

"Of course," said the governor. "In his line of work, those kinds of identification would cripple him. And you should talk. You're not carrying any identification at all. Either of you. I think you should both get out."

Not far off, the wail of police sirens grew closer.

"I guess that's our cue," Remo told Chiun. "What about you, pal?" he asked the man in black.

"I will return to the shadows. If the governor needs me, he has only to whistle."

"I think I'm going to throw up."

"Then throw up for me too," said Chiun. "I do not think this circus clown is worth the effort."

Giving a short bow, the ninja stepped behind the screen.

"Oh, give me a break," Remo said, whipping the screen

aside. He found himself looking at old wallpaper. There
was no place the ninja could have gone, no door or window
behind the screen.

"How did he do that?" Remo asked no one in particular.

"Who cares?" said Chiun. "Ninjas always cheat. Let us
be gone."

As they slipped out the back door, Governor Princippi
called after them, "And don't think I'll forget this. If this
is the caliber of operative Smith employs, the sooner he's
shut down, the better."

"Smitty is sunk, Little Father," Remo said glumly as
they got into the Lincoln.

"The governor is merely distraught," Chiun said worriedly. "He may change his mind after the election."

"Not when he finds that letter is missing," Remo retorted, starting the engine. "He's going to want our heads.
And the line forms behind the Vice-President."

17

It was on nights such as this that Dr. Harold W. Smith wished that CURE security was not so critical.

He stood looking out the big picture window. A steady rain pelted the waters of Long Island Sound. Although he was in his office, the sight of that remorseless rain made Smith shiver in sympathy and yearn for home, with a nice crackling pine log in his fireplace.

But tonight Smith had to stand by the CURE telephones waiting for word from Remo and Chiun. If CURE's very existence had not been a national-security secret, Smith could have installed a private extension in his house. He could now be waiting in the snug comfort of his Rye home, instead of dreading the drive home through the rain. A drive that he might not be able to make for many hours yet. Maude would not be waiting up for him. Smith's wife had long ago given up on waiting up for her husband. Sometimes he wondered what kept them married.

Smith dismissed his gloomy thoughts. What was keeping Remo from calling bothered him more. Obtaining a simple letter from Governor Princippi could not be so difficult. Not for people with Sinanju powers. He hoped that this last mission had gone better than the botched attempt to safeguard the Vice-President's life.

Tired of watching the rain, Smith took his seat and called up the CURE terminal. Message traffic on CIA and Secret Service levels was busy. The Service was still trying to explain the deaths of the detail that had been slaughtered while protecting the Vice-President. Newspapers screamed about Middle Eastern terrorist interference with the American election, just days away.

Smith had been in touch with the President. The President had received another call from the Vice-President.

Oddly, this time the Vice-President had called to thank the Chief Executive for sending a new bodyguard, a martial-arts expert known by the code name Adonis.

The President had not told the Vice-President the truth—that he had not sent for this Adonis. Had Smith?

"No, Mr. President," Smith had replied. "I have no idea who this person is."

"But your person was on the scene?" the President had asked.

"Yes, he was."

"The Vice-President claimed that there were two CURE operatives at Blair House," the President said slowly.

"Ah, he must have been mistaken," said Smith, mopping his brow with a handkerchief.

"Yes, he must have been," said the President. "We lost our American enforcement arm last year during that fiasco with the Soviets."

"Yes," said Smith uncomfortably. A year ago, when CURE had been compromised by the Russians, it had nearly ended for all of them. Thinking that he would never see Remo or Chiun again, Smith had allowed the President to believe that Remo had been liquidated by Smith's own hand. It had been Smith's way of atoning to Remo for past injustices, now that Remo had decided to settle down in Sinanju. For the past year Smith had lived in dread that the truth would come out.

"People under stress are often confused," the President agreed slowly. "And the Vice-President has escaped two assassination attempts now."

"I have a new lead on the leak," said Smith. "There is a man named Tulip who has sent a letter detailing our operation to the Vice-President. There is reason to believe that Governor Princippi has also received an identical letter. The Master of Sinanju is trying to verify this right now."

"Who? Why? It sounds as if this person is bent on shutting you down, Smith."

"If so, his approach is inefficient. He could have easily leaked what he knows to the press. I would have no choice but to terminate operations if this broke publicly."

"I know one thing. I did not send anyone named Adonis to protect the Vice-President. I told the Vice-President otherwise only because he was yelling for your head. He wants you placed under arrest.''

"Sir, it may be possible that a rival intelligence agency, having learned about CURE, is copying its methods in an effort to replace us.''

"I doubt the KGB would detail a man to protect an American politician.''

"I meant a domestic rival group. The CIA or the Defense Intelligence Agency. Or possibly someone on your National Security Council.''

"Don't start that with me, Smith. The NSC is not involved with this.''

"I'm sorry, Mr. President, but I cannot ignore any possibilities.''

"Just don't stir up any unnecessary mud. As far as I'm concerned, you remain sanctioned to operate. Don't give me a reason to change my mind.'' And the President hung up.

That had been hours ago. Smith had pondered the situation without respite. His CURE computers showed no strange activities on any level of America's regular intelligence agencies. And Smith had many people on his payroll who worked for the CIA, the DIA, and the NSA but who actually reported to him without realizing it.

If it was not any of those agencies, who then?

By the time night fell and the rain started, Smith was still lost in the imponderability of it all.

Hours later, Remo and Chiun walked in unannounced.

"Remo,'' Smith said in surprise. "And Master Chiun.''

"Hi, Smitty,'' said Remo. "I've got good news and bad news.''

"He means good news and better news,'' corrected Chiun.

"Let me tell it, will you, Chiun?''

"Ignore him,'' said the Master of Sinanju, lifting the crease of his trouser legs delicately and settling into a chair. "He is tired from our long journey. And his memory may be failing him.''

Remo turned to Chiun. "I tell you, Little Father, I saw him as plain as day. He had Western eyes.''

"Nonsense. His eyes were Japanese. I know a Japanese when I see one.''

"Japanese don't normally stand over six feet tall."

"Nor did he," insisted Chiun. "He was much shorter than that. He was short even for a Japanese, who walk with their legs bent like monkeys."

Smith interrupted wearily. "What are you two arguing about now?"

"Nothing important," said Chiun.

"The bad news," said Remo.

"Give me the good news," sighed Smith, grateful that this was his final operation involving Remo and Chiun.

Remo scaled a letter across the room. It landed between fingers of Smith's upraised hand. An observer would have sworn Smith had plucked it from his sleeve like a magician.

"I wish you wouldn't do things like that," Smith said, looking at the envelope. It was addressed to Governor Michael Principi. The letter bore Korean stamps and a Seoul cancellation mark.

"The letter?" Smith asked, plucking the contents out and unfolding them. There were three sheets of paper covered with small spidery handwriting. Smith scanned the contents all the way to the end, where it was signed "Tulip."

"Whoever this Tulip is, he knows everything about us," said Smith, his face sagging like candlewax reaching its melting point.

"Hey, that was supposed to be the good news," said Remo. "You wanted the letter. We got it for you. Don't break the furniture in your rush to thank us."

Smith let the letter fall from unfeeling fingers. He ran his hands through his thinning hair once and buried his face in them. He felt numb.

"What is the bad news?" he asked hollowly.

"Someone tried to kill Governor Principi when we were at his house."

"When you were—"

"I personally dispatched three of the vermin," said Chiun, leaping to his feet. "You should have been there, Emperor Smith. You would have been proud of your servant. Though alone and outnumbered, bullets flying all about my aged head, I dispatched them one, two, three."

"Alone? Where were you, Remo?"

"I was in the governor's bedroom stealing the letter."

"The governor did not know you were there, of course."

"He didn't see me steal the letter," Remo said quickly.

Smith relaxed. "Excellent. You recovered the letter and prevented an attempt on the governor's life without anyone being the wiser."

"Not exactly," said Remo.

"Not exactly? Please don't tell me that—"

"Smitty, something strange is going on," Remo said. "When the shooting started, the governor came downstairs to see what was happening. Chiun had killed most of the killers, but there was still one running loose."

"And you got him?"

"No, some screwball in a ninja suit beat me to it. I would have had him easy but I lost a few seconds when the guy drew aim on the governor. I had to step in front to protect the governor's body. Otherwise I would have been all over the ninja. Honest."

"The governor saw you." It was not a question, but a sick statement of fact.

"Sorry, Smitty. When he discovers the letter's gone, he's going to know it was us. We tried asking for it earlier in the day, but it was no go."

"Oh, my God," said Smitty.

"Smitty, there was another thing. This ninja popped out of nowhere. He said he was from the President. It was just like the situation with the Vice-President, only instead of a kung-fu beach boy, it was some white guy in a ninja suit."

"He was Japanese!" shouted Chiun. "His eyes were Japanese."

"I stood closer to him than you and I say he was white," insisted Remo.

"Are you saying that my eyes are fading?" bristled the Master of Sinanju.

"I saw what I saw. Something's fishy here, Smitty. The President doesn't employ ninjas."

"I had a call from the President," said Smith dully. His eyes were focused in on themselves, like those of a man who had been told he was terminal. "According to him, your Adonis had represented himself to the Vice-President as an official presidential bodyguard. The President denied it, but now I don't know. Anything is possible. Anything."

"I am glad to hear that anything is possible," said the Master of Sinanju, floating out of his chair. He stepped up to Smith's desk and set a plastic card on it. "If anything is possible, then it will be possible for the Master of Sinanju to obtain a card such as this one."

"I told you," said Smith, picking up the card idly. "American Express won't do business with you anymore. But perhaps I can work out something with one of the other credit-card companies." He stopped speaking and stared intently at the card.

"Hah!" said Remo triumphantly. "It's a phony, isn't it? I can tell by your face. I knew that fake ninja was spinning a story."

"This card is blank," said Smith, turning it over several times.

"Give it here," demanded Chiun, taking it back. He looked at the card. Remo leaned over his shoulder to look at it too.

The Master of Sinanju held a black plastic card. Both sides were blank, without writing of any kind.

"But this was the card," Chiun exclaimed.

"Yeah, it was," said Remo, recognizing the shape and texture. "Smitty, the ninja flashed this thing at all of us. It was covered with gold letters saying that it belonged to an agent of a secret government agency. And it was signed by the President. At least, it was the President's name. I don't know if it was his handwriting."

"This card?" asked Smith.

"Yes!" said Remo.

"That's rubbish!" said Smith. "No secret agency with any sense would issue such a ridiculous piece of identification."

"That's what I tried to tell the governor, but would he listen? No. He swallowed the ninja's story whole. He wasn't even a real ninja. He was white."

"Japanese," muttered Chiun, looking at the card with puzzlement.

"There's no lettering on either side," Smith said, holding it up to the fluorescent ceiling lights.

"Maybe he used invisible ink that works on plastic," said Smith slowly.

"Does this mean I cannot obtain a card like it?" Chiun asked unhappily.

"How can I duplicate it if I don't know what was written on it?" Smith asked in a reasonable voice.

"That Japanese thief," snapped Chiun bitterly. "He will rue the day he tricked the Master of Sinanju."

"What did he look like?" asked Smith.

"His face was masked, ninja-style," Remo said.

"And with good reason," said Chiun. "Did I ever tell you about the ninjas and the Masters of Sinanju, Emperor Smith?"

"I don't believe so," said Smith.

"You will like this tale," said Chiun, drawing up a chair so he could be closer to Smith. "And I have many more besides."

"While you're regaling Smith with tales of Sinanju, I'm going for a walk," said Remo. "And for the record, Smitty, the ninja was six-foot-one, white, and had blue eyes."

"He was my height, Japanese, with beady black eyes," insisted the Master of Sinanju.

"And I'm Kris Kringle," snorted Remo, slamming the door behind him.

'Do not mind him, Emperor," said Chiun after Remo had gone. "Obviously he is not well."

"What makes you say that?"

"Any man who would mistake a Japanese ninja for a fat white man in a ninja costume is obviously sick. I think Remo's mind is going soft. After all, he is the first white to learn Sinanju. For years I have been concerned that his weak white mind could not endure the strain of perfection, and now I am sure of it. I only hope he does not reject his training entirely. All the more reason for us to reach a new agreement."

"Didn't Remo say the ninja wore a mask? It's possible that one of you was thrown off because his face was obscured," said Smith, turning the black plastic card over and over in his hands, as if its secret could be worried from it.

"All ninjas wear masks," spat Chiun. "It is a curse that Sinanju has placed upon them. Let me tell you that story."

"Yes, of course," said Smith absently. The plastic card held his attention.

"Once," said Chiun, striding to the center of the room, "a Master of Sinanju was hired by a Japanese emperor. The year was A.D. 645 by Western dating."

"What was the Master's name?"

Chiun paused in his pacing of the room. "That is an excellent question," he complimented. "A very excellent question. Remo has never asked such an intelligent question in all the years I have worked with him."

"Thank you," said Smith. "But I was just curious."

"Master Sam was his name," said Chiun, bowing in recognition of the wisdom of Emperor Smith in asking such an insightful question. "Now, Sam was summoned to the court of Japan by its emperor of that time."

"His name?"

"Sam. I have said it already," said Chiun, his face stung.

"No, I meant the Japanese emperor."

"Pah! What matter his name? That is not important to the legend."

"Keep talking while I look it up," said Smith, reaching for his computer keyboard. After a moment he looked up. "It was Emperor Tenchi."

"Possibly," said the Master of Sinanju vaguely. Why did Smith always insist upon wallowing in foreign trivia? he wondered. "Now, this emperor," Chiun went on, "whose name might have been Tenchi, told the Master Sam that he had enemies. And the emperor told where his enemies might be found, in their homes or in their places of business. And one by one, the Master swooped down upon each of these enemies and they were no more. And each time Master Sam returned to the ruler of Japan to report success, the emperor said unto him, 'Go not yet, for I have discovered a new enemy. Attend to him as you did the others before him and I will increase the tribute to be paid to Sinanju.'

"And because the Master Sam did not wish to leave his work undone, he took responsibility for each new victim as they were brought to his attention by the emperor. Until with the fifth victim, the Master of Sinanju grew suspicious because some of these men were simple peasants, without wealth or will to plot against the chrysanthemum throne."

"I see," said Smith, his eyes drawn to the greenish light of his computer terminal as a steady stream of news digests flashed on and off.

The Master of Sinanju ignored his emperor's rudeness. The legends of Sinanju were traditionally shared between Master and pupil, not Master and emperor. Did Smith not understand why he was being told this story? Still, he would ignore Smith's inattentiveness this time. The white mind was congenitally incapable of focusing on one thought for very long.

"And so, charged to eliminate a sixth victim, the Master went early to the place the emperor had told him the plotter would be found. Arriving there, he discovered concealed high in a tree a spy who had been sent there to watch the Master Sam work his art.

"Taking the spy by the scruff of the neck, Master Sam demanded of this man his true business. And the spy, knowing full well the power of Sinanju, trembled and said, 'O Master, my emperor seeks the wisdom of Sinanju, which I was to observe and report to him, just as I have observed you kill the others.' And the spy also revealed that the emperor had no known enemies. The Master had been slaughtering peasants."

"That's terrible," said Smith.

"Not as bad as it could have been." Chiun shrugged.

"I fail to see how it could have been worse."

"Master Sam was paid for his work in advance."

"Oh," said Smith.

"Now," Chiun continued, "having learned these things, the Master had a final question for the spy of the Japanese emperor, and it was this, 'What have you learned, spy?' And the spy replied in a suitable quavering voice that he had learned from watching the Master of Sinanju how to move stealthily by wearing clothes the color of night, how to climb sheer walls like a spider, and certain ways of killing with openhanded blows."

"And Master Sam killed him, naturally," said Smith, thinking that he understood how the mind of Sinanju Masters worked.

"No, of course not," Chiun said irritably. "The Japanese emperor did not pay him to kill that man." Why was Smith so dense? It must be a white trait, he decided. Remo was like that too.

"He let him go, even though he had learned Sinanju?"

"Imperfectly," corrected Chiun. "He had learned Sinanju imperfectly. His blows were weak, and in order to climb walls he needed artificial aids. Like spikes and grappling hooks. No, he did not learn Sinanju. He stole the inspiration, but in practice he was like a mechanical man pretending to be human. So Master Sam said to this man, 'Return to your emperor and tell him you have learned naught but how to skulk and steal, and also tell him that the Master of Sinanju kills for payment, not for the enlightenment of emperors.' "

"What was his name, this man?" wondered Smith.

"Why would you ask such a question?" demanded Chiun in an exasperated voice. "What has that to do with anything?"

"Historical curiosity," said Smith. "That man was the founder of ninjutsu."

"Founder!" spat Chiun. "He did not find anything, he stole it! Have you not listened to a word I have said? You whites are all alike."

"Er, never mind," said Smith hastily. "I'll look it up later. But you haven't told me why the ninjas go about masked."

Chiun subsided. "Very well," he said in a controlled voice. "It happened years later, after word came out of Japan of a new sect of assassins who dressed in black and were known as ninjas. And Master Sam ventured back into Japan, unsummoned and unknown, in order to evaluate this new competition. And he found a tiny band of these ninjas, and their leader was this unimportant thief from years before, who had trained others. Of course, they were as clumsy as monkeys, but that is not the point. They were taking work that should have gone to Sinanju."

"So naturally Master Sam killed them all this time," said Smith, who knew that Sinanju Masters stopped at nothing to guard their livelihood.

Chiun froze in the middle of a grand flourish and fixed his brittle hazel eyes upon Dr. Harold W. Smith.

Smith felt a chill, as if the cold rain had somehow penetrated the great picture window to run down his back. He shook his head in a silent negative.

Chiun shook his head in response, and went on, the edge in his voice glittering. "Master Sam stood before this thief and his face was wrathful. But he did not slay him. Instead, he said to him, 'You have stolen that which lasts longer than rubies. You have stolen wisdom. I could kill you, ninja, but you are a child imitating his elders, and I will not kill you. Instead, hear my curse: you are a thief, and I curse you, and all who follow in your path, to forevermore conceal your faces in shame. And should any of your number in succeeding generations ever go about his skulking work with his face uncovered, the Master of Sinanju will no longer suffer your existence. And that is why to this very day these so-called ninjas go about with their heads covered.''

Chiun folded his long-nailed hands into the belled sleeves of his suit complacently.

"There is one thing I still do not understand," Smith said cautiously.

Chiun's forehead gathered in wrinkles. "I believe I covered everything."

"Why didn't the Master Sam kill the ninjas?"

"He was not paid!" screeched Chiun like a teacher before a recalcitrant child.

"But not killing them took money and employment away from future Masters," Smith pressed on. "Wouldn't it have been better to have killed the ninjas?"

"That is the way the story is written in the histories of my ancestors," Chiun returned defiantly. "To ask for information not written in those scrolls is impertinent."

"I'm sorry," said Smith stubbornly. "I thought it was a reasonable question."

"Reasonable to whom? I am sure Master Sam had a good reason for handling it the way he did. He must have forgotten to write it into his scrolls."

"Scrolls," said Smith suddenly. He was looking at the letter signed "Tulip." The envelope had been mailed from South Korea. Smith had been puzzled by that, but his full attention had been captured by the contents of the letter itself. Now the significance of the postmark was beginning to sink into his mind.

Looking up, he asked the Master of Sinanju a question.

"You mentioned the scrolls of your ancestors," said Smith. "Might I assume that you regularly transcribe the history of your service to America in similar scrolls?"

"In great detail," said Chiun proudly.

"I see. And where are these scrolls now? Yours, I mean."

"In Sinanju. In past times I kept them with me, but I was unable to bring them back with me when I last returned to these shores. But do not worry, Emperor Smith, I have an excellent memory. When I am free to send for my scrolls, I will duly record this most recent year of service to your highness. And while I am on the subject,'' he said, removing a blue-ribboned scroll from his coat, ''I have completed the latest contract. It only needs your signature to guarantee that you will be served well in the coming year.''

''Leave it on the desk,'' said Smith. ''I will read it and we will discuss it later.''

''It is exact in every detail of our last negotiation,'' protested Chiun.

''I am sure that it is,'' said Smith. ''But if you'll look out the window, you'll notice that the sun is coming up. We've been here all night. I really need some rest before I can deal with such a weighty matter.''

''Let me read it to you, then,'' said Chiun. ''There is no need for you to strain your royal eyes.''

''I'd rather read it at my convenience, if you don't mind,'' insisted Smith, gesturing for the scroll to be left on his desk.

The Master of Sinanju hesitated, but he had already snapped at the Emperor Smith twice this night. There was no need to push the matter. What was another few hours?

Reluctantly he set the scroll on the desk and bowed from the waist.

''I will await your decision,'' he said.

''Thank you,'' said Smith.

When the Master of Sinanju had gone, Smith considered the envelope on his desk. Yes, it made sense. There was no way for CURE's existence to leak out of the American government, whether from past or present administrations. In all his years at the helm of CURE, Smith had overlooked the simple fact that all along the Master of Sinanju had been recording his every assignment for posterity. The events of the last year had caused those scrolls to be left unguarded, and now it had come to this.

There was no telling what the consequences might be, but CURE was not necessarily doomed. It all hinged upon whether the next President kept his campaign promise. And Smith, knowing politicians, would not bet on that.

Smith looked at his watch and decided to wait another hour before he reported his findings to the President. No need to wake him. And noticing also that his secretary was due to arrive for work at any moment, Smith sent the CURE terminal slipping back into its desk well.

Smith's secretary was as punctual as always. She knocked on Smith's door before entering. She was a bosomy middle-aged woman in bifocals, her hair tied into an efficient bun.

"Good morning," she said, setting a container of prune-whip yogurt and a can of unsweetened pineapple juice on the desk. "I picked up your usual breakfast from the commissary."

"Thank you, Mrs. Mikulka," Smith said. Taking from a desk drawer a disposable plastic spoon with which he had eaten his yogurt for the last twenty years, he dug in.

"I see you've been working all night."

"Er, yes," Smith admitted, puzzled by his secretary's overly familiar tone. She did not normally remark on matters outside of her duties. "Important matters," he said.

"I imagine curing the ills of the world is worth losing a night's sleep here and there," she said, closing the door behind her.

Smith's mouth hung open. Yogurt ran down his chin and dripped, unnoticed, onto his wrinkled trousers. He had completely forgotten he was eating.

"Figure of speech," Smith assured himself huskily. "Yes. A figure of speech. She couldn't know. Not Mrs. Mikulka. I've got to relax. This thing has me jumping at shadows."

18

The President of the United States was already awake when the special telephone rang. He had been lying in bed enjoying a few minutes of extra rest before having to get up, when the muffled ringing started.

"Not again," cried his wife.

"Could you excuse me, dear?" the President said, maneuvering himself into a sitting position on the edge of the bed. The phone rang again.

The First Lady mumbled something under her breath and climbed into a sheer nightgown. "If that's World War III, I'll be in the shower."

When she was out of hearing, the President opened the end-table drawer and lifted the receiver of the red phone.

"Good morning," he said cheerily.

"I'm sorry to wake you, Mr. President," said the voice of Dr. Harold W. Smith.

The President's voice hardened. "I've been awake for several minutes. Why does everyone assume I'm not awake at this hour? It's already nine o'clock."

"Yes, Mr. President," Smith said stiffly. "If I may make my report."

"Fire away," said the President.

"As you may know, there was an attempt on Governor Princippi's life last night."

"A gang of street punks," said the President. "Probably copycatting the attacks on the Vice-President."

"There's no reason to believe otherwise at this point in time," Smith said, "but we should not assume anything."

"The gang members are dead, I'm told."

"Yes, my special person accounted for most of them."

"That should impress the governor."

"Mr. President, the governor knows about our operation. And he's not happy with it, or with me."

The President's hand tightened on the receiver. "How?"

"It appears that an unknown person signing himself 'Tulip' has sent letters describing CURE operations to both the governor and the Vice-President. The governor's letter is in my hands. It's postmarked South Korea. From that, I believe I can infer the source of Tulip's knowledge."

"Yes?"

"He seems to have accessed personal diaries of our special person which have remained in the village of Sinanju since the incident with the Soviets last year."

"I remember it well," the President said bitterly.

"A fluke, sir," Smith said uncomfortably.

"Well, this makes two flukes in one year."

"I am aware of that, sir. If it's your wish that I cease operations, I can be shut down within the hour. I should have been aware of this possibility."

"I'm not prepared to do that, Smith," said the President without hesitation. "After that last incident, you'll recall we decided that you could operate without an enforcement arm. You'd be doing that if your special person, the Korean, hadn't returned to America and offered you another year of service. Isn't it about time for your contract with him to lapse?"

"Yes, he handed me a new one just this morning. Its terms are quite generous. Of course, I explained to him that if I sign it, I may not be able to guarantee its terms after you leave office."

"What the next administration decides is their business. For now, you will continue operations."

"And our special person?"

"Have him destroy his records. Make that a stipulation of this new contract. If he refuses, terminate his employment. Is that all?"

"Not quite, sir. There was another player in the Governor Principi incident. A ninja master. He claimed that he was protecting the governor at your behest."

"I have no such report, Smith."

"No?" said Smith vaguely.

"You do believe me, don't you?"

"Yes, of course. I have no reason to think otherwise."

"Thanks for the vote of confidence," the President said acidly.

"I apologize for my tone, Mr. President, but you have to understand my confusion. Two martial-arts experts have preempted separate assassination attempts. Both claimed to be working for you."

"Governor Princippi has said nothing about any ninja. His story is that the assassins were stopped by persons unknown. I assumed that it was your unknown person."

"It was, but this ninja was also on the scene. I don't understand how he could have known of an assassination attempt ahead of time, unless he is sanctioned, or. . ."

"Or what?"

"Or he's part of the plot."

"I'll have the Secret Service look into it."

"I could handle it, sir," Smith said hopefully.

"Stick to your computers, Smith. For now. That's all." And the President hung up.

In his office at Folcroft Sanitarium, Dr. Harold W. Smith rose from behind his desk and locked the door. From a closet he removed a gray three-piece suit identical to the one he wore. Changing out of the wrinkled suit, Smith plugged in an electric razor and efficiently scoured the stubble from his face. He checked himself in a hand mirror and adjusted his rimless glasses. When he was done, he buttoned his fresh white shirt and knotted his Dartmouth tie. Putting away the razor and hand mirror, Smith tripped the intercom.

"Mrs. Mikulka, could you ask that Mr. Chiun and Mr. Remo come to my office?"

"Yes, Dr. Smith."

Minutes later, Remo and Chiun entered.

"Please close the door," requested Smith.

"Sure, Smitty," said Remo.

Seeing that his new contract lay open before Harold Smith, the Master of Sinanju burst into a broad smile.

"Perhaps Remo need not attend this meeting inasmuch as it concerns matters between you and me," Chiun said pointedly.

"I'd prefer that Remo remain."

Chiun's face fell.

"Thanks, Smitty," said Remo.

"I'll be brief," began Smith. "I've looked over your contract, Master Chiun. It is accurate, insofar as the terms we discussed yesterday go."

"Excellent," said Chiun, puffing out his chest. "It just so happens I have with me the ceremonial goose quill. Here."

Smith raised his hand. "One moment, please."

"Two moments," interrupted Remo. "Don't I have some say in this?"

"None," said the Master of Sinanju. "You are not part of this contract. You are dead. Smith has led the President to believe this. And dead people do not sign contracts."

"I'm not signing anything," said Remo hotly. "I'm returning to Sinanju. You promised that you'd return with me."

"I promised no such thing."

"You didn't say you wouldn't."

"And I did not say that I would. Emperor Smith has graciously offered me another year of employment in this land, and I have decided, because you are unwilling to accompany me on my Sinanju World tour, that this is the only way I can continue to support the starving villagers of Sinanju."

"Bulldookey," said Remo. "You wouldn't let me marry without attending the ceremony, would you?"

"No, of course not," retorted Chiun. "But would you marry without me being present? That is the true question."

"We'll find out. I plan on setting the date as soon as I hit the beach."

"It might be that the Emperor Smith will allow me a week off for that purpose. Say, next summer, perhaps?"

"Actually I'd like you both to return to Sinanju immediately," said Smith.

Chiun's parchment face collapsed. "Return?" he squeaked.

"I'm already packed." Remo grinned, pulling a toothbrush from his back pocket.

"It has to do with one last stipulation upon which I must insist if we are to come to an agreement here," said Smith.

Chiun looked at Smith. Then he looked at Remo's pleased
face.

"Very well," he said decisively. "Name it. Whatever it
is, I am certain it will be agreeable, for you have been recorded in the histories of Sinanju as Generous Harold the
First."

"You must destroy every record of your service to America that you have in Sinanju."

The Master of Sinanju froze. His head flinched as if from
a blow. He said nothing for long moments. Finally, in a
low, too-quiet voice, he asked, "Why would you ask me to
do such a thing?"

"This letter from Tulip. It is postmarked South Korea."

"Another place entirely," said Chiun. "Sinanju is in
North Korea."

"I believe this Tulip has stolen or accessed your records.
It is the only explanation for the precise knowledge he pos-
sesses."

"Impossible," sputtered Chiun. "The scrolls of Sinanju
are kept in the House of the Masters. It is guarded contin-
uously. The door is double-locked."

"That's right, Smitty," Remo put in. "I locked it myself
when I left Sinanju."

"Yes, that is correct," Chiun said. He froze. Suddenly
he wheeled upon Remo. "You! You were the last one to
leave Sinanju! If my scrolls are missing, it is your fault!"
he shouted, leveling a shaking finger at Remo.

"Hey, Chiun, lighten up. You just got through telling
Smitty that it's impossible for the scrolls to be missing."

"It is impossible! But if they are missing, it is no doubt
your fault, clumsy white who cannot properly lock a door
after him. You probably left the water running too."

"Not me," said Remo, folding his arms defensively. He
turned to Smith. "Are you sure about this?"

"My computers are secure. They have not been accessed.
The only other possible leak is the President. And he denies
it. And there's no reason for him to go to the extreme of
masquerading as this Tulip. He could shut us down with a
phone call."

Remo turned to Chiun. "He's got a point, Little Father."

"Nonsense," snapped Chiun. "If anyone had dared to
defile the House of the Masters, my faithful servant, Pull-

yang, would have seen it and reported it. His last letter to me said nothing of such a crime."

"Isn't this the same Pullyang you once called a barking dog without teeth?" Remo inquired.

"Do not listen to him, O Emperor. He cannot tell a Japanese from an American at three paces. No doubt his hearing is going also."

"It will, if you keep shouting like that," complained Remo.

"Please, please, the both of you," Smith pleaded. "Master Chiun, I'd like your answer."

"My answer is no, no one could have rifled the scrolls of my ancestors. That is a certainty."

"I meant: will you agree to return to Sinanju to destroy your scrolls?"

"This is an unfair thing you ask of me," said Chiun hotly. "No emperor in history has ever placed such a ridiculous demand upon the House of Sinanju. My answer is no."

Smith nodded grimly. "Very well," he said, standing up. He picked the contract scroll off the desk and studiously tore it down the center.

"Aaaieee!" wailed Chiun. "I worked for days on that scroll."

"I'm sorry. I cannot sign this document without your agreeing to that stipulation."

"I said no, not definitely no," Chiun complained.

"Then you will agree to destroy the scrolls?" Smith asked.

"Definitely not!" Chiun shouted.

Smith tore the scroll again. Chiun's mouth hung open.

Remo grinned broadly. "Looks like we're going home."

Chiun turned on him. "Do not be so smug! This may be your fault for leaving the House of the Masters unlocked."

"I assume," said Smith, "that if you find the scrolls in question are missing upon your return to Sinanju, you will do everything in your power to track them down and eliminate the culprit."

"Aha!" screeched Chiun, his eyes flashing. "I see your game now, Smith. You have tricked me! You are expecting service without payment. Yes, I will track down this thief, if such exists, but do not count upon my eliminating him. Remember the story of Master Sam and the ninjas."

"That is your privilege, Master Chiun. I have my orders."

"And my contempt," snapped Chiun, striding out the door. "And be assured that this perfidy will be recorded in my scrolls and your name disgraced for all generations to come."

"I'm sorry it had to end this way," Smith told Remo in a quiet voice.

"I'm not," said Remo, taking Smith's hand. "It couldn't have worked out better. Thanks, Smitty. You want to come along? I'll let you dance at my wedding."

"I don't dance," said Smith, shaking Remo's hand.

"A party pooper to the bitter end," sighed Remo. "It's okay. I don't think you'd fit in anyway. Can we count on the usual transportation by submarine?"

"Of course," said Smith, letting go of Remo's hand.

And without another word, Remo skipped out the door, whistling. Watching him go, Smith thought that he had never seen Remo so happy before.

Remo found the Master of Sinanju in his room, writing furiously.

"What are you doing, Little Father?"

"Are you totally blind? I am writing, fool."

"Don't be like that."

"What should I be like? I have been terminated by my emperor."

"You should be happy. Like me."

"To be happy like you I would have to be an idiot like you. Thank you, no. I will forgo that illustrious experience."

"Then be happy for me. And Mah-Li."

"I am writing to Pullyang now, telling him to prepare for our return. Do not fear, Remo, your wedding will take place as you wish."

"What's that other letter for?" Remo asked, nodding at a sealed envelope.

"It is a wedding invitation," said Chiun.

"I already asked Smith. He says he's tied up."

"I wish never to see that man ever again. He is a base trickster and a taker-back of Gold Cards."

"Then who?" Remo asked.

"No one you know. I have friends who are not known to you."

"I hope they bring a nice wedding present."

"It will be one that you will never forget, I am sure."

"Sounds great," Remo said pleasantly. "But hurry up, will you? The helicopter is waiting."

19

Dr. Harold W. Smith watched the helicopter lift off from the old docks that reached out like skeletal fingers from the patch of Folcroft land that fronted Long Island Sound. The air was still moist from the evening rain, and a chill fog rolled in off the water.

Smith stood before his big office window. For some reason, he felt a need to watch them go. To see Remo and Chiun leave his life forever. It had been a long twenty years. It was strange that it would end on this difficult note, but perhaps that was for the best.

As Smith watched, Remo helped the Master of Sinanju, who had reverted to his traditional Korean dress, into the medical helicopter. Smith had summoned the helicopter on the pretext that Mr. Chiun, an Alzheimer's patient, and his guardian, Mr. Remo, needed immediate transportation to another facility. The helicopter would drop them off at Kennedy Airport, from where they would take a commercial flight to the San Diego Naval Air station, where the submarine *Harlequin* was waiting to take them back to the shores of Sinanju for the final time.

The door closed and the helicopter, its rotors beating the air, lifted. It disappeared into the fog as if swallowed.

"It's over," breathed Smith. He returned to his familiar desk terminal. From now on, CURE was just him and his computers.

There was a tentative knock on his door.

"Yes?"

The bespectacled face of Mrs. Mikulka poked through the door.

"They're gone?" she asked.

"Yes," said Smith, not looking up.

"Back to Sinanju?"

"Yes, back to—" Smith froze. "What did you say?" he croaked. He was staring at his secretary, who had served him loyally for over five years, who ran Folcroft as capably as himself, and who knew nothing—or should know nothing—about Sinanju.

"I asked if Remo and Chiun had returned to Sinanju."

"Come in, Mrs. Mikulka," Smith said coldly. "And close the door behind you, if you would."

When Smith saw that his secretary had seated herself on a long divan, he asked in a tight voice, "How do you know about Sinanju?"

"I know about CURE too."

"Oh, God," said Smith. "Did you receive a letter from Tulip too?"

"No."

"Then how?"

"I am Tulip."

"You!"

"Tulip is not my real name, of course."

"You are Eileen Mikulka. Before you were a secretary, you taught high-school English. I did a thorough background check before I hired you."

"No," said the voice of Eileen Mikulka. "Eileen Mikulka is locked in a patient's room on an upper floor. She met with an accident as she carried your yogurt and fruit juice from the commissary this morning. Oh, do not worry, she is not dead. It was an effort for me not to kill her, but if I killed her, I might not have been able to stop killing. And then where would my plans be?"

"You look just like her. Plastic surgery?" Smith let one hand drop to his lap. He tried to be casual about it. His gray eyes locked with those of this woman, so that his gaze would not betray any surreptitious movement.

"Plastic surgery would not give me her voice, her manners. And do you really think I—or anyone—would go to the ridiculous extreme of becoming a middle-aged woman permanently to achieve a goal?"

"What you say is logical," admitted Smith, tugging open the middle-left-hand desk drawer with two fingers. He hoped it would not squeak before he could reach into it for his automatic. "May I ask why you wish CURE terminated?"

"I wish no such thing," said the voice of Eileen Mikulka. "You are not my target, nor is your operation. Nor were the presidential candidates I ordered assassinated."

"You?" blurted Smith. He was so shocked he let go of the drawer handle. "You were the person behind the attempts upon the Vice-President and Governor Princippi? Why, for God's sake?"

"So I could stop the assassins."

"You?"

Abruptly the figure of Eileen Mikulka shimmered. Smith squinted. Instead of the familiar bosomy plumpness of his secretary, a man sat on the divan. He was blond and bronzed, and wore a white karate *gi*. He smiled broadly.

"Call me Adonis."

"What?" Smith croaked. Then he remembered his weapon. He had the drawer open a crack. He tugged on it again. He dared not look down to see if it were open wide enough. He fumbled with his fingers. The opening was too narrow.

"Or call me ninja master."

And the handsome face melted and ran, tanned skin turning into black folds of cloth. The figure on the divan was garbed in ninja black now, his face concealed by the flaps of his mask. Only his eyes showed. Smith saw that they were blue.

"Chiun was mistaken," he said in a stupid voice. "He thought you were Japanese."

"The Master of Sinanju is never wrong," said the figure, and his words were in the singsong accents of Japan. Smith looked closer. The ninja's eyes were black and almond-shaped. And his robust physique seemed to have shrunk.

Smith forced himself not to react. With an effort he kept his voice level. "I suppose I would be wasting my time if I asked you to identify yourself?"

The ninja stood up and came toward Smith.

"You have the letter before you," he said. "You saw my signature."

Smith's hand touched cold metal. He had the automatic.

"It says 'Tulip.' That means nothing to me."

"That is because you have not thought about it, Smith."

"I'll think about it later," said Harold W. Smith, whipping up the automatic. He held it at desk level, resting the butt on the desktop to keep it steady. ''Please stop where you are.''

But the ninja kept coming, his body swelling and running like a million multicolored candles melting together. Suddenly it was the figure a young man with a flowing mane of yellow hair and purple garments who came toward him on quiet, confident feet. His eyes were so blue it hurt to look at them.

Smith steeled himself and fired.

The purple figure kept coming. Smith fired again. This time he saw, incredibly, the afterimage effect as the figure returned to its path of approach. The figure had dodged the bullets. Had dodged them so fast that it looked to the untrained eye as if he had allowed the bullets to pass through him.

Smith knew he was looking at a being trained in the ancient art of Sinanju, and suddenly the significance of the name Tulip was clear. He knew whom he faced. What he faced. But his knowledge came too late, far too late for Harold W. Smith.

''I have no quarrel with you, Smith,'' a different voice rang in his ears. ''I want Remo. I want to destroy him. You have helped me with the first phase. Do not think I am not grateful—or unmerciful. You will feel no pain, I promise.''

And for Harold W. Smith, the world went black. He never saw the hand that struck him.

20

The letter arrived in Sinanju the next day. It had come via Pyongyang, the capital of North Korea, and was delivered to Sinanju by a People's helicopter. It was left in an iron mailbox at the edge of the village, for it was forbidden for any who were not of Sinanju to enter Sinanju without permission.

When the helicopter departed, a boy was sent to the mailbox. He came running back and gave the letter to Pullyang, who was again at his post, guarding the House of the Masters.

Old Pullyang placed the letter in the dirt while he got his pipe going. After a few preliminary puffs he opened the letter, which he recognized as from the Master of Sinanju. His tiny eyes took in the message of the Master eagerly.

"Summon Mah-Li," Pullyang told the boy, who would not go until he had heard the news from America.

"Is it good news?" the boy asked.

"Joyous news. But I must tell Mah-Li myself."

Mah-Li climbed the low hillock to the House of the Masters, expectation on her radiant face.

"What word from America?" she called.

Pullyang waved the letter. "It is from Master Chiun. He returns soon. He bids us to prepare for the wedding of the white Master, Remo, and the maiden called Mah-Li."

Mah-Li's hands flew to her throat in surprise. "Remo," she breathed. "And what word from him?"

Old Pullyang shook his head. "None."

Mah-Li knit her smooth brow. "None. No message for me?"

"The Master wrote, not Remo."

"Oh," said Mah-Li, her face clouding. "It is not like Remo. You do not think he has changed his mind, do you,

Pullyang? After all, it has been a year since we last saw him.''

"The Master Chiun would not order the wedding preparations if the groom had changed his mind. Why would you say such a foolish thing, child?''

"I do not know," said Mah-Li, dropping to her knees beside Pullyang. With nervous fingers she picked at a clump of coarse grass. "It is just that ever since the purple birds came to us in the night, my sleep has been troubled and I know not why.''

"You are a child still. And children are often subject to strange fears," Pullyang said tenderly.

"You yourself called them a bad omen, Pullyang. What did you mean by that?''

And because Pullyang did not himself know, he shrugged and tried to look sage. He took a long draw from his pipe and hoped that Mah-Li would not press the point.

"I think you were right about their being a bad omen," said Mah-Li after a time.

"They are gone," said Pullyang.

Mah-Li looked up into the morning sky. It was gray and troubled. "I know, but my dreams tell me that they will be back." And she folded her arms and shivered.

21

The USS *Harlequin* broke the slate waters of the West Korea Bay and settled in the trough of a wave. Water crashed over the submarine's hull and ran out the deck gunwales.

Sailors popped open a hatch and set about inflating a collapsible rubber raft. When they had it inflated, one called down the hatch, "All set on deck, sir."

Remo came up first. The moon was high, a crescent moon that shed little illumination. Remo saw the Horns of Welcome jutting up from the shore. They framed the low hill on which the House of the Masters stood, like some arcane emblem of antiquity. But to Remo the forbidding sight was a happy one.

He called down the hatch, "Shake a leg, Chiun. We're home."

The Master of Sinanju's head emerged like a squirrel peering from its hole. "Do not rush me, Remo. I am an old man. I will not hurry just because you are in heat."

"I am not in heat," said Remo, taking Chiun by one elbow as he clambered out of the hatch.

The sailors were lowering the raft into the water.

"Better hurry, gentlemen," one of them called. "These seas are running high."

Remo and Chiun climbed down the submarine hull until they were safely on the raft. Two crewmen manned oars. There was an outboard motor but it was not used because of the fear that the sound would attract North Korean patrol craft and create an international incident.

The raft got going.

"Sure seems strange to come back without any gold, huh, Little Father?" Remo said quietly.

"Do not remind me of my failure," Chiun said morosely.

"I was just making small talk. Why are you on my case?

You haven't said a civil word all the way across the Pacific.''

"If my scrolls are missing, it will be your fault."

"Christ, Chiun. I told you and told you. I did not leave the door unlocked."

"We will see," warned Chiun.

The raft bumped one of the natural stone breakers that jutted from the Sinanju beach, and Remo stepped out to help Chiun onto the slick tumble of rock.

"Thanks," Remo told the sailors.

"Do not say thanks," said Chiun. "Tip them."

"I don't have any money, remember?"

Chiun told the sailors, "You may keep this person if you wish, in place of a proper tip. He is not of much use, but perhaps you can put him to work peeling potatoes."

"Next time, guys," Remo said. And the raft shoved off.

The Master of Sinanju strode from the bleak rocks to the stretch of sandy beach. He looked around him, his face unreadable.

"At least I am home, where I am respected by my people," he said solemnly.

"You've got a short memory, Little Father."

"No, it is my villagers who have short memories. In the past, they thought well of you because you had agreed to care for the village and uphold its traditions when I am gone. But a full year has passed. Their memory of your promises has faded from their hardworking minds. Instead, they will remember the great accomplishments of Chiun, who has brought new glory to their lives."

"We'll soon know, because I see people coming now."

A small group of villagers stumbled down to the beach. Remo recognized old Pullyang in the lead.

"Pullyang will know if there has been a problem," Remo said confidently.

"Yes," agreed Chiun. "Pullyang will know." He closed his eyes and stuck out his hand so that his worshipful villagers could kiss it as they sang adorations. In a moment, he heard the traditional Korean words in all their glory.

"Hail, Master of Sinanju, who sustains the village and keeps the code faithfully. Our hearts cry a thousand greetings of love and adoration. Joyous are we upon the return of him who graciously throttles the universe."

But his hand remained cool, unwarmed by adoring touches.

"Cut it out," complained Remo. "You're drooling all over my hand. Chiun, how do you get them to stop?"

The Master of Sinanju's hazel eyes blazed open. The sight was a shock to his aged heart. There were the villagers—his people—clustered about Remo, kissing his hands and offering him the traditional greeting.

Chiun stamped a sandaled foot. A nearby barnacled rock split and fell in two sections. Chiun yelled in Korean.

"He is not Master yet! I am still Master! I, Chiun. Do you hear me? You, Pullyang, speak to me. Has there been any trouble since last you wrote? Is the treasure safe?"

"Yes," said Pullyang, scurrying to fall at Chiun's feet.

"And are my scrolls still in their resting places?"

"Yes, O Master," said Pullyang.

"Pullyang deserted his post," said a pinch-faced woman, running to Chiun's side. "He fled when the devil herons came."

"Herons?" asked Chiun, not understanding.

Pullyang threw himself at Chiun's feet. "I only left to call the villagers back after they fled the coming of the purple birds. They had all deserted the village for the hills. I went after them when the birds were gone."

"You left the House of the Masters unguarded!" shrieked Chiun.

"For minutes only," protested Pullyang.

"Minutes! An empire can fall in seconds."

"No harm was done," Pullyang promised. "I examined the door. It was locked."

"Did you enter?"

"No, I would have had to break the door. That is forbidden."

"Not when it assures that all my property is safe. Come, Remo, we must see to the treasure."

"What's the rush?" Remo said testily. "If it's gone, it's gone. The trail won't get any colder. I want to see Mah-Li. Why isn't she here?"

"Do not be a complete fool. It is forbidden for you to see her. You are to be married."

"What does that have to do with anything?" asked Remo.

"The bride is always placed in seclusion before she is

wed. It is traditional in this country. You will see her at the ceremony.''

"When? Next year?"

"No, tomorrow. The wedding is scheduled for tomorrow," snapped Chiun. "Now, are you coming?"

"Tomorrow? Really, Chiun? No tricks?"

"No tricks. Now, will you come?"

"I'm with you," said Remo.

At the door to the House of the Masters, Chiun examined the wood with a critical eye.

"There," said Remo. "It's still sealed."

"We shall see," replied Chiun, pressing the top panels, which released the inner locks. Then he removed the bottom panel, undid the dowel, and pushed the door open.

Remo followed him in. Old Pullyang lit tapers on the floor. Light swelled in the main room, revealing stacks of gold and treasure surrounding the low teak throne of the Master of Sinanju.

"The treasure's still here," Remo pointed out.

"There is more than one treasure of Sinanju," sniffed Chiun, stepping into the next room, where his steamer trunks reposed. Chiun fell upon these and snapped open each lid until all seventeen displayed their contents.

"Looks fine to me," said Remo.

"Someone has been in here," Chiun said softly.

"Says who?" Remo demanded.

"Say I. Look," Chiun said, lifting pinched fingers to Remo's nose.

Remo looked. Something like a silver thread hung from Chiun's fingertips.

"A hair," he said. "So what?"

"Not just any hair, but the hair of the Master Wang."

"Wang?"

"Yes, it is customarily stretched across the receptacle of the oldest, most sacred scrolls of Sinanju and anchored at either end by the saliva of the current Master. It is an honored Sinanju tradition."

"I think it's gotten around since then," Remo said dryly.

"It lay loose, not anchored."

"Maybe it came loose on its own," suggested Remo.

"The adhesive power of Sinanju Masters' saliva is legendary," said Chiun. "This hair was pushed aside by an intruding hand. I must count my scrolls to see if any are missing. Meanwhile, it is your duty to inventory the treasure.''

''And what shall I do, Master?'' asked Pullyang.

''You sit in the corner, facing the wall. Your carelessness may have cost Sinanju a priceless relic. I will decide your punishment later.''

''Hey, don't be so hard on him,'' said Remo. ''It sounds like he had a good reason for going.''

Chiun simply glared at Remo.

''Why don't I check on the treasure?'' Remo said, slipping out of the room.

When Remo returned to report that the treasure seemed intact, Chiun nodded absently.

''It is as I thought,'' he said. ''Nothing was taken. Not treasure, not scrolls. But some of the histories of Sinanju have been read, for the ribbons are not tied correctly.''

''What do you make of it?'' Remo wanted to know.

''Tulip has been here.''

''Yeah, I guess we can assume that. Let's get Pullyang's story.''

Old Pullyang squatted in a dark corner of the House of the Masters, his face to the wall.

''Arise, wretch, and face your Master,'' Chiun commanded.

Pullyang got to his feet and faced Remo. He trembled.

''No, not him. I am Master here,'' spat Chiun.

Pullyang turned like a dog. ''Yes, Master.''

''Your story,'' Chiun demanded.

And Pullyang babbled a long, convoluted tale of the devil herons which had come down from the stars because poor old Pullyang had foolishly looked up at them. He told about their leathery purple wings and their baleful green eyes and how they perched on the Horns of Welcome, casting no shadows, and how the villagers fled their gaze. All but poor loyal Pullyang, who waited and waited until at last the birds were gone and it was safe for the villagers to return. But the villagers did not know that, and so Pullyang had to go and seek them out.

''I was gone but a few minutes,'' he finished piteously.

''In which direction did these birds fly away?''

''I did not notice, O Master.''

"If they stared at you, and you at them, how could they depart unseen by you?" Chiun demanded.

"It may have been that I closed my eyes momentarily, for their gaze was awful. It seemed to freeze my very soul."

Chiun placed his hands on his hips and turned to Remo.

"What do you make of his prattling?"

"I don't think they were herons, Little Father," Remo said.

"Of course they were herons. This man knows herons when he sees them."

"They were too big for herons," muttered Pullyang.

"Then what were they?" challenged Chiun.

"I do not know," Pullyang quavered. "I have never heard of birds such as these, even in tales of old."

"Nor have I. Therefore they must have been herons—very large herons."

Remo shook his head. "He wasn't describing herons. He was describing pterodactyls."

"I have never heard of birds called that," Chiun countered.

"Pterodactyls aren't birds," said Remo in a strange voice. "They are lizards, I think. But they have wings, like bats."

"There is no such thing in all of Sinanju history," snapped Chiun.

"Were they like bats?" Remo asked Pullyang.

"Their wings, yes. But they had heron-demon faces. I did not know what they were."

"Whatever they were," Remo said, "they sure didn't sneak into this place while the villagers were up in the hills. That means somebody sent them—probably to scare everyone off so he could slip in unseen and go through your scrolls."

"There are no such birds as you describe, Remo," Chiun insisted. "I think Pullyang is making this up."

"Didn't the villagers admit they saw the birds too?"

"It is a conspiracy, then. The villagers themselves stole in to read the histories. And they will all be punished," added Chiun, looking at Pullyang severely.

"I don't think so," said Remo.

"I say again, there are no such creatures as this wretch describes."

"That's the weird part, Little Father. Pterodactyls don't

exist anymore. They haven't existed in millions of years. They're dinosaurs. They all died out before Sinanju came along.''

"If that is so, how would you know of them?" demanded Chiun.

"I read about them when I was a kid. Every American kid knows about pterodactyls and dinosaurs.''

"My ancestors would have mentioned such creatures if they existed," said Chiun with finality. "But just to be certain, I will look through my histories for mention of these terrorbirds. How do you spell the name?''

"Got me. But it starts with a P," Remo said.

"P?" sputtered Chiun. "You mean a T, do you not?''

"No, it's P, then T. The P is silent.''

"You are making this up, aren't you?''

"No, honest," Remo insisted.

Turning to Pullyang, the Master of Sinanju said, "Go. I will decide your fate later.''

Old Pullyang lost no time in finding his way out of the House of the Masters.

"If there's nothing missing," Remo said after some thought, "then there's no real harm done.''

"Yes, there is. Whoever entered this dwelling knew how to work the locks. That is a secret reserved for Masters of Sinanju only.''

"I didn't do it," protested Remo.

"Nor did I.''

"Then who?''

"I know not. But I will find out. Perhaps as early as the morning. But for now, I am weary and require sleep. Tomorrow will be a stressful day, for I must watch helplessly while the white upon whom I have bestowed the gift of Sinanju weds a maiden he barely knows.''

"I'll ignore that crack," said Remo. "But only because I'm in a good mood.''

"No doubt you would tell jokes at your own execution.''

22

He changed planes in London for a KAL flight to Seoul.

He had been a Spaniard during the first leg of his journey, with haughty Castilian features and an inner composure that made people hesitate to intrude upon his thoughts. The simulacrum kept the couple occupying the adjoining seats from bothering him with tourist chatter. For good measure, he had held a paperback book open on his lap, focusing on it, but not reading. It kept the beast inside of him under control.

The flight was uneventful.

Phase One was complete. Remo and Chiun were cut off from their American employer. They would never again work for that country.

At the KAL counter he insisted upon a window seat. The ticket girl was happy to oblige.

"Here you are, Mr. . . ." She paused to look at the ticket. "Mr. Nuihc," she said smilingly.

"Thank you," he said. His name was not Nuihc. Nor was it Osorio, the name he had used on the earlier flight. Now he was a moon-faced Korean, impassive and soft of voice. In the men's room he checked himself in the mirror. Even the mirror reflected the lie that was his face. Yes, it was a good face. No one would bother him during the flight. And that was good, because if the beast started killing, it would kill them all, including the flight crew. And that would be suicide because he did not know how to pilot the big airliner.

As it happened, the seats next to him were empty. He relaxed. This was better than he had hoped. He shut his eyes and dozed.

He awoke when the stewardess screamed.

Smoke boiled from the forward galley. Yellow oxygen masks dropped from the overhead compartments.

A steward in a neat uniform grabbed a dry chemical extinguisher from an overhead rack and doused the flames. After a few minutes the captain came over the intercom and joked that he shouldn't have turned off the no-smoking signs so soon. He explained that a microwave in the galley had shorted and caught fire. An accident.

"Mr. Nuihc" did not think it was an accident. It must have been the beast, the beast inside him that wanted everyone on the plane dead. It had caused the short.

He decided not to sleep for the remainder of the flight.

The blond woman came down the aisle after lunch had been served. He had not noticed her during the preboarding wait at Heathrow. She had been seated in front. She was tall and athletic, her blond hair braided in coils on either side of her womanly face. Her eyes were cornflower blue, but as she passed down the aisle they shifted color like a turbulent sea, going from blue to green and green to gray and back again.

She led a small child—who was practically her image except for some residual baby fat in the cheeks—to the rest rooms at the rear of the aircraft.

He recognized the mother, but not the little child, who was bundled up in a snowsuit and parka hood.

Averting his gaze, he gripped the seat armrests tightly. No, not now, he told himself. Please, not now. This was too good, too perfect. You can have her later, beast. Not now. Later. I promise. Later.

But the beast was raging within him. It would have to be unleashed. Below, the ocean sparkled. Desperately his eyes sought a target, a release for the unstoppable force building within. An oil tanker slid into view. Perfect. He focused on it. Silently, it went up in a ball of fire. The plane vibrated in the turbulence of the shock wave.

The blond woman and the child passed him, clutching the seats to keep their balance. Satiated, the beast allowed them to live.

He closed his eyes tightly and kept them shut until the faint natural scent of the woman passed him on the return trip and he knew they were seated and out of his line of sight.

He relaxed again.

In Seoul he would hire a vehicle and see how far north the driver would take him. If necessary, he would walk across the demilitarized zone. It would not be hard. He would walk all the way to his destination if he had to. There was no rush. In North Korea the beast would be fed. And there would be plenty of food for the beast within him, because he knew that the tall woman's ultimate destination, like his own, was the village of Sinanju.

23

Mah-Li wept.

She knelt in the middle of the floor of her house, her eyes downcast, regarding the bamboo floor. Rice-paper squares were pasted over her eyes to inhibit her vision. Her long black hair had been put up at the back of her neck and her face was powdered the traditional bridal white. Her tears soaked the rice paper and cut channels through the face powder.

"I long so to see my Remo," she said.

"Hush, child," cautioned one of the elder women of the village, a crone name Yuli, as she repaired the streaks in Mah-Li's makeup. "Custom must be observed. You will see your husband tomorrow at the wedding. You have waited a year. Is one more night too much?"

"I must know if he still loves me," Mah-Li said plaintively. "He did not write. He always writes. What if he rejects me? What if he has found a new lover in the land where he was born?"

"Master Chiun has proclaimed that the wedding will take place tomorrow. Is that not assurance enough? Think upon your fortune, to marry the future Master of the village. That he is white is not important. After all, you are an orphan. You would have no dowry without Master Chiun, and no prospects for marriage."

Mah-Li bowed her head low. Not in shame, but because custom demanded a bride-to-be feign humility on the night before her wedding.

"I know," she said.

"A year ago you were Mah-Li, the orphan. Tomorrow at this time you will be Mah-Li, the next Master's wife."

"I know," repeated Mah-Li. "But a feeling of dread has come over me ever since the purple birds came. Something clutches at my heart. I know not what it is. I wish Remo were here.''

"He is not far. Think on that. I must go now."

After Yuli had gone, Mah-Li tried to keep the rice-paper squares in place over her eyes, but she could not. Her tears had soaked into the flour adhesive.

Mah-Li did not hear the footsteps approach the house. The door was not locked, because in Sinanju ordinary homes were never locked. Out of the corner of her eye Mah-Li saw the door open, and she caught a glimpse of a tall figure.

Her indrawn breath was quick and sharp. Remo she told herself. But why had he come? It was against tradition for the groom to invade the bride's quarters before the wedding.

Mah-Li kept her eyes riveted to the floor. Her peripheral vision told her that the man was white. It must be Remo. There were no other whites in all of Sinanju, and no whites in all the world, so far as Mah-Li knew, who walked with the soft cat-padding step of a Master of Sinanju.

Mah-Li's heart pounded within her, wild and uncertain. Whatever Remo wanted, she decided, it was up to him to speak first. Even if it was to tell her that he no longer wanted to marry Mah-Li, poor Mah-Li, the orphan.

Mah-Li closed her liquid eyes and held her breath, waiting.

24

Remo Williams awoke to the sound of impatient clapping.

"Up, up, lazy one," barked the Master of Sinanju. "Would you sleep through your wedding day?"

"Oww, not so close to my ear, okay, Chiun? I'd like to be able to hear the ceremony." Remo sat up on his sleeping mat, blinking the sleep from his eyes. The Master of Sinanju stood dressed in a flowing white jacket over white cotton trousers. He wore a black stovepipe hat on his nearly hairless head. It was tied under his chin with string.

"What are you supposed to be?" Remo asked, getting up.

"The father of the groom," snapped Chiun, turning to rummage through a pile of clothes heaped on a *tatami* mat. "But perhaps if I stand in the back during the ceremony, no one will recognize me."

"Very funny," said Remo. "What's that stuff?"

"Your wedding garments."

"There's enough cloth in this pile to outfit the Bolshoi Ballet. I can't wear all that."

"These are the wedding vestments of past Masters," said Chiun, holding up a green-and-blue costume that might have suited a geisha girl. "We must find one that will fit you."

"This isn't exactly my style," commented Remo, examining the cloth. It was pure silk.

"You have no style. But with the proper garments that sad fact might go unnoticed long enough for you to get through the ceremony. Ah, here is a worthy one."

Remo took the offered garment.

"Very colorful," he said dryly. "In fact, I don't think there's a single color in existence not on this thing. Hmmm, wait a minute, I don't see puke yellow. Oh, here it is, in the shape of a cat. See? Under the left armpit."

"That is a badger," snapped Chiun, ripping the cloth from Remo's hand and tossing it onto a second pile. "And you are obviously not worthy to dress in the garment I wore at my wedding."

"That was yours?" said Remo, dumbfounded.

"Try this one. It belonged to Master Ku."

"I've never looked right in snakeskin," protested Remo. "Besides, this would just about fit a midget if he didn't button it."

"That is exactly the problem," said Chiun, throwing the garment of the Master Ku onto the second pile. "All past Masters of Sinanju have been properly sized. You, on the other hand, are a big clod-footed freak. None of these will fit you."

"How about if I go as I am?" suggested Remo, spreading his arms.

Chiun looked Remo up and down. Remo was dressed in the white T-shirt and black slacks he'd worn to Sinanju. Chiun made a sour face.

"I will work something out," he said, returning to the piles of clothes.

Remo, seeing that this was going to take some time, assumed a lotus position in the middle of the floor and cupped his chin in his hands.

"You don't seem happy, Little Father."

"I am not," said Chiun, taking a frilly yellow garment and tearing off long strips.

"I know you wanted to stay in America, working for Smith. I know you're not happy that I'm getting married, but couldn't you, just for today, pretend my happiness isn't a conspiracy against your well-being? For me?"

"For you, I will see that you are properly attired for your wedding. Is that not enough?"

"Okay," said Remo in a light voice. "Why don't you tell me about the wedding ritual? That pile of rags leads me to believe I'm not being prepared for a quickie civil ceremony. What do I do?"

"After you have properly dressed, you will go to the bride's house riding a suitable steed. There you will meet and drink wine, and promise devotion to your bride, and she to you. It is a simple ritual. Even a white could not mess it up."

"I can't drink wine, you know that. The alcohol would short-circuit my system."

"I take back my rash words. You may be the exception that proves the rule. Never mind, we will worry about that part when we get to it. Ah, this one is good. It matches your eyes."

"It looks like shit, color and texture."

"Yes, your eyes exactly," agreed Chiun, winding the cloth around Remo's forehead and tying it off so that it nearly obscured Remo's vision. He stepped back. "It is a beginning," he said, and with his long fingernails he loosened the seams of a pair of green trousers. "Put these on," he ordered.

Remo climbed into the green trousers.

"The cuffs barely cover my knees," Remo complained. "I look like some twerp whose idea of a day at the beach is to go wading up to his ankles."

"I will take care of that. Stand still!" And kneeling, Chiun wound strips of different-colored cloth around Remo's bare calves with furious motions.

"Not so tight, huh?" Remo pleaded.

"Now the jacket," said Chiun, offering Remo a tigerskin tunic.

Remo held it up. "Too small," he pronounced.

"Try it."

Remo did. Without removing the T-shirt, he slipped his arms into the tigerskin jacket. It smelled of must. When he got it on, he tried to close it in front with loop-and-button fasteners.

"No, do not strain it," warned Chiun. "It is fine just like that."

Remo turned. Behind a tapestry was a gold-framed mirror. Remo swept the tapestry aside and looked at his reflection.

"No way," he said firmly. "I look like Elvis Presley as a bag lady."

"I am sure her wedding garment was equally memorable," Chiun pronounced happily.

"I'm not going to be married dressed like this."

"If you would prefer to have a wedding vestment made specially for you, that could be arranged. But we would have to postpone the wedding two, perhaps three, weeks."

Remo considered. "Okay. But only because you might change your mind if I wait any longer. What's next?"

A timid knocking came from the outer door.

"Enter," proclaimed Chiun.

A dirty-faced boy rushed up to the Master of Sinanju and tugged on his trousers. Chiun bent an ear and the boy whispered.

"Excellent, thank you," said Chiun, shooing the boy off.

"What's the secret word?" asked Remo when the boy was gone.

"I am informed that wedding guests have arrived."

"Must be your relatives. I don't have any."

"Do not be so certain," said Chiun.

"What's that supposed to mean?"

"It means that it is time for the wedding feast."

"Now? This early?"

"This early? This early?" said Chiun, his hazel eyes blazing. "For a year you have carped and complained, complained and kvetched, because you cannot get married. Now that the day has come, you recoil as from a serpent's tongue. We can call it off if that is your wish. I would be shamed forever, but it could be done."

"Now, I'm not trying to call it off, it's just . . . it's just . . ."

"Yes?"

"Well, after a year of your stalling, it seems strange that you're suddenly rushing me into this."

"Who is rushing?" said Chiun, pushing Remo out of the room. "Come, your steed awaits."

Remo, trailing loose strips of cloth, followed Chiun to the throne room of the House of the Masters. Outside, a bullock was uprooting stones with his nose.

"I thought you said a suitable steed," Remo said, looking at the bullock.

"Normally it is a pony," explained Chiun. "But if you mounted one of our delicate Korean ponies, you would break its spine. This is the next best thing."

Reluctantly Remo climbed onto the bullock's bowed back. The bullock moaned a low protest.

"I don't think he's used to being ridden," said Remo.

"It is just a short ride. Now, sit still, and whatever you do, do not fall off."

"Tell that to the bullock."

And Chiun took up the azalea-garlanded rope and led the bullock down into the village, crying, "Come all, come all, the day of the wedding of Remo the Fair is at hand. Come to the house of Mah-Li."

"You sound like the town crier," Remo whispered, trying to keep his balance. He noticed that Chiun carried something under one arm. It was a wooden duck.

"Going duck hunting?" Remo asked.

"The duck is part of the ceremony. Among my people, the duck is venerated as a symbol of marital fidelity. Fidelity is very important in a marriage. We value it highly."

"Thank you, Dr. Ruth."

Out of the peak-roofed houses of Sinanju, men, women, and children poured out in the bullock's wake. They laughed and danced and sang. Mostly they laughed, Remo noticed. And they pointed. At him.

"You know, Little Father," Remo whispered tersely, "if I didn't know better, I'd say they're all laughing at me."

"Who wouldn't laugh at a too-tall white man dressed like a ragamuffin and riding a bullock," said Chiun smugly.

"You're doing this on purpose," hissed Remo. "You're trying to make me a laughingstock."

"No, you *are* a laughingstock. I did not make you."

Remo almost lost his balance as the bullock picked its way down to the shore road, which led to the house of Mah-Li on the outskirts of the village.

"What's the deal here, Chiun? You're still jealous that the villagers are paying too much attention to me, so you dress me up like a clown to take me down a peg in their eyes. Honk if I'm getting warm."

"Would I do that to you, and on your wedding day?"

"You'd do it to me at my freaking funeral if it served your purposes."

"Hush," warned Chiun. "We are nearly to the house of your bride. Try to compose yourself. You have the pleasant expression of a pig stuck in a tree."

Remo took a deep breath. It felt hot in his throat. Here it is, he thought to himself, my wedding day and I look like Bozo the Clown. Behind him, the villagers of Sinanju formed a ragged noisy line like revelers at a Mardi Gras.

"Hold," said Chiun in a voice loud enough to carry into

South Korea. The bullock snorted and stopped at the court-yard of Mah-Li's modest hut.

Two Sinanju maidens dressed in finery stood on either side of Mah-Li's door and bowed as Remo dismounted clumsily.

"What do I do now?" Remo whispered to Chiun.

"Go and bow to the table three times," he said. "And try not to trip over your big feet."

"I'm nervous," Remo whispered, his heart pounding.

The courtyard was decorated with long rice-paper strips on which Korean wishes of good fortune were marked in black ink. A wooden table stood in the middle of the court-yard. A bottle of wine had been placed between a plate of jujube fruit and an empty bowl.

Remo bowed three times before the table.

"Now what?" he asked Chiun.

"Stand still. If that is possible."

Off to one side, Remo saw a stack of gold ingots. Mah-Li's dowry—a gift from Chiun. It was the final CURE payment made to Chiun, one year ago, by Harold Smith.

"Where is she?" asked Remo, looking around.

"Hush," said Chiun.

The two bridesmaids in blue-and-white kimonos opened the hut door. Mah-Li, attired in a splendid bridal costume of red silk, emerged from within. The bridemaids escorted her to the table and Mah-Li stood, her head bowed as if in shame.

The wedding party gathered around. Those who could not fit into the courtyard peered in from outside the little gate. There was some snickering among the solemn faces.

"Look at her, Chiun," Remo whispered. "She's ashamed of me. How could you do this to her?"

"Korean maidens always stand modestly before their hus-bands-to-be. It is our way. Now, go and stand with her."

Remo went around the table and the bride lifted her face. Once again Remo felt that familiar stab of desire in his stomach. The face staring back at him was radiant with a youthful innocence. Her dark eyes were haunting.

"Hello, kid," Remo breathed. "Long time no see."

Remo was rewarded by a shy smile and downcast eyes.

Officiously Chiun stepped up to the couple and waved the

bridesmaids back. Taking a long strip of white cloth, he bound Remo's wrist to those of Mah-Li.

"I bind their hands, this man and this woman, to signify that they are forever united."

Chiun faced the audience, his hands raised as if in invocation. Remo noticed that his birdlike eyes searched the crowd worriedly.

"As the father of the groom, not by blood, but by ties of Sinanju, I hereby accept the dowry of Mah-Li," Chiun proclaimed gesturing to the stacks of gold ingots.

The old pirate, thought Remo. After all that, he ends up with Smith's gold anyway.

"Now all that remains is to join these two in wedlock," said Chiun, who Remo saw was up on tiptoe, trying to see over the heads of the wedding audience. Chiun's face wrinkled concernedly. "Now all that remains is to join these two in wedlock," he repeated in a louder voice. The crowd fidgeted. Chiun pressed on. "But first, I must speak of what it means to be married. Being a husband, like being a wife, means devotion to spouse. But unlike in certain barbarian countries, it requires more than a spouse to make a family. Or a happy marriage. Others should be considered. Especially the elder relatives of the married couple. Some people, in some lands," said Chiun, eyeing Remo closely, "think that marriage means leaving their families. Not in Korea. Not in Sinanju. Here, when a man takes his bride, both are welcomed into the groom's family, making for a larger, happier family. Let us not, because we see this day a new era dawning in our village, abandon the old for the new."

"Pssst," hissed Remo. "I get the message, okay? Can we wind this up?"

"Cast the old for the tried and true," added Chiun, pleased that he had made part of his speech rhyme. His neck bobbed this way and that, scanning the stolid faces of the wedding party.

"By custom, the groom will spend the next three days here, in the bride's house," Chiun went on distractedly. "At the end of the third day, the newlyweds will be obligated to come and live in the house of the male line. Because the groom is from a foreign land and not one of us by birth, I will now ask him to agree to our honored custom.''

And Chiun turned to face Remo, grinning like a cat.

"Yes," Remo said, brittle-voiced. Under his breath he added, "You always get your way, don't you?"

"Only when it counts," Chiun answered, turning his back on the bride and groom so that he again faced the wedding party. Remo saw his shoulders lift, a sure sign of a deep breath and the beginning of another long-winded oratory. Remo wondered if Chiun intended to stretch the ceremony over the whole three-day honeymoon.

Abruptly Chiun turned to face them again.

"I now ask the bride to say that she accepts the groom."

Remo heard, for the first time since he had returned to Sinanju, Mah-Li's sweet voice whisper a breathy, "Yes."

"I now ask the groom," intoned Chiun, "if he accepts the maiden as his bride, today and forever."

"I do," said Remo.

Chiun faced the crowd one last time. He raised his hands so that the sleeves of his costume fell back, exposing spindly arms.

"I now ask those assembled here to witness this marriage. And before I pronounce them wed, I further ask if there is anyone present who objects to the joining of these two."

The crowd gasped with one voice. Such a question had never before been asked at a Sinanju wedding. Was it some strange American custom? How were they to respond? The members of the wedding party looked at one another blankly.

And through the crowd, a tiny face pushed out from between the legs of Pullyang, causing the old village caretaker to cackle with surprise. Tiny brown eyes fixed on Remo Williams and widened suddenly.

"Daddy, Daddy!" a childish voice said, a smile breaking over a cherubic face.

Remo blinked. A tiny figure bundled in a blue snowsuit toddled up and wrapped stubby arms around his right leg.

"What's this?" Remo asked awkwardly.

The Master of Sinanju hurled the wooden duck to the ground, causing its head to snap off. He clapped his hands once, sharply.

"There has been a mistake," he proclaimed. "This man is not pure. I declare this marriage invalid because the groom is not a virgin."

"Not a . . ." sputtered Remo. "Since when is that news?"

"The bride did not know," said Chiun. "Only one who is pure in mind and body may take a Sinanju maiden to wive. Remo, I am ashamed of you for leading her to believe otherwise when the proof of your unchaste behavior clings to your leg for all to see."

Remo turned. "Mah-Li, I don't know what this is all about," he said, anxiously. "Honest."

"You do not?" a woman's crisp voice asked from the crowd.

Remo's head snapped around. The voice. It was familiar.

Standing at the front of the crowd, drapped in a forest-green cloak, was a tall blond woman with coils of hair on either side of her face. Her eyes shone an angry green, and then darkened to a flat unfriendly gray.

"Jilda!" gasped Remo.

25

It had all happened so fast that Remo Williams was para-
lyzed by surprise.

Jilda of Lakluun stood before him, throwing back her long
cloak to reveal a Viking warrior costume of leather and chain
mail. She wore a short dagger clipped to her belt.

"How?" Remo sputtered. "I mean, hi! Uh, what are you
doing here?"

"Before you wed this woman," Jilda said frostily, "you
should look upon your child. Then if it is your wish to wed,
so be it."

Remo looked down. Troubled brown eyes stared up at
him. The child hugged Remo's leg tightly.

Remo looked up, his face stricken. "Mine?"

Jilda of Lakluun nodded severely. "Ours."

Remo turned to his betrothed. "Mah-Li, I . . ."

But she was no longer standing there. Remo saw that the
white strips of cloth that had bound their wrists together
dangled loosely from his arm. And the door to Mah-Li's
house slammed shut after a scarlet train of silk.

The Master of Sinanju stepped to Remo's side and lifted
the child from Remo's leg. He faced the wedding audience,
holding the child above his head with both hands.

"Do not feel sad, my people. For although no wedding
will take place on this day, behold the son of my adopted
son by the warrior woman Jilda of Lakluun!"

The people of Sinanju started to cheer. But the cheering
died in their throats.

"White," they whispered. "It is white. Are no Koreans
ever again to take responsibility for our little village?"

Remo stepped in front of Chiun.

"You did this," he said. "You told Jilda about the wedding."

Chiun stepped around Remo so the audience could see the child, who stared wide-eyed and uncomprehending at the wedding party.

"Later," he hissed. "This is the crucial moment. The village must accept your son as Sinanju."

"What am I going to tell Mah-Li?" Remo said hotly.

"She will find another. Mah-Li is young; her heart is resilient. Now, be silent!" Again Chiun addressed the crowd. "You call this child white," he cried. "It is white—now. But within a year he will be less white. In five, you will not be able to tell him from a village child. And in twenty, he will be Sinanju in mind and body and soul."

"His eyes are round," a boy said.

"He will grow out of it," insisted Chiun. "Already the sun source burns within him. After Master Chiun, there will be Master Remo. And after Master Remo, there will be this one, Master . . . What is his name?" he asked Jilda from the side of his mouth.

"Freya, daughter of Remo," Jilda said.

"Freya, daughter o—" Chiun's mouth froze on the open vowel.

The villagers broke into howling laughter. They pointed at the little girl and openly mocked Remo's tattered figure.

Remo looked at Freya, at Jilda, and again at Freya. He mouthed the question: Daughter? Jilda nodded.

Abruptly the Master of Sinanju handed the child to her mother, his face bitter. He waded into the crowd.

"Away! Away with you all! What follows here is not for the ears of common villagers."

Reluctantly the village people started to drift off. Curiosity slowed their feet. But at an angry exhortation from Master Chiun, they broke and ran. The Master was beside himself with fury. They understood it was not safe to remain.

Chiun waited until the last flop of sandaled feet had faded from hearing. He faced Remo and Jilda.

"You tricked me!" Remo said.

"And me," added Jilda. "Your letter told me nothing about a wedding. Only that my presence was urgently required."

Chiun dismissed their complaints with flapping hands. "Trivia! I will not hear of it! Do you not realize what has happened here?"

"Yes," Remo said bitterly. "You ruined my life."

"Your life! Your life! What about mine? I am shamed. You are shamed. We are all shamed."

"What have I to feel shame for?" asked Jilda, patting Freya's head. Frightened by Chiun's strident voice, the little girl had buried her face in Jilda's shoulder.

"For this!" said Chiun, pulling back the hood of Freya's snowsuit. It came off like a golf-club cover, revealing hair like new gold.

Remo and Jilda looked at Chiun blankly.

Seeing their expressions, Chiun stamped a foot and spoke his shame aloud, which only made it worse. "A female. The firstborn of my adopted son, the next Master of Sinanju, is a lowly female."

"So what?" said Remo.

"Yes, so?" agreed Jilda.

Chiun pulled at the hair tufts over his ears in frustration. "So what! So what! She is useless. Masters of Sinanju have always been male."

"I have not given permission that this child be entered into Sinanju training," Jilda said firmly.

"Your permission is not needed," snapped Chiun. "This does not concern you, only Remo, the child, and me."

"I am the child's mother."

"Has she been weaned?"

"Of course. She is nearly four years old."

"That means your work is done. Remo is the father and I the grandfather—in spirit, of course. We make all decisions concerning the child's future. But it does not matter now. Everyone knows that females are uneducable. Their bodies cannot handle Sinanju. They are good only for cooking and breeding. In that order."

"Have you forgotten, old man, that I was the representative of my people at your Master's Trial? Only Remo and I survived that ordeal. I am female and a warrior too."

"A warrior is not an assassin," Chiun spat. "My people will never again look upon us with respect. It is your fault, Remo. You gave this woman the wrong seed. You should have given her a good male seed, not an inferior female seed."

"I'm a father," Remo said bewilderedly. He reached out to touch the little girl's hair. It felt soft and fine.

"You sound surprised," snorted Chiun. "You knew that she bore your seed when you and this woman parted after the Master's Trial."

"I asked that you not tell him," Jilda said accusingly. "You promised to keep this child our secret."

"He had to know. The child bears the spirit of Sinanju. Or at least I supposed it had. Why did you not tell me it was a female?"

"This is Remo's child. The rest does not matter."

And at that particular piece of white imbecility, the Master of Sinanju threw up his hands.

"I give up! I am ruined. Disgraced. And no one understands."

But neither Remo nor Jilda was listening. Remo was stroking his daughter's head as Jilda looked on tenderly. The tension seeped from her face, to be replaced by a mother's contented pride.

"Hi, there," Remo said quietly. "You don't know me, but I'm your daddy."

Little Freya looked up. "Daddy," she giggled, reaching for Remo's face. "I missed you."

"May I?" Remo asked. Jilda nodded.

Remo took his child in his arms. She was heavier than he had expected. Freya had most of Jilda's features, but her face was rounder. Her eyes were as brown as Remo's, but not as deeply set.

"How could you miss me?" Remo asked. "You've never met me before today."

Freya hugged Remo's neck. "Because you're my daddy," she answered. "All little girls miss their daddies. Don't they?"

"Awww," said Remo, hugging her tightly.

"Uggh!" said Chiun, turning his back disdainfully.

"Little Father, maybe you should go for a walk or something," Remo suggested. "Jilda and I have things to discuss."

"If anyone wants me," Chiun muttered, "I will be committing suicide. Not that anyone cares." He strode up the shore path, his stovepipe hat rocking to his angry gait.

Jilda took Freya from Remo and placed her on the ground.

"Play, child," she bade her daughter.

"Why didn't you tell me about her?" Remo asked, watching Freya playing with the good-luck streamers.

"You know my reasons."

"I want to hear them from you."

"After the Master's trial, when I knew that I carried your child, I understood that there could be no place for me in your life. Nor you in mine. I did not belong in Sinanju. I could not be with you in America. Your work is dangerous. You have many enemies—and one enemy in particular. I could not risk this child's life. Keeping my own counsel was the only way I knew to avoid our facing an impossible choice."

"I almost went after you, you know."

"I would have fled," Jilda said.

"But you're here now," Remo pointed out.

"I received a letter from Master Chiun, bidding me to come to Sinanju. I was told you were in danger, and that only my and our child's presence would save you."

"Yeah," Remo said bitterly. "From matrimony."

"Do you love her?" Jilda asked, nodding toward the closed door of Mah-Li's house.

"I think so. I thought I did. Seeing you here again has me all confused. I thought we'd never meet again. And now this."

"I, too, feel mixed emotions. Seeing you about to wed was like a sword sliding into my belly. I hold you to no promises, Remo, for we made none to each other. Your life is your own. As is mine."

"It's different now. I don't work for America. I'm planning on settling here."

"Then perhaps it is time that we face the hard choices we fled from when last we were together," said Jilda, smiling tentatively.

Impulsively Remo took her in his strong arms and kissed her.

Freya broke out in bubbly laughter. "Mommy and Daddy like each other!" she said, clapping her hands with glee.

"Let's go for a walk," Remo suggested. "The three of us."

"What about her?" asked Jilda.

Remo shot a guilty glance at the house of Mah-Li.

"One insurmountable problem at a time," he said, reaching out to take Jilda by one hand and Freya with the other. It felt right somehow.

26

The Master of Sinanju sat amid the splendor of his treasure. His parchment face was strained. Before him the scrolls of Sinanju stood upright in glazed celadon holders. Chiun went from one to another, searching for guidance.

There was no precedent in all the history of Sinanju for such a thing. Never before had a Master failed to produce a male on the first try. Masters of Sinanju, being absolute masters of their bodies, possessed the ability to produce males at will. Remo had been taught the exercises that built up the male seed so that there was no chance for error. But of course, Remo, being lazy, had complained about the exercises.

And now this. Chiun hoped to discover guidance in the writings of his ancestors. Perhaps the child should be sacrificed to the sea, as was done in past times when the village was without sufficient food. The infants were drowned in the cold waters of Sinanju harbor.

But there was no record of that ever being done with the offspring of the Masters. Perhaps, Chiun thought, that meant that he was free to create his own solution. It had been a rare thing, these last five centuries, for a reigning Master to inaugurate new traditions, and a faint smile tugged at his dry lips at the thought of entering another first in the records of the Master Chiun.

But that still left the problem.

Chiun heard Remo's approach before the knocking started.

"That door is thousands of years old," Chiun said. "If you break it with your ridiculous knocking, I will hold you personally responsible."

The door opened with a splintering crash. Wood chips flew everywhere.

"Are you mad?" cried Chiun, horror wrinkling his face. "This is a desecration!"

"Look, don't give me any of that crap," Remo shouted back. He had changed out of his makeshift wedding costume. "It's all your fault I'm in this mess."

"I am the one who is in a mess. I have to decide what is to be done about the daughter you have inflicted upon me."

"Inflicted? What kind of talk is that?"

"Sinanju talk. Men are born into the world. Women are inflicted upon it."

"Not in my book," Remo said.

"No, but in my scrolls. How could you sire a female? Had I taught you nothing? You knew the exercises."

"Those weren't exercises. They were torture."

"A minor sacrifice to ensure a male is produced."

"I don't call drinking fish oil for a week before I do it, holding a pomegranate in my right hand and poppy seeds in my mouth while I'm doing it, and plucking my eyebrows afterward minor sacrifices."

"The eyebrow plucking can be dispensed with," Chiun said dismissively. "It is only for luck."

"Look, Jilda and I have been talking. There's a chance we can come to an understanding about our future."

"I might agree to that."

"Might?"

"On one condition. She sells the baby."

"No chance. How could you even ask that?"

"According to Sinanju tradition, the firstborn is trained in Sinanju. But never women. She must be trained, but she cannot be trained because she is female. It is a conundrum I cannot resolve."

"Solve it later. I've got a problem too. What about Mah-Li? I love her, but after what's happened, she probably hates me."

"I will speak with her."

"I think I should be the one. But I don't know what to say to her. I need your help."

"Help?" muttered Chiun, picking through his scrolls. "Ah, this one covers that eventuality," he said, unrolling it. "Listen, 'In the event that the Master must break off his betrothal to one woman because he has stupidly sired a female first born by another, matters can be brought to a balance by offering said child to the jilted one and trying for a boy with the other.' ''

''What? Let me see that,'' demanded Remo, snatching up the scroll. He ran his eyes down the parchment. ''It says no such thing. This is all about lineage.''

Chiun shrugged. ''It was worth a try,'' he said.

''I really like the way you play fast and loose with my life.''

''I was not the one who got one woman with child and tried to marry another one.''

''I hadn't seen Jilda in over four years. I didn't even know where to find her. And she didn't want to be found. What was I to do? It took me long enough to get over her the first time.''

The Master of Sinanju replaced the scroll thoughtfully.

''We must deal with this one unpleasant step at a time,'' he announced. ''Come, we will visit Mah-Li.''

''Fine,'' said Remo. But as he followed Chiun along the shore road, his heart beat high in his throat. He forced his breathing lower in his stomach, trying to get a grip on his emotions.

The decorated courtyard was deserted when they arrived. Wind plucked at the good-luck streamers forlornly. A loon flew up from the tipped bowl of jujubes, and the wine had been spilled.

Remo knocked at the door. There was no answer.

''Maybe we'd better come back,'' he suggested nervously. ''It might be too soon.''

''It will only be harder tomorrow,'' said Chiun, pushing on the door. Remo followed him in.

The main room was empty of all but a low table and some sitting mats.

''Mah-Li?'' Remo called. His voice bounced off the bare walls.

Chiun raised his nose. His nostrils clenched. ''Smell,'' he commanded.

''What is it?''

''Death,'' said Chiun. ''Come.''

In the next room, the bedroom, Mah-Li lay on her sleeping mat, still in wedding costume. She lay with her face turned to the ceiling, pale hands folded upon her breast. Her eyes were closed. The room was still. Too still.

Remo pushed past Chiun. He knelt and tapped on Mah-Li's shoulder.

"Mah-Li? It's me," he whispered.

There was no response. And Remo suddenly, shockingly, recognized why the room was too still. He could not hear Mah-Li's heartbeat.

"Mah-Li!" he cried, lifting her head in his hands.

Mah-Li's head lolled to face him. Her cheek was cool to the touch, her face the flat color of antique ivory. From the corner of one closed eye a dried tear had streaked down her cheek and under her chin. The tear was red.

Although he knew what the tear meant, Remo touched her throat. His trembling fingertip detected no pulse.

Remo looked up into the stern face of the Master of Sinanju. His expression was stricken.

"She's dead," he said hoarsely.

Chiun knelt and felt her face.

"What could have happened?" Remo asked, his voice cracking. "She was fine at the ceremony. That was only an hour ago. Little Father, can you explain this?" And Remo's mouth drew into a thin line.

The Master of Sinanju undid the high collar at Mah-Li's throat, disclosing a purple bruise no larger than a dime.

"A blow," he said. "Look."

The bruise was over the larynx. Remo felt it. One touch told him that the windpipe had been collapsed. He looked up.

Chiun nodded. "A single finger stroke did that."

"Whoever did this knew what he was doing. If it wasn't for the blood, I would suspect Sinanju."

Remo looked down at the face of the woman he was to have married. Even in death, it was a peaceful face.

"Little Father," Remo said in a faraway voice. "Did you do this?"

Chiun came to his feet, girding his kimono about his waist.

"I will assume that your grief has caused you to ask that question, and not you," he said. "Therefore, I will answer it and not take offense. No, I did not slay this poor child of my village. Such a thing would be sacrilege."

"Well, if I didn't do it, and you didn't, who did?"

"The murderer may still be about. Come, let us hunt the dog."

Carefully Remo lifted Mah-Li's head off his lap and set it on the sleeping mat. Unable to tear his eyes from her face, he stood up.

"Whoever he was, he couldn't get far in an hour," he said.

"Your grief has blinded you, Remo. Did you not see how the blood has dried on her cheek? That poor girl was slain last night."

"But the wedding was only an hour ago. She was there."

"Not her. Someone who looked like her."

"Something's not right here," said Remo.

"Come." Chiun beckoned. "There are answers to be sought."

The Master of Sinanju stormed out of the house of Mah-Li, his face grim. Remo started after him, stopped, and dropped to one knee beside the body of Mah-Li. He kissed her once, on her slightly parted lips. They were cold and tasteless.

"I wish—" Remo started to say, but his voice choked off and he hurried from the house.

The Master of Sinanju waited for him in the courtyard. "We will accomplish more if we go our separate ways," he said.

"After this is over," Remo said grimly, "we may go our separate ways in more ways than one." His eyes were the color of a beer bottle that had been left out in the elements, dull and devoid of sparkle.

"If that is your wish, then so be it," said Chiun proudly. "I am content that I have done only what is right for my people and my village."

"Yeah, I noticed," Remo muttered, starting off.

Chiun watched him go. Remo's hands were clenched into white fists of rage. His back was straight and defiant, but the Master of Sinanju saw that his pupil walked with his head bowed, like a man who did not care where he was going—or one who had no place to go.

Shaking his head sadly, he turned to the shore road. And saw the man standing on the rocks.

The man was short. He stood with his hands on his hips, defiantly. His face was swathed, like his body, in black folds of cloth. And from the patch of uncovered skin at his face, slanted black eyes laughed insolently.

"You are not content to be a thief, ninja," Chiun hissed under his breath. "Now you are a murderer as well."

And as if the ninja could hear him across the rocks, he laughed out loud. The laugh was a rattle of contempt.

"Remo!" Chiun shouted. "Behold!"

Remo whirled, his eyes following Chiun's accusing finger.

The ninja jumped back and disappeared behind the tumbled rocks of the beach.

Without a word, Remo burst into motion. He flashed past Chiun like a wild wind. The Master of Sinanju leapt after him.

"It is he, the thief from America," said Chiun.

"He did this," Remo bit out. "And he's going to suffer for it."

Together they topped the rocks and swept the beach below with their eyes.

"He is not here," said Chiun in a puzzled voice.

"Must be hiding," Remo decided, jumping onto the sand. "He couldn't have gotten far."

"But where?" said Chiun, following. "There is no place to hide."

Remo didn't answer. He ran along the beach, looking for footprints. But there were none.

Remo doubled back. "Other way," he said, passing the Master of Sinanju.

Chiun reversed direction too. Remo was running so fast his toes, touching the ripples of beach sand, left almost no mark. Chiun nodded. Remo was almost good enough to be Master now. Even in his grief he remembered to control his feet.

Chiun looked back to see the marks his own sandaled feet left. There were none. Good. Chiun was still Master.

Chiun caught up to Remo at the base of one of the towering Horns of Welcome. Remo was talking to someone. Chiun recognized the wizened form of old Pullyang, the village caretaker.

"You didn't see anyone?" Remo asked incredulously. He told Chiun, "Pullyang says nobody came this way."

"Impossible," Chiun insisted. "There are no tracks going the other way,"

"And none this way," said Remo. "Except Pullyang's."

"He was in black, a thief of ninja," Chiun told Pullyang. "You must have see him."

The old man shrugged helplessly as if to say: Is that my fault?

Chiun said, "Away with you, then, useless one."

He noticed Remo staring at him, an odd expression on his face.

"Remo? What is it?"

"You said ninja," Remo muttered.

"So?"

"Chiun," Remo said slowly, "I saw him clear as day. He wasn't a ninja. He was that kung-fu beach bum from Washington—Adonis."

"He was the ninja. His eyes were Japanese."

"That's not what I saw."

"Perhaps both thieves have come here," suggested Chiun.

"I saw you point at a man on the rocks, and it was Adonis."

"I pointed at a ninja. That is what I saw."

"And we both saw him jump behind the rocks," Remo said. "You know what I think? I think we saw what someone wanted us to see."

"I think that you are right."

Remo looked around. "Hey, where'd Pullyang go?"

Chiun looked about angrily. Pullyang was gone. Chiun frowned.

"Are you thinking what I'm thinking?" Remo asked.

"I am thinking that Pullyang's footsteps start at the rocks and end at our feet," Chiun said, gesturing to the sand, "as if he ascended into the sky."

"We'd better get back to the village. There's no telling what this phantom—whoever he is—is up to."

"Then we are together on this?"

"Until I say different," said Remo.

27

The Master of Sinanju summoned his people to the village square with a bronze gong that was held in a hornbeam frame by springs so strong that no known mallet could make it ring.

Chiun stepped up to the gong and tapped its center with a single finger. Its deep reverberations caused the scavenging sea gulls to fly from the square in fright.

The villagers came running. Never in the memory of the village of Sinanju had the Gong of Judgment been sounded. Never had there been a crime in the village while a Master was in residence.

They came, the old and the young, their faces etched in lines of shock, and clustered around the gong.

"Assemble before me, my people," commanded Chiun. His eyes seemed to fix every face, so that each felt that the Master of Sinanju was probing his own innermost thoughts.

When the villagers had formed a ragged semicircle before the Master of Sinanju—the adults holding their children before them with hands on their shoulders and the infants slung on their hips—Chiun lifted his voice to the sky.

"Death has come to Sinanju," he proclaimed.

The villagers hushed as if the sky were slowly pressing down upon their heads.

"Mah-Li, the betrothed of Remo, has been murdered."

The faces of the villagers took on a stony quality. It was as if they had suddenly become one emotionless, extended family.

"I seek her murderer among you," Chiun said.

Remo came up behind Chiun.

"I checked every hut," he said quietly. "Empty. They're all here."

177

Chiun nodded without taking his eyes off the crowd. "Jilda and the child?" he asked.

"I put them in the treasure house. I fixed and locked the doors too."

"Then our murderer is among those assembled."

"Maybe," Remo whispered. 'How can we tell if he can make himself look like anyone he wants?"

"Pullyang, step forward," Chiun commanded.

From out of the crowd, walking like a dog that expected a whipping, came old Pullyang, the caretaker. He stood before Chiun, his legs trembling inside dirty trousers.

"Were you down at the beach today?" Chiun asked.

"No, Master," Pullyang quavered.

"At all?"

"No, O Master," Pullyang repeated.

"I saw you at the beach not five minutes ago," insisted Chiun. "I spoke with you, and you with me."

"I was not there."

"My son says that you were," Chiun said sternly.

"That's right, I saw you," agreed Remo.

Pullyang fell to his knees. "Not I! Not I! I have been with my grandchildren all day," Pullyang cried.

Chiun looked down upon the pitiful figure, but no pity crossed his wrinkled countenance.

"If my words are not true," Chiun intoned, "you must call me a liar, and my adopted son a liar too, before the village. Will you do this?"

"Not I. I cannot call you a liar, but neither would I lie to you."

"You lied about the purple herons," Chiun said.

"I saw them!"

"And I saw you at the shore," said Chiun distantly. "Arise, Pullyang, faithful caretaker, and see to your grandchildren."

Remo asked Chiun, "If the murderer is here, he could look like anyone. How are we going to tell him from the others?"

"We will find a way. This crime will be punished."

"Just remember," said Remo, "who's going to do the punishing."

"We will see. It is against Sinanju law for a Master to harm a villager, no matter the reason."

"Try to stop me," said Remo, looking at the blank faces watching him fearfully.

"I may do that," Chiun said softly, stepping around the clot of villagers, his hands clasped behind his back like a general reviewing troops.

"You, Pak," said Chiun, pointing at a young man. "Name your father."

"Hui, O Master."

"Good. Go stand beside the Gong of Judgment. I will ask each of you a question. My question will be easy. Those who answer correctly will stand with Pak. And woe to him whose face is not known to me."

For an hour the Master of Sinanju inquired of each villager, from the oldest man to the youngest speaking child, a question of family tradition or Sinanju history. All answered correctly. And all went to stand with Pak until the village square was empty of all but the blowing plum-tree leaves.

"He's not here," said Remo impatiently. "He got away."

"All my villagers are accounted for," admitted Chiun.

"Let's leave them here and search the entire village."

"Agreed," said Chiun. "But beware, my son. We may be facing sorcery. Our abilities are not always proof against such things."

"I don't believe in that crap," said Remo, stalking off.

Chiun followed him. "You saw that crap with your own eyes, heard the words with your own ears. Was that not Pullyang's voice you heard coming from a mouth that looked like Pullyang's?"

"It wasn't black magic."

"What it was we have yet to discover. But it was. You know that as well as I. Come, let us speak with Jilda."

"Why?"

"Did you test her to see if she was truly who she seemed?"

"I know Jilda when I see her."

"And I have known Pullyang since I was a child. We shall see."

The door to the House of the Masters was closed, but not locked. Chiun's sharp vision told him that much even from a distance.

"I thought you locked the door," he said, picking up his pace.

"I did," Remo replied sullenly.

"It is not locked now."

Remo broke into a run. He went through the door like a thunderbolt.

"Jilda!" Remo's cry was strangled with anguish.

The Master of Sinanju swept into the throne room, taking in the treasure with a glance. Satisfied that it was undisturbed, he joined Remo in the guestroom. Remo was trying to shake Jilda awake.

"Remo," she said thickly, stirring from a sitting mat.

"What happened?" Remo asked.

Jilda of Lakluun looked around dazedly. Her eyes were a milky, confused gray.

"I do not recall. Was I asleep?"

"Yeah," said Remo. "Don't you remember?"

"I waited here as you bade me to do. Freya wanted to play with the other children. She grew cranky. The last thing I recall is telling her to mind her manners. There my memory stops." As she looked around the room and saw only Remo and Chiun, Jilda's voice shrank. "Freya . . ."

"Check the other rooms," Remo said.

The Master of Sinanju disappeared like steam from an open valve. When he returned, his cold expression had melted into the frightened face of a grandparent.

"Remo! She is gone!"

Jilda of Lakluun drew her cloak around her as if the room's temperature had dropped. She said nothing, her eyes growing reflective.

"Come on, Chiun," Remo said. "We're going to find her."

"Remo!" Jilda called suddenly. Remo paused at the door.

"My Freya is a guest of your village. If anything has happened to her, it will be upon your head."

Remo said nothing, and then he was gone.

Outside, it had grown dark.

"Something is wrong here," Chiun said ominously. "It should not be dark for two hours yet."

"Forget the Sinanju almanac," Remo snapped. "We have to find my daughter."

In the square, the villagers huddled together. They, too,

knew that it lacked two hours to sunset, but darkness mantled the little village like a doom.

"Look!" quavered Pullyang. "See! I did not lie. They are back."

Remo looked. Down by the shore, two creatures circled on their purplish-pink bat wings, their hatchet faces twitching on gooselike necks.

"Pterodactyls," Remo breathed. "I was right."

"I have never seen such things," said Chiun. "But I understand this much. They are circling prey."

"Oh, no," groaned Remo. He flashed to the rocks that ringed the shore and hit the sand running as the pterodactyls dipped lower, their spiky tails whipping excitedly.

On the beach, running on tiny legs, was a little girl with blond hair.

"Freya!" Remo called. "Hang on, babe. I'm coming."

The pterodactyls swooped down like blue jays worrying a cat. Freya kept running, her face haunted.

Remo ran after her, his feet blurring as he concentrated on his breathing. In Sinanju, proper breathing was all. It unlocked the latent powers of the human body. Remo's breathing flattened as he ran and his feet picked up speed until he was running faster than the pterodactyls could fly.

Freya's little legs churned. She glanced back in fear just as a rock was coming up in her path.

Remo yelled, "Watch the rock!"

He saw Freya trip. He leapt for her.

But the pterodactyls were closer. One twisted away and came at Remo, talons grasping. Remo chopped once, but the claw was somehow faster than his lightning reflex. He ducked under a billowing wing and came up behind the ungainly thing. About to launch a kick at the back of its saclike body, Remo suddenly forgot his situation.

The other pterodactyl landed where Freya had fallen and folded its beating wings in a quick gathering motion. It returned to the sky, its long neck straining. Clutched in its hanging talons, a tiny figure wriggled like a worm.

"No!" Remo screamed.

The pterodactyl glided out over the water.

Remo plunged after it. His feet did not kick up any sand as he ran. And when he hit the water, he did not plunge in, but kept running, his feet moving so fast they did not break through the heaving waves. He was running on top of the waves, his momentum so great that gravity could not pull him down.

Remo narrowed his focus. Only the pterodactyl existed for him now. The pterodactyl with a little girl in its claws—Remo's daughter. He wasn't going to lose her too. All the awesome power that was Sinanju burned within him, forcing every muscle to function in perfect harmony.

He was only dimly aware of Chiun's voice behind him.

"I am with you, my son."

Remo didn't answer. He was gaining on the ugly reptile. Its tail lashed tantalizingly within reach.

"Yes," said Chiun, as if reading Remo's mind. "The tail. If you can snare it, you may bring him down. Do not worry about the child. I will catch her when the devil heron lets go. Or I will plunge into the sea and rescue her. You stop that monstrosity. Trust the Master of Sinanju to preserve the life of your child."

The tail danced closer. Remo knew he would have only one shot. Once he went for the tail, he would lose the momentum that kept his feet from sinking. One shot. He wasn't going to blow it.

Remo took his shot. He saw his right hand close over the purple tail. Then the sea rose up to swallow him. Still hanging on, he let himself sink. He'd drag the pterodactyl to the ocean bottom and tear it to pieces. Please, God, he prayed as the cold clutched his muscles, don't let Chiun fail.

The water was like a wall of ice. It numbed his body. He could not tell whether he still had the tail. His fist felt like a rock. Remo reached out, found his wrist, and reached up toward his clutching hand. No way that thing would shake a two-handed grip.

But Remo felt nothing. The sea was too dark. He couldn't see if he still had the tail. God, do I have it? I couldn't have missed. Please don't let me have missed.

And suddenly, as if the sun had been turned on, the sea flooded with light. Remo saw that his fists were clutching seaweed. Frantically he kicked his feet, trying to get back his equilibrium. There was no sign of the pterodactyl.

The Master of Sinanju, his cheeks puffing air bubbles, swam up and tapped him on the shoulder. He shook his head no.

Remo kicked free. When he broke the surface, he saw the sun was out again. It was low in the horizon. The skies were clear.

Chiun's wrinkled face surfaced beside him.

"She is gone." Remo thought tears streamed down his wrinkled face, but it might have been seawater. "My beautiful granddaughter is gone!"

"I don't see the pterodactyl. It's got to be down there!"

Remo slipped under the surf, Chiun following.

Grimly they searched, their lungs releasing pent oxygen in infinitesimal amounts. A half-hour passed without their breaking for air. The ocean floor was rocky and forbidding. Few fish swam. And although they scoured the ocean floor for more than a mile around, they found no bodies. Only the green crabs of the West Korea Bay, which had been known to eat the flesh of drowned villagers.

Fearfully Remo dived into a group of them feeding on the ocean floor, scattering them with his hands. He uncovered a fragment of white meat. A flat silver eye stared at him. A fish.

When the sun disappeared beneath the waves, they gave up.

"I am so sorry, Remo," Chiun said chokingly. "I saw you grasp the tail, and when the bird fell, I reached out for the poor innocent child. I thought I had her. But once underwater, my arms were empty."

"I couldn't have missed that tail," Remo said.

"You did not," Chiun told him.

"I had the tail and you saw the bird come down. But there's no bird down there."

"What does it mean?" asked Chiun.

"Come on," Remo said grimly, settling into the overhand swimming stroke that was favored by Sinanju. He made for the shore.

Jilda was waiting on the beach. She stood tall and grim, her hands clutching the seams of her cloak. Her womanly face reflected neither grief nor resignation. She was too proud a warrior for either emotion.

"You failed," she said in an arid voice.

"You watched us. What did you see?" asked Remo.

"You fell on the ugly bird. It crashed into the sea. And

the two of you come back empty-handed. Could you not have at least returned my child's body to me?''

''She's not out there,'' Remo said flatly. And he struck off for the village.

Jilda spun on Chiun. ''What does he mean? I saw—''

''You saw a darkness fall and lift in an hour's time,'' said Chiun. ''Did you believe that?''

''I do not know.''

''Distrusting your senses is the first step toward truly seeing,'' said Chiun, taking Jilda by the arm. ''Come.''

''And what should I trust, if not the evidence of my eyes?''

Chiun nodded in the direction of Remo's purposeful figure.

''Trust in the father of your child, for he is of Sinanju.''

28

Jilda of Lakluun caught up with Remo.

"Tell me," she said.

"Quiet," snapped Remo as they approached the village proper. "He can hear us."

Jilda grabbed Remo by the arm. The muscle felt like a warm stone. "I care not about who can hear," she said. "Are you so cold that you do not care about your own child?"

Remo took Jilda by the shoulders. He put his face close to hers. "The pterodactyls weren't real," he whispered. "I grabbed the tail and ended up with air. There was nothing there."

"I saw my child fall into the sea."

"You saw what someone wanted you to see. Someone who is close enough to influence our minds and manipulate the images we all see. And if he's who I think he is, we've got our work cut out for us."

"You know who it is?"

"I have an idea," Remo said, looking toward Chiun, who stood with his hands resolutely folded in his kimono sleeves.

Chiun nodded. "For once, my son has reached a truth before me," he said proudly. And he bowed in Remo's direction.

"Save the grease," Remo said sharply. "We have things to settle between us, you and I."

"Tell me one thing," Jilda said anxiously. "Is my daughter dead or alive?"

"I don't know," Remo admitted. "But forget what we saw at the beach. That wasn't Freya. An illusion can't lift a flesh-and-blood child and carry her out to sea."

"Illusion?" said Jilda. "You mean it is—"

"The Dutchman," said Remo. "There's no other explanation. He knew how to unlock the treasure house. Probably learned that from Nuihc, the bastard. He got into Chiun's scrolls, learned about CURE, and used that information to make as much trouble for us as possible. Now he's followed us back to Sinanju to finish the job.''

''I remember him from the Master's Trial,'' said Jilda. ''He is as powerful as you in Sinanju, and his evil mind can make us see any witchery he cares to conjure.''

''He's the reason you fled from me in the first place,'' Remo said bitterly. ''It's because of him you and I couldn't be together. And now he's killed Mah-Li. He's going to pay for that.''

''Remember, Remo,'' Chiun interjected. ''He is like you, a white who is trained in Sinanju. But he is also the Other, the yin to your yang.''

''And I can't kill him, because if he dies, I die,'' Remo said grimly. ''I haven't forgotten that. But I'll tell you this, Chiun. I may not kill him, but I'm going to bring him right to the damned edge. When I'm done with him, he's never going to kill anyone again. Ever.'' Remo headed back toward the village.

A faraway-sounding voice stopped him.

''Remo.''

Remo's sensitive hearing fixed on the voice. It was Mah-Li's voice, light and silvery. But the line of rocks from which the voice came was empty.

''Remo.'' It was her voice again.

Remo looked around, and saw her. She was standing beside the house that Remo had started to build a year ago. She wore her high-waisted scarlet bridal costume and she smiled at him warmly, gesturing to the open door of the unfinished house.

''Come, Remo. Come, it is your wedding night. Don't you want me, Remo?'' The voice was Mah-Li's, but the tone mocked him.

''You son of a bitch,'' said Remo.

The Master of Sinanju tried to stop his pupil, but Remo Williams moved too rapidly. Chiun's fingers brushed Remo's bare arm impotently.

''He is baiting you, Remo,'' Chiun called. ''Do not forget your training. No anger. Anger gives him the edge.''

Then the music started, the dissonant music that came from

the diseased mind of Jeremiah Purcell, who had become known as the Dutchman during his years of solitude on the island of Saint Martin after the death of his trainer, Chiun's evil nephew, Nuihc. The air filled with colors and Remo found himself caught in a psychedelic tunnel of light. There was no road, no sky, and no house with the Dutchman standing there invitingly. It was all bands and swirls of colored light. Remo kept running anyway, but he was stumbling through a world that did not exist except in his own mind. His foot struck something hard—a rock or a tree root—and he went sliding on his chest, dirt spraying into his open mouth.

Remo shut his eyes. At the end of his slide he got to his feet, spitting to clear his mouth. But even with his eyes closed he saw the colors and heard the music.

"Eating dirt on the wedding night," said the voice that sounded like Mah-Li. "Is that a new Sinanju custom?"

"You can't hide behind your illusions forever," Remo warned.

Abruptly the colors spun into a coalescing dot and exploded like fireworks. The last sparks faded and Remo could see again. Chiun and Jilda were standing not far from him, their eyes blinking stupidly. They, too, had been made to see the colors.

"I am not afraid to face you." The voice was that of Adonis. He walked calmly toward Remo, a smug smile on his wide tanned face.

"Remo. Beware," warned Chiun.

"But you are afraid of me." And suddenly he was a ninja in black costume with one round blue eye and one slanted black eye.

"Not me," said Remo.

"If you kill me, you die," crowed the Dutchman, reverting to his natural form. His blond hair swished like a lion's mane.

"He is baiting you," said Chiun.

"So what?" barked Remo, setting himself. "If he kills me, he dies too. It goes both ways—doesn't it, Jeremiah?"

"Do you not see?" Chiun said. "Look at his eyes. They are full of madness. He wants to die. He has nothing to lose."

The Dutchman stopped in his tracks and set his fists on his

hips. A sea breeze made his purple fighting costume flap against his arms and legs. He opened his mouth and a laugh rattled out as if it were produced by a mechanism keyed to the throwing-back of his head. It was not a human sound.

From the yellow sash girding his waist he plucked a pair of rimless glasses and tossed them at Remo's feet.

Remo looked down. They were Smith's glasses.

"I have killed your intended bride, your daughter, and your former employer. Take your revenge now, if you dare."

"I dare," said Remo, leaping into the air. He executed a magnificent Heron Drop, rising over thirty feet into the air. At the apex of his leap, he dropped sharply toward the lifted face of the Dutchman. But the Dutchman stood his ground, prepared to receive a death kick in the face. And Remo knew, too late, that Chiun was right. The Dutchman wanted to die.

But at the last possible moment the Dutchman shot out a hand and caught Remo's right ankle as it came down. Spinning like a discus thrower, he redirected the energy of Remo's descent into a wide arc. He let go. Remo flew in a straight line, smashing against the side of his unfinished house. He landed in a tangle of splintered bamboo and teak.

The Dutchman's voice filtered into his mind. "Come, Remo. We have all night to die. Perhaps I will kill your Viking dyke of a lover before I extinguish your life."

Remo jumped to his feet. He came out the door like a cannonball, hitting the door with his palm. The door flew ahead of him and bounced along on its corners like a square wheel.

The Dutchman stood laughing. Behind him Jilda lifted the dagger from her leather belt. She crept up behind him.

Remo caught the bouncing door and flipped it like a Frisbee. It sailed high, then sank like a pitcher's fastball. Remo hoped it would distract him just long enough.

The Dutchman watched the door lift and then plunge in his direction. It would be easy to avoid. Had Remo learned nothing in the years since they had last clashed?

He saw the hands a split-second before the dagger slid under his jaw. So that was it. It had almost worked too.

"My child. Speak of her fate," Jilda of Lakluun hissed, pulling his hair back to expose his throat.

"Your hands are so gnarled, Jilda," he said smoothly. "How can you even use them?"

Jilda recoiled. The dagger dropped. Her fingers stiffened as if petrified. She held them up, and saw with widening eyes that they were like dried wood, as if tree limbs had grown into the rough shape of her hands.

The Dutchman turned. "Old dry wood," he mocked. "Not warrior's hands. Good for firewood only."

The fingers ignited first. The flames were blue and ethereal but they crept toward her wrists and then raced toward her elbows, which had also turned to wood.

"An illusion! It is only an illusion!" Jilda cried.

"Not the flames," corrected the Dutchman.

"Yes! Illusion!" she said, squeezing her eyes against the pain.

The Dutchman stepped back as the Master of Sinanju took Jilda and forced her to the ground, rolling her in the dirt to smother the fire.

"The flames are real," Chiun said. "It is one of his true sorceries."

"Now watch, old man," called the Dutchman, "and you will see who is truly worthy of becoming the next Master of Sinanju." He turned his attention to Remo Williams once again.

Remo's face was warped with pain and rage. He was only yards away now, and coming like an angry arrow.

"You are looking well," said the Dutchman. "I only wish your wedding—excuse me, our wedding—had not been interrupted. I had in mind for you a most memorable honeymoon."

Remo came in with both hands held open. He grasped thin air. The real Dutchman materialized behind him.

"Pitiful," said the Dutchman. "You have learned nothing. I am still your superior. Nuihc trained me as a child, while you came to Sinanju as an adult. I will always have that advantdge."

And to show his contempt, he turned his back on Remo.

"Now we are equal," he said, folding his arms.

Remo sent out a sweeping kick. The Dutchman jumped in place, expertly avoiding it. He spun with the jump and sent out a stiff-fingered blow. Remo parried it with crossed wrists. Hooking the back of his enemy's knee with a toe, Remo sent the Dutchman into a spinning cartwheel. He landed on his back.

"Who's superior now?" asked Remo, placing a conquering foot on top of the Dutchman's heaving chest. Remo pressed down until he heard the crackle of straining cartilage.

The Dutchman's unreal blue eyes flared.

"I underestimated you, Remo. Very well, slay me, if that is your wish."

"No, Remo," Chiun said. The Master of Sinanju leapt to Remo's side.

"Stay out of this, Chiun," Remo warned. And while he glared at Chiun, the Dutchman saw his opportunity. Steel-hard fingers took Remo's ankle and twisted once. Remo cried out. He floundered away in pain, hopping on one foot.

The Dutchman pushed himself erect and said, "Your powers of concentration are pathetic. How did you survive your initial training?"

Remo found his feet. "Some people think I'm pretty good," he answered. When he leaned on his right foot, it hurt. But he felt no grinding from broken bones. The pain wasn't important.

"Mah-Li does not think so. She is in the Void now, her spirit crying out that you could not protect her. Your child, your employer, they are eternal testaments to your incompetence."

"Get ready to join them," said Remo, advancing menancingly.

"No, Remo." It was Jilda's voice. "He knows where my Freya is, whether she is dead or alive. Do not kill him. Please."

"Listen to her, Remo," Chiun said. The Master of Sinanju stood over Jilda, his hands fluttering helplessly. He could not kill the Dutchman without killing his pupil. It was between the two white Masters of Sinanju now.

"Listen to me," cried the Dutchman. "You will only beat me by killing me. I want you to do that, Remo. I have killed those closest to you. I could kill you. I prefer that you kill yourself by killing me."

Remo said nothing. His eyes were focused on that open mocking face. Nothing else mattered now. It was just him and the Dutchman. The warning cries of Chiun were faint in his ears, as if all Remo's energies had been diverted from his surroundings to his enemy. The Dutchman was only four paces away, then three, then two, then . . .

Remo's fist blow went to the solar plexus. It would have felled a strong tree, but the Dutchman had hardened his stomach muscles in anticipation of the blow. He bounced back several feet, but retained his balance.

The Dutchman grinned at him. "A poor blow. Your elbow was bent. But that has always been your problem, hasn't it?"

Remo came on, silent and purposeful. There was something in his eyes, the Dutchman saw. Something that was not anger, something that did not belong in the eyes of a human being, even one trained in Sinanju.

"You're going to tell me where Freya is, scum," Remo said levelly.

"Where?" mocked the Dutchman. "Why, she is all around us. I fed one piece to a sea gull, some to the snakes, and the rest to the crabs. I don't believe in wasting good meat, do you? Especially such tender, sweet meat."

Remo's hand was quicker than the Dutchman's eye by the merest of microseconds, but it was enough. He snared the Dutchman's long hair and twisted his head around. Remo shoved him down on one knee, his hands locking about the Dutchman's smooth neck from behind.

Remo began squeezing. "Tell-me-where-she-is," he said through grinding teeth. "Tell-me-where-my-daughter-is."

Jeremiah Purcell strained for Remo's hands. His pale fingers were frantic, but it was as if they struggled with stone. Remo's death grip on his throat was unshakable. He twisted and fought in vain, and as his field of vision began to redden like boiling blood, he panicked. He hadn't expected it to end this way. Remo had cut off the oxygen flow to his lungs, disturbing his breathing rhythms. For the first time, the Dutchman felt fear. He realized he did not want to die, but Remo was squeezing the life out of him. Darkness rolled across his vision even with his eyes open wide.

The Dutchman tried to summon up an image, but the beast would not respond. Instead, there was a voice, cold and metallic.

"You can fight or you can beg," Remo was saying into his ear. "But I won't let go until you tell me where my daughter is. Can you hear me, Purcell? You'd better be serious about dying because I'm serious about killing you."

No, no, Jeremiah said wordlessly. It can't end like this. I'm not done. O beast, help me. But the beast in him was cowed, as helpless as he was before this true Master of Sinanju.

Finally, with his sight darkening like a falling curtain, Jeremiah Purcell relaxed his clawing fingers and spread them out in an unmistakable gesture of surrender.

"You giving up, huh?" demanded Remo, still squeezing. "You want me to let go. Is that it? Maybe I'm not ready. Maybe I don't want to let you go at all. Maybe I want to finish the job, you scum."

"No, Remo," Chiun said. His voice was suddenly close. "If you must kill this man, do it with a clear mind. Listen to me. Should he die, he takes not only your life but also the truth of Freya's fate with him."

With a final savage shake of the Dutchman's neck, Remo let go. His hands were like claws as he stood up, his fingers clenched so tightly they could not fully open.

"Where?" demanded Remo, his chest heaving.

The Dutchman curled up like an insect that had been set afire. His hands held his throat. He coughed rackingly. It was many minutes before the coughing subsided and he was able to speak.

"She is in the House of the Masters. While you were busy chasing my images, I placed her in one of the steamer trunks."

"You son of a bitch," hissed Remo, going for the Dutchman's throat again.

"No," Jeremiah Purcell said, cowering. "I did not kill her. Think of me what you wish, but like you, I am Sinanju. To kill a child is forbidden. The illusion of her death was only to provoke you."

"All right," said Remo. "We'll check it out. You be here when I get back."

"Why?"

"I still want a piece of you. Isn't that what you want?"

"Yes," said the Dutchman in an unconvincing voice. "It is what I want."

Chiun stood over the huddled figure in purple silk.

"I will stand guard over this one while you see to your child, Remo."

29

The Master of Sinanju waited until Remo and Jilda of Lakluun disappeared from view. He bent over the Dutchman's cringing form.

"Forget the pain in your throat," Chiun said softly. "Focus on your breathing. My son has robbed you of breath, disrupting your inner harmony. Take slow sips. Hold them deep in the stomach before releasing the bad air. That is it. Good."

The Dutchman found the strength to sit up. His eyes were glazed like a birthday cake.

"He was. . ." The words rattled in the throat. The Dutchman coughed painfully.

"He was stronger than you expected," finished Chiun. "Yes. He is a different Remo now. He knows who he is. He understands that he is the avatar of Shiva on earth. The knowledge troubles him, but he has taken an important step in his development. I sometimes think he is almost as powerful as I. Almost."

"My powers are greater."

"Your capacity for destruction is greater, that is all. Nuihc has taught you well. Although he is long dust, I still rue the day I taught him Sinanju. Are you able to walk?"

The Dutchman nodded. "I think so."

"Stand up, then. You will follow me into the village."

"No. I will wait here for your pupil's return."

"You no longer wish death. I saw it in your face. And Remo will surely kill you when he returns."

"I'm not afraid of him," the Dutchman said sullenly.

"You are, whether you admit it or not. And I am afraid for my son. If you agree to follow me into the village, I will see that you live to see another day."

"You slew Nuihc, who was like a father to me," said the

Dutchman in a bitter voice. "I will make no deals with you."

"And I will make none with you, carrion who murdered a child of my village," blazed Chiun. He slapped the Dutchman across the face. "If it were within my power to snuff out your base life without extinguishing Remo's with the same stroke, you would now be so much scavenger food. Arise!"

The Dutchman stumbled to his feet. His face was red where Chiun had slapped him. His eyes were strange.

"You will come with me to the village."

The Dutchman nodded numbly.

The Master of Sinanju walked two paces behind the Dutchman so that he could watch him at all times. The Dutchman walked unsteadily. His confidence was gone, Chiun knew. He had allowed himself to be manhandled by Remo. That was bad enough. But he had also displayed cowardice in combat—a trait that was considered un-Sinanju. The discovery that he feared death in spite of his boasts had shaken this white youth. He was still turning the realization over in his mind. What was left of it. For Chiun knew that the Dutchman walked along the edge of madness. It had been his lot ever since he discovered his mutant powers. They had always been accompanied by a strange desire to kill, which the Dutchman called the beast. It had never been fully controllable.

As they descended into the sheltered village, Chiun began speaking quietly.

"You see the square below?"

"Yes," the Dutchman said woodenly.

"You see my villagers there?"

"Yes."

"When we reach the square, we will walk among my people. They will be curious. They will come close to see you better. Can you still use your mind powers?"

"I think so."

"Be certain. Imagine for me a butterfly. A pretty summer butterfly."

The Dutchman concentrated. About his head, black wings fluttered in the moonlight. A butterfly. But Chiun saw that the butterfly, although having a beautiful pattern to its veined wings, had a flaming skull for a head. Despite himself, Chiun shuddered.

"You will use your power of mind," Chiun went on, "in this fashion. . . ."

Remo found Freya in the first trunk he opened. His ears had zeroed in on her heartbeat as soon as he entered the House of the Masters. Surprisingly, the heartbeat was very calm.

"Are you okay?" Remo asked, lifting her into his arms.

Freya looked at him seriously, but her face was unafraid. "I'm okay. Are you okay?"

"Yeah," Remo laughed. "I'm okay."

"Hi, Mommy."

"I would hug you, my child," Jilda said warmly, holding out her seared arms, "but I cannot. Your father will hug you for me."

"What happened to your hands, Mommy? Did you burn them?"

"Never mind, child. It is nothing."

"She takes after you," Remo said admiringly.

"How do you mean?"

"Brave. The both of you. Locked in a trunk for a couple of hours. I'll bet you didn't even cry, did you?" Remo asked Freya.

"Nope," replied Freya. "Why should I cry? I knew you'd come to get me out. Isn't that what daddies are for?"

"Yes, sweetheart," Remo said. "That's what daddies are for."

"Did I tell you about my pony?" Freya asked. "His name is Thor. I ride him every day."

"Hush," said Jilda. She turned to Remo. "As long as the Dutchman lives, none of us are safe. What can you do with him that will not cause your own destruction?"

"I don't know," answered Remo. "I'll think of something, because no one is ever going to lay a hand on this little girl again. Right, Freya?"

"Right," Freya said stoutly, making a little fist. "We'll beat him up. Pow!"

Remo set Freya down. He searched Jilda's face.

"We gotta talk," he said seriously.

"My arms need attention," she said, holding them up.

The skin was singed to the elbow. Remo examined her carefully.

"Not good," he decided. "But not bad. Chiun knows a lot of healing stuff. I'll bet he can have you swinging a sword again inside of a month."

And Remo smiled. Jilda smiled back.

"I think he wants to be kissed again, Mommy," said Freya, looking up with innocent eyes.

Remo and Jilda laughed.

Their laughter was cut short by the sound of commotion from outside.

"Sounds like a riot," Remo said. He made for the door.

"Stay, Freya," Jilda warned, and followed Remo.

Remo stepped out of the House of the Masters and almost fell over the figure of the Dutchman. Reflexively he grabbed him by his long hair. A thin scream—not the Dutchman's—pierced his ears.

"You're not fooling me, Purcell," said Remo, tossing the Dutchman to the ground. He fell like a rag doll. He must still be weak, Remo thought.

Remo had set himself, in case it was an act, when another Dutchman came around the corner.

Remo took the second Dutchman by the arm. Again there was no resistance. But the second Dutchman pointed to the first and in an old woman's voice cried, "The evil one. I must escape." The sounds of confusion down in the square grew more frantic.

Dragging both Dutchmen to the edge of the hillock on which the House of the Masters stood, Remo saw a hundred figures in purple silk running wildly through the village, bumping and stumbling in a frenzied effort to escape each other.

In their midst, the Master of Sinanju danced about like a chicken running amok.

"Chiun?" Remo called. "What the hell happened?"

"Are you blind? Can you not see?" Chiun shouted back.

"I see a million Dutchmen everywhere."

"That is what I see too," said Jilda.

The gabble of Korean voices told Remo that each villager saw the others as Dutchman. They ran from one another, not knowing which one—if any—was the real Dutchman.

"Damn!" said Remo. "Chiun, here's what you do. Knock 'em out. Knock them all out. We'll sort them later."

Remo took the two Dutchmen in his hands and squeezed nerves in their necks. They collapsed like deflated party balloons.

"You watch Freya," Remo told Jilda, and leapt down to the square.

It was easy work. Remo simply ran through the village, taking necks at random. No one fought back. Remo was too fast, and every neck he squeezed was as unresisting as a kitten's. Remo worked his way toward Chiun, who was busy performing the same operation, except that Remo let them lie where they fell and Chiun made little piles of purple-clad Dutchmen.

They ended up back-to-back in the village square, Dutchmen falling all around their feet.

"What happened?" Remo demanded.

"He got away and worked his magic. As you can see," Chiun explained.

"You were supposed to keep him under guard," Remo said, gently lowering a Dutchman to the ground.

"He recovered more swiftly than I expected," Chiun complained, taking two necks at once. Two identical Dutchmen closed their neon-blue eyes and joined other heaps of purple-clad figures.

"Dammit, Chiun. You know how dangerous he is," Remo said.

"Yes," Chiun said evenly. "I know how dangerous he is."

After the entire square became littered with unconscious Dutchmen, Remo and Chiun worked their way out to the huts and hovels of the village. They found other Dutchmen cowering under the raised floors and in darkened rooms.

They dragged every last one into the open.

"I think this is the last," said Chiun, lugging a body over his frail shoulders and depositing him in a pile.

"How can you tell?" asked Remo, joining him.

"Because I count 334 Dutchmen."

"So?"

"That is precisely the number of villagers in Sinanju."

"That means we don't have the right one."

"Really, Remo," said Chiun, surveying his handiwork

with a certain pride. "That should be obvious to you. If the true Dutchman had succumbed, his illusion would have vanished with his consciousness."

"Yeah, you're right. What do we do now?"

"I think I saw someone running toward the East Road. Did you intercept one of the false Dutchman going that way?"

"No," said Remo.

"Then I suggest you go swiftly along the East Road if you wish to settle with your enemy."

"You seem awfully eager to see me go," Remo said suspiciously.

Chiun shrugged. "I cannot stop you if you are bent upon your own destruction."

Remo hesitated.

"Or you can help me sort my villagers. Perhaps the Dutchman is among them."

"I'll see you later," Remo said evenly, taking off.

"I will guard your woman and your child while you are gone," said Chiun loudly. Under his breath he added, "On your wild-goose chase."

Remo Williams took the inland road away from the village of Sinanju. A simple dirt road, it ran for several hundred yards and suddenly diverged into three superhighways that were bare of traffic. Beyond the horizon, the smoky glow of the most heavily industrialized section of North Korea obscured the stars. The bite of chemical wastes abraded Remo's lungs. Although the East Road was deserted, Remo set off at a dead run. If the Dutchman had taken this road, Remo would catch up with him. But somehow Remo didn't think the Dutchman had taken the East Road at all. He had known Chiun too long and he figured this was one of his tricks. But Remo was not sure, so he ran and ran, eating up miles of black asphalt with his feet and getting further and further away, he suspected, from his ultimate enemy on earth.

In Sinanju, the villagers began to wake up. Their resemblance to the Dutchman faded slowly, like a double exposure. The phenomenon told the Master of Sinanju that the Dutchman had escaped safely.

Chiun roused some of the slow ones with massaging fingers applied to their necks. It increased the flow of oxygen-carrying blood to their brains, reviving them faster than a shot of stimulant.

Jilda watched with Freya at her side.

"What if Remo does not come back?" she asked.

"He will," Chiun said absently.

"Not if he finds the Dutchman."

"He will not. I told Remo that the Dutchman took the East Road. If he decides to believe me, he will take the East Road and waste his time. If he chose not to believe me, he will take either the North or South road."

"I understand," said Jilda. "There is only a one-in-three chance that Remo took the correct road."

"No," said Chiun, whispering encouragement to a waking villager. "The chance is none in three. The Dutchman took the shore road."

"Then why did you send Remo along the East Road?"

"Because I have spent two decades training him and do not wish to lose him foolishly."

"He will know he has been tricked."

"Remo is used to being tricked. If his mind were as strong as his body, he would be the greatest Master Sinanju has ever known."

"None of us are safe as long as the Dutchman lives."

"I do not claim to have achieved a solution to this problem," Chiun said, shooing the last of his villagers away. "Only that I have postponed one tragic result."

The three stood alone in the silent village square. The only light came from the moon. Chiun took in a deep breath of sea air. It was cold and bitter.

When Remo returned, his shoulders sloped dejectedly.

"He got away," he said.

"Is that a bad thing?" asked Chiun.

"We gotta get him. Now. Today. This can't go on. We can't have him hanging over our lives like this."

"I think it is not my life he hangs over," said Chiun. "I think it is yours. And are you so eager to end your life that you will pursue your inevitable mutual destruction with this man?"

"If we're going to die because of one another, I'd rather get it over with," Remo said seriously.

"How white," Chiun remarked nastily. "Oh, it is too

much of a burden to wait and plan a solution to my problem. I would rather commit suicide than live in such uncertainty.''

"It's not that way, Chiun, and you know it.''

"Oh? Then how is it, Remo? You cannot kill this man. Let him go lick his wounds. You are stronger than he is. He knows that now. Perhaps he will never return.''

"You're forgetting that he killed Mah-li.''

"And you are forgetting that beside you stand your child and the woman who bore her.''

"That's exactly why I have to take care of the Dutchman,'' Remo said. "Don't you see that? They're not safe as long as he's alive. He won't stop until he's murdered everyone in my life. I'm going after him. Are you going to tell me which way he went—or am I going to have to waste a lot of precious time?''

"Very well,'' Chiun said, drawing himself up proudly. "He took the shore road.''

"See you later, then.''

"If that is your wish. You will miss the funeral. But it does not matter. A person so bent on self-destruction that he would leave without saying good-bye to his only child and the child's mother is obviously above pausing to pay his respects to the woman he almost married. The woman he claims to have loved.''

Remo stopped in his tracks. He did not turn around. "Postpone the funeral,'' he said.

"Sinanju law. Burial must be on the evening of the passing of the villager. I cannot bend Sinanju law, not even for you. But go. I will tell the villagers that you would not attend the funeral because you did not truly love her. I have been saying it for months, and now you are proving it to me.''

Remo turned to face the Master of Sinanju. The resolve vanished from his face. "You always have an answer, don't you, Chiun?''

"No,'' said Chiun, turning his back on Remo. "It is you who always have a problem. But I like that in you. It makes life so interesting. Now, let us bury our dead.''

30

Cold moonlight washed the funeral of the maiden Mah-Li like an astringent solution.

The funeral procession began in front of the House of the Masters. The entire village wore white, the traditional Korean color of mourning. Villagers carried the rosewood coffin on a palanquin. Remo and Chiun walked just ahead of the litter, the remaining villagers trailing behind, carrying incense burners and making no more noise than the sea mists rolling off the bay.

Jilda walked in the rear, her arms bandaged, Freya beside her.

The procession followed the shore road to the plum-tree-shaded burial ground of the village of Sinanju. Every Sinanju villager was entitled to a mound of dirt in the burial plot, with a small stone or pillar to mark his or her life.

The palanquin was set on the ground beside an open hole. After a moment of silence in which the villagers were allowed a final view of the face of the deceased, the coffin was closed.

The Master of Sinanju watched his pupil, Remo Williams, as the lid closed on the face of his beloved for the final time. There was no expression on his face. No shock, no grief, no nothing. Chiun's parchment countenance frowned.

Chiun stepped before the villagers.

"Think not that Mah-Li is dead," he said, looking squarely at Remo. "She was a flower whose perfume has made our lives sweeter, but all flowers wither. Some with age, some by disease, and others by cruel acts. So it was here. But let this be said of Mah-Li, if nothing else. That she was a flower who left us while her perfume was still fragrant in our nostrils, and our last sight of her face gave us the pleasure of her smooth skin and her innocent nature. No one will remember this child as stooped or wrinkled or infirm. I decree that future generations, when they speak of Mah-Li, will know her as Mah-Li the Flower.'' Chiun paused.

The villagers wept silently. Only Remo stood unmoved.

''Before we let the maiden Mah-Li settle into her final rest, I will ask her beloved, my adopted son, Remo, to speak of her memory.''

Remo stepped forward like a robot. He looked down at the coffin.

''A year ago I took a vow to protect this village and everyone in it,'' Remo said. ''My vow to you today is that the man who did this will pay dearly. No matter what it costs me.'' And Remo stepped back.

Chiun, unsettled by the raw edge in Remo's voice, signaled for the coffin to be lowered into the ground. Shovels began cutting into the mound of loose dirt beside the hole, and with dull, final sounds, clods of barren earth fell upon the coffin.

The people of Sinanju stood respectfully as the coffin was covered. Except Remo Williams. Without a word, he stormed off.

Chiun lowered his head sadly. Tonight, he thought, felt like the end of so many things.

Remo took the shore road, the wind whipping the loose cotton of his white funeral costume. He had no destination in mind. He was just walking.

He came to the house he had built with his own hands and never finished. The doorway gaped cavernously like the eye of a skull. There was a hole in one wall, where the Dutchman had hurled him, and no roof. It was the final touch he had not gotten around to.

Remo stepped inside. The interior was a single square room filled with starlight so bright Remo could see the hairs on the back of his hand clearly. He squatted in the middle of the room and lifted his face to the sky. It was brilliant with stars. They lay in wreaths and pools, like diamonds awash in celestial milk. In all his years in America, Remo had never seen such a beautiful night sky. Its haunting glory made him want to cry. But he knew that if he shed tears now, they would not be in tribute to the beauty of creation, but over the waste of earthy dreams.

The Master of Sinanju appeared in the doorway. He said nothing. Remo did not acknowledge his presence, although both men knew that each was aware of the other.

Finally Chiun spoke.

"It is customary to speak of the cherished memory of a loved one at a funeral, not to voice vengeance."

If Chiun expected an answer, he was disappointed. Remo continued to ignore him.

Realizing that his pupil was not going to take the bait, Chiun asked in a gentler voice, "What is it you do here, my son?"

Remo's throat worked as he struggled to answer. His words were thick.

"I was trying to visualize how it would have been."

"Ah," said Chiun, understanding.

"I'm trying to imagine the furniture," Remo went on in a distant voice. "Where the cooking fire would be, how the noodles would be drying out in the courtyard with the radishes in their big rattan bowls. The sleeping mats would be over there. How every morning she would wake me up with a kiss. I keep trying to see the children we won't ever have. And you know what, Chiun?" Remo said, his voice cracking.

"What?"

"I can't," Remo said, choking on the words.

Chiun frowned.

"I can't imagine it. No matter how hard I try, I can't imagine how it would be. For a solid year I daydreamed about it all the time. I knew exactly how it would feel and smell and taste, but now I can't even bring back the memory of that dream."

Remo buried his head in his arms.

Chiun stepped inside and settled into a lotus position before his pupil. He waited.

"Why can't I do that, Chiun? Why can't I bring back the memory? It's all I have left."

"Because you know it was only a dream, and you have awakened from it."

Remo looked up. For the first time since the funeral procession, his face registered emotion. Anguish. His eyes were like old pennies, worn and impossibly sad.

"I had such plans, Chiun. Sinanju was going to be my home. No more Smith, no more killing. No more of any of it. Why couldn't I be happy? Just once. Finally. After all the shit I've had to live through."

"Let me explain something to you, Remo," the Master of Sinanju said quietly. "That which you call the 'shit,' that is life. Life is struggle. Do you think happiness can come to one such as you by living peacefully in a small ugly village surrounded by backward peasants? No. Not you. Not I. Why do you think I have lived in America these last two decades? Because I enjoy breathing brown air? To live is to struggle. To continue to exist is to respond to challenge."

"My life is screwed up," said Remo.

"You are the finest example of human power to walk the earth in our time—next to me, of course—and you say that your life is screwed up. You belong, not to me, not to Mah-Li, not even to Jilda and little Freya, Remo, but to a greater destiny. You act as if your life is over when truly it is just beginning."

"I grew up in an orphanage. Having a family I could call my own was my greatest dream. I'd give up Sinanju for a normal life, a house with a white picket fence, and a wife and kids."

"No, you would not. You say it, but in your heart you do not mean it."

"How would you know what I mean?"

"I know you. Perhaps better than you do yourself."

"It's such a simple dream," Remo said. "Why can't it come true for me?"

"I remember when I married," said Chiun. "I, too, was filled with such yearnings. I married young, and my wife, although beautiful on our wedding day, grew shrill and old before her time. Have I ever told you about my wife?"

"Yeah. And I don't want to hear it again."

"Too bad. I am going to tell you anyway. In the past, you heard the lessons of past Masters of Sinanju from my lips. Of Wang, of Kung, of little Gi. But I have never told you the great lesson of the Master Chiun."

"Wrong. I know that one by heart," Remo said bitterly. "Never accept checks."

"I will ignore that," said Chiun, his squeaky voice dropping into the dramatic tone he used when telling lessons of past Masters. "I have always told you that my wife was barren, and having no heir, I was forced to train the son of my brother-in-law, Nuihc, in the art of Sinanju."

"Yeah," interrupted Remo. "And Nuihc went off to freelance for himself, sent no tribute back to the village, and you were left without a pupil. Until Smith hired you to train me. And even though I was a white who couldn't keep his elbow straight, you made do. And we took care of Nuihc. But he had trained Purcell, so now we have the same old problem of a renegade Master. He just wears a different face. Did I leave anything out?"

"How eloquent," Chiun said tartly. "But I have never told you the full story. About the time I had a son of my own. I will tell you that story now."

"Go ahead. I'm not going anywhere," Remo said resignedly, but the Master of Sinanju recognized the first stirrings of interest in his voice.

"The son who was born to me was named Song. He was a fine boy, lean of limb, with skin like tallow and intelligent eyes. I took him as my pupil, of course. And as the years passed, my heart swelled with pride as he learned, first the breathing, then the early exercises. He learned quickly, and the quicker he learned, the faster I pushed him along the path to greatness."

"Sounds familiar," said Remo.

"Oh, do not think that I have trained you hard. I have trained you rigorously, but compared to my dead son, Song, you have been loafing through the stages of Sinanju. In truth, I pushed too hard. I have never admitted this to anyone, but I killed my own son."

"You, Chiun? That's terrible."

"I did not kill with a stroke, or a blow, or a kick. I did not spill his blood with my own hands. I killed with pride. It was the first day of the spring, when the villagers were flying their kites to welcome the season. My son wished to join them. He was but eight. His ninth summer lay ahead of him, but it would be a summer as dark as night—although no one knew that on the day I tore his kite from his hands and marched him to Mount Paektusan.

"We stood at the bottom of Mount Paektusan. And I said

to my son, 'If you are truly the son of my wife, you will climb Mount Paektusan in one day.' And my son say to me, 'O my father, I cannot. It is too high and my hands are too small.'

"And I said to him, 'The Master Go climbed Mount Paektusan when he was nine. Before him, no Master had climbed Mount Paektusan before his twelfth summer. I see greatness in you, and unless you wish to give the lie to my judgment, you will climb this peak before your ninth birthday. Begin now.' ''

The Master of Sinanju smoothed the lap of his mourning kimono with thoughtful hands before going on.

"Reluctantly my son began his climb. I sat in the melting spring snows to await him. I knew he would not make it on his first try, but I was determined that he would one day succeed, and if necessary, I would bring him to the base of Mount Paektusan every day until he succeeded or the summer rains made me a fool.''

"He didn't make it," Remo said.

"On the first day," continued Chiun, "I watched him ascend until he was a spider speck against the snows of the high mountain and he disappeared into the upper mists. He had gone very high. I could tell, because at times falls of snow indicated that he was nearing the summit. I remember a moment on that day when I was very, very proud. But time passed, and my son did not descend from Mount Paektusan. I waited, determined that if he reached the summit on his own, he would descend on his own. I was stubborn. The sun set on my pride and it arose upon a stubborn young man—for I was young in those days—and when my son did not return, I scaled the peak to reach him, angry and intending to berate him for his lack of resolve.

"I found him near the summit," Chiun said softly, looking at his hands in his lap. "To this day, I do not know if he fell trying to reach the summit or while climbing down from it. The last of the snow had melted that morning, and there were no traces of his climb. My son lay on a wet outcropping, where he had fallen and dashed his head. He had been dead for many hours, but it had taken him many hours to die. Had I been less stubborn, I might have found him in time. I carried his body home to his mother, and from that day on she never had a civil word for me, nor would she allow me to enter her so that I would have another son and an opportunity for atonement. In time, age did make her barren, as I have told you in the past. But in truth, she did not trust me with another child.''

''Why didn't you divorce her and remarry?''

''In Sinanju, one marries for life.''

''Life sucks sometimes,'' said Remo.

''When you are Master you may write that in the scrolls of Sinanju, if that is your wish. But there are worthier thoughts.''

''I can't help how I feel.''

''How do you feel?''

''How do you think I feel? I lost my bride-to-be, and the woman who mothered my daughter is afraid to have me around. All because of one man.''

''And so you will seek revenge, even though it costs you your life.''

''What else do I have?''

''Me.''

''What?''

Chiun searched Remo's face hopefully. ''You have me. Have I meant nothing to you, that you would kill yourself and deprive an old man of his last chance for atonement?''

''I don't owe you anything. Especially after that trick you pulled at the wedding.''

''I saved you from a horror. Had you married what you thought was Mah-Li, the Dutchman would have revealed himself to you at a moment of great intimacy. I spared you that.''

''You didn't know it was the Dutchman at the ceremony. Don't you take credit for that. Don't you dare take credit for that.''

Chiun smiled to himself. Anger. Good. Remo was coming out of his depressed self-absorption.

''I do not claim to have prior knowledge of the deception, true,'' Chiun admitted. ''But the good I did still stands. You cannot disagree with that.''

''You always twist things around so that they turn out in your favor,'' Remo said.

''True,'' agreed Chiun. ''After I lost my son, I learned to transform defeat into victory, errors into detours, not endings. I promised myself that I would never feel such bitter disappointment again in my life."

"I always wondered why you did some of the things you did."

"Because I am Chiun," said the Master of Sinanju. "But do not think that because I did not know of the Dutchman's deception, my motives were selfish."

"Here we go again," said Remo bitterly. "Here's where you do it to me again. Okay, Chiun, give me your explanation. Tell me how wrecking my wedding was for my own good. And make it good, because if you don't convince me, I'm walking out of this place and you're never going to see me again. You understand? End of partnership. We're through."

Chiun drew himself up so that his sitting posture was perfect, the spine aligned with the pelvis and the head sitting square to the upper vertebrae.

"Remember this time a year ago, when you brought me back to Sinanju?" Chiun asked.

"You were sick. Or faking sickness. You wanted to come back to Sinanju for good."

"Faking or not," said Chiun, "you thought I lay near death. And in your grief, you sought solace. Do you remember your first meeting with Mah-Li?"

"Yeah. She wore a veil to hide her face because the other villagers thought she was ugly. They called her Mah-Li the Beast. She was gorgeous, but by the screwed-up ideals of Sinanju beauty, she was homely."

"When did you first fall in love with her?"

"Almost immediately. It was love at first sight."

"Yet you did not see her face on that first meeting. How could you love at first sight when you had no sight of her veiled face?"

"I don't know. It was her voice, the way she made me feel good all over. She was lonely, an orphan like me."

"Precisely," said Chiun.

"Precisely what?" Remo asked.

"You were lonely. You thought the Master of Sinanju—the only person you cared for in life—was dying. You reached out to the nearest person you saw to fill the void in your existence."

"You'd better not be saying that I didn't love her."

"I am not saying that. Love is learned. This love at first sight is a Western concept. A rationalization of a necessary but inconvenient urge. How long did you know Mah-Li?"

"A few weeks. I don't know."

"Less than a month," said Chiun. "And you knew her only a day when you came to me to ask my blessing for your marriage. Yet a month later when I stole away from Sinanju in the night, you left your love-at-first-sight and followed me to America. And when I told you I intended to remain in America for a full year, did you return to your betrothed? No, you chose to remain with me."

"I was worried about you. I thought of Mah-Li every day."

"Did you send for her? Did you say, 'Mah-Li, come to America where we will be wed'?"

"No," said Remo slowly. "I wanted to be married in Sinanju."

"So you say. But I say that had you met in other circumstances, had Mah-Li been a Korean living in America and you passed her on the street, you would not have given her a second look. You thought I was dying and you found a Korean maid who, in her sweetness and intelligence, was appealing to you. And so you took her for your betrothed to fill the coming void. When my health miraculously improved, that void was healed and there was no need for her in your life."

"I loved her!" Remo shouted.

"You came to love her. You started to love her. You saw her as the fulfillment of your dream of happiness. But in truth, you barely knew her. This is why you did not cry at her funeral. I watched you, Remo. No tears fell from your face. There was anger, yes. But not true grief. In fact, she was nearly a stranger to you. Deny this if you dare."

"Her death hasn't sunk in yet," said Remo. "Hey, I loved her."

"You loved the dream. You loved what Mah-Li represented to you—your silly white house and picket fence. I understood this even if you did not."

"And you think that gave you the right to bust up the wedding? That's lame, Chiun. Even for you. I'll be seeing you around," added Remo, heading for the door.

Remo stopped at the threshold with Chiun's next words.

"I interfered with your wedding because you had a daughter you did not know. If it was your wish to marry, I would not have stopped you, even believing as I did that it was a mistake. But you had to see your own child first. You had to confront the reality that you had caused life to be brought into the world and weigh your new responsibility against this fantasy of yours."

Remo stood at the doorway unmoving.

"The love you had felt for Jilda of Lakluun was a casualty of the Dutchman. Did you think that living in Sinanju would have protected Mah-Li from his wrath? That is a lesson you have learned in the bitterest way imaginable. Just as I learned one of my own long before you were born."

"As soon as Jilda came back," Remo said weakly, "all my old feelings for her returned."

"Because now she represents your dream. And can you say whom you loved more, of these two women?"

"I never slept with Mah-Li, you know. I wanted to do it the old-fashioned way. Wait for the honeymoon."

"What are you saying? That because you had lain with one and not the other, you cannot compare them? That is unworthy of you, Remo."

Remo shook his head. "No, it's not that. I was just thinking out loud. I don't know, I'm all confused. I've got to clear my head. I have decisions to make."

"Yes," said Chiun, climbing to his feet. "You have many decisions to make. Whether to live or to die. Whether to be a father or to walk away from fatherhood. Whether to continue as my pupil or to go your way. But either way you choose, Remo, you will have to walk through shit. For that is life."

Chiun stepped out into the cold night.

"I am going to my home," he said solemnly. "If you wish, you may come with me. There will be a fire."

"I'd rather be alone right now," said Remo, looking at the house that was all he owned in the world.

"Just as long as you understand that your decision affects more than you alone. If you make the wrong decision, little Freya is an orphan—and I am once again sitting at the bottom of Mount Paektusan, a stubborn and childless man."

"I'll let you know, Little Father," said Remo. "You

know what hurts the worst? The last time I saw Mah-Li alive, it wasn't her. It was that bastard Purcell.''

''And my son was dead even as I berated him in my mind for his failure. We have that emptiness in common, you and I.''

And Chiun walked off, grateful that whatever Remo decided, he had once again called him Little Father. It still felt good, even after all these years.

Remo watched the Master of Sinanju go and turned his attention to the house. He had built it bare-handed, breaking the bamboo with deft chops, splitting it with his fingernails to make the floor. It was only a shell. It had never been more than a shell, roofless and solitary. Like my life up to now, Remo thought bitterly.

Remo kicked at one wall. It wobbled, then crashed mushily. He attacked the remaining walls, tearing them apart, ripping up the floor and hurling shoots of bamboo high into the air. One by one, they splashed into the barren waters of the West Korea Bay and were borne away like the fragments of a dream. His dream.

When he was done, Remo stood on the bare earth where the house no longer existed. The tears came then. Finally. They flooded out and he sank to the ground sobbing.

When they stopped, Remo got up and scuffed the dirt smooth until there was nothing to show that a dream had ever been built on the site.

Remo took the shore path, back into the village of Sinanju. Everything was clear now.

31

Sunrise found the Master of Sinanju inscribing a fresh scroll. He heard Remo Williams climbing the hill, and noticing his firm and confident step, continued writing.

"I've decided," Remo said from the open door.

"I know," replied the Master of Sinanju, not looking up from his calligraphy.

"I'm going back to America," Remo announced.

"I know," said Chiun.

"You couldn't know that."

"I knew it a year ago."

"No way," said Remo. "Don't try to con me with that tired Oriental-wisdom routine. That went out with Charlie Chan. You couldn't know."

"Remember a day last year when you barged in on my meditation? You had great plans for Sinanju, you said. You wanted to put in electricity, running water, and—ugh!—toilets."

"I thought they were improvements. There's plenty of gold. The village can afford it."

"For thousands of years the village of Sinanju has been considered the pearl of Asia," Chiun recited. "Long before there was an America. Men have come here seeking power and gold and jewels. Instead, they find a ramshackle fishing village where the men do not fish, the woman are no better than scullery maids and the children uncouth. They find squalor. And they move on, convinced that the legends are false or that the true Sinanju lies beyond the next horizon. And so my people and my treasure have remained safe for centuries."

"Thanks for the lesson, but that doesn't explain how you could know a year ago that I would decide to return to America."

"By the very act of intending these so-called improvements, my son, you were showing me that you were already homesick. It was your intention, whether you realized it or not, to remake this village in the image of your place of childhood, Newark, New Jersey." Chiun's nose wrinkled distastefully. "How clever you are. If there is a less desirable spot on the crust of the earth than my little village, it is there."

Remo considered. "Improvements," he said at last.

"I will not argue. You wish to return to America. Is that all?"

"The Dutchman said he killed Smith. I want to know if it's true. I owe him for that, as well as for Mah-Li. Then I'm going to bring him to American justice."

"Sinanju justice is more absolute."

"I'll only kill him if I have no choice."

"Why don't you simply sit down and slit your throat? You will be dead, and the Dutchman, being entwined with your destiny, will die. This will save you a long journey, not to mention plane fare."

"After I take care of the Dutchman," Remo went on, "I'm going to ask Jilda to marry me."

"I doubt that. After you take care of the Dutchman you will be dead. Even if a dead man can propose marriage, I doubt a living woman will accept. But she is white. Who knows? You can still hope."

"What about you?"

"What about me? I am like an onion that awaits peeling. There are so many fascinating layers. Where shall I begin?"

"You can come if you want. To America, I mean."

"Why would I want to? I have already carried one dead son home to Sinanju. I think that is my allotment in life."

"Well, if you don't want to . . ."

"I did not say that," Chiun said abruptly, putting down his quill. "I asked. It was a rhetorical question."

Remo's face brightened. "Then you're coming?"

"Only to see if Smith is in truth dead. It is a minor fact, but necessary if I am to finish the scrolls pertaining to my service in America."

"Whatever," Remo said nonchalantly. He pretended to examine a Persian wall hanging so that Chiun could not see his relieved expression.

"But I have another, more important, reason."

"Yeah? What's that?" Remo asked.

"You are an orphan."

"What kind of cockamammie reason is that?"

"The best kind. Who else is there to bury your miserable carcass after you have squandered your life?"

"Oh," said Remo. After a pause he said, "I'd like to leave as soon as possible."

"What is stopping you?"

"Don't you have to pack?"

"I have been packed for the last year, in anticipation of your decision. You will find my steamer trunks in the storage room. Be so good as to carry them to the edge of the village. A helicopter from Pyongyang is already on its way to transport us to the airport. I have purchased the airline tickets with my own money. First class for me and coach for you."

"Bull!" said Remo. "Even you couldn't be that sure of yourself." Then he heard the whut-whut-whut of a helicopter in flight. Remo subsided.

"You had best hurry," suggested Chiun, blotting the writing on his scroll. "I have chartered the helicopter by the hour."

The village came out to watch the Master of Sinanju depart. The lazy whirl of the helicopter blades fanned their stricken faces.

"Do not fear, my people," Chiun called from the helicopter's side. "For I will return sooner than you think. Until then, faithful Pullyang will head the village."

Remo loaded the last steamer trunk into a hatch on the helicopter's skin. Then he looked around for Jilda. She stood a little off from the villagers, holding Freya's tiny hand. The helicopter blades picked up speed.

"Come, Remo," Chiun said, climbing aboard.

"Hold your horses," said Remo, walking toward Jilda.

"I have to go," Remo told her. "But I'll be back. Will you wait for me?"

"Where do you go, Remo?"

"America. I'm going to end the Dutchman's threat once and for all."

"Remo, hurry," Chiun called querulously. "The meter is running."

Remo ignored him. "I have to go. Please wait for me."

"I do not think so, Remo. I do not think you will return."

"Look, I promise to come back."

"I do not belong here. Neither do you, I think."

"Remo!" Chiun's voice was strident.

"I'm coming," Remo snapped. The backwash of the helicopter blew Jilda's green cloak open. "Look, if you won't wait for me here, come with me. Now."

"That I will not do."

"Then meet me in America. We can talk there."

"Are you going, Daddy?" asked Freya.

Remo picked her up. "I have to, little girl."

Freya started to cry. "I wanted you to meet my pony," she cried. "I don't want you to go. Mommy, don't let Daddy go. He may never come back."

"It can't hurt to meet me in America," Remo pleaded. "You don't have to decide anything just yet."

"I will consider it," said Jilda.

"That's something," said Remo. "Here, stop crying, Freya."

"I can't. I'm scared."

Remo set Freya down and knelt in front of her. He brushed a tear aside with his finger. "Let Daddy show you how never to be scared."

"How?" Freya asked petulantly.

"By breathing. Take a deep breath. That's right, hold it in. Now, pretend this finger is a candle. Quick, exhale!"

Freya blew on Remo's upraised finger.

"Okay," said Remo, touching her heart. "That was breathing from the chest. But you want to breathe from down here," he said, tapping her round stomach. "Try it again."

Freya inhaled. This time, at Remo's instruction, she let it out slowly.

"Didn't that feel better?" Remo asked tenderly.

"Oh, yes! I feel all tingly. Not scared at all."

"That's Sinanju. A little hunk of it anyway. Keep practicing that way," Remo said, getting to his feet, "and you'll grow up to be big and strong. Like your mother."

Jilda smiled. She kissed Remo slowly, awkwardly, her bandaged arms held away from her body.

"In America," Remo said, and he whispered the where and when in her ear.

"Perhaps," said Jilda.

"Good-bye, Daddy. Can I have the hug you can't give Mommy? I'll give it to her later for you."

"You sure can," Remo said, squeezing her tight.

Then, walking backward because he wanted to hold their image in his mind as long as possible, Remo returned to the helicopter. It lifted off before his feet left the ground.

Remo settled in beside Chiun. He waved out the open door. Jilda and Freya waved back until long after they had become dots that disappeared under the helicopter's wheels.

"What were you doing with that child?" Chiun asked, pulling his unfinished scroll from his kimono.

"I was just showing Freya how not to be afraid."

"You were showing her early Sinanju breathing. You were wasting your time."

"How do you know that?"

"Because women do not know how to breathe. And never will," said Chiun, untying the scroll's blue ribbon.

"What's that?"

"You tell me, trainer of females."

"Looks like a scroll. Blue ribbon. A birth announcement?"

"You have the mind of a grasshopper," said Chiun, starting to write.

"Quick, and leaps high?"

"All over the forest," said Chiun. "And seldom landing in the correct place."

32

He maintained his control until he came to a little fishing village. He did not know the name of the village, only that it lay below the thirty-eighth parallel and therefore was in South Korea.

The village reminded him of Sinanju, and because he had kept it penned in too long, the beast burst free.

The village caught fire, every hut at once. The people screamed as they fled their homes. Then they too caught fire. The flames were blue. Pretty flames. The flesh that burned under the flames was pretty. Then it shriveled and blackened and slid off the bone as the helpless screaming peasants rolled in the dirt in a futile attempt to put out their roasting bodies.

The beast satiated again, the Dutchman continued his slow march to Seoul.

In the South Korean capital he bought a pair of wraparound sunglasses and a Sony Walkman headset. He also purchased a brush and jar of flat black enamel paint. And a cassette of the loudest rock music he could find.

He paid for the airplane ticket with a credit card that was an illusion and went through customs with a passport that was a product of his imagination. Everyone saw him as a portly American businessman in a cable-knit gray suit.

In the airport men's room he painted the inside of the sunglasses with the black paint.

The Dutchman put on the glasses immediately after take-off. And although it was against airline rules, he donned the Walkman. He hoped the sounds of the overproduced music and the fact that he could not see past the painted-over sunglasses would keep the beast in check. Just long enough. Just until he was safe in America.

Where he could kill again.

Because there was nothing left for him.

33

The President of the United States had never felt more helpless.

The ornate walls of the Oval Office seemed to press in on him. As commander-in-chief of America's armed forces and vast intelligence apparatus, he should have been able to find the answers he so desperately needed.

The CIA had assured him that they had no special operative detailed to guard the Vice-President. So did the DIA, and the FBI, and even though it hurt him to have to ask, he inquired of his National Security Council. And the Secret Service.

He was assured that only normal Secret Service agents guard the Vice-President. Not fancy martial-arts practitioners.

Not even the Secret Service could say that they were guarding Governor Michael Princippi. He still refused protection. In fact, for a man who had escaped one assault on his life, he seemed serene.

In desperation the President had put in a call to Dr. Harold W. Smith. And for the first time in his memory, Smith did not pick up the red phone. The President tried calling at all hours.

It was obvious something had happened to Smith. It was impossible for the President to learn what. An average citizen could have made a normal phone call to Smith's Folcroft office. But the President could never get away with it. The phone company would make a record of any ordinary long-distance call. Nor could the President ask his staff to investigate the disappearance of a certain Dr. Harold W. Smith. Someone might ask why. And the President could never answer that question.

So he sat alone in the loneliest office in human history, trying to put the pieces together himself.

He did have one new fact, courtesy of the Secret Service. It had taken them two days to uncover it. Two critical days in which the news media and editorial writers of the nation had whipped themselves into a frenzy attempting to link all the loose ends into some sinister skein.

The Secret Service had interrogated surviving members of the Eastie Goombahs. They learned that the gang leader had boasted of having been paid to assassinate Governor Principi. Okay, thought the President, so maybe it's a conspiracy. Who runs it? Who could know about CURE and use it to topple the American electoral system or even the entire government?

Over and over the President chased the possibility around in his mind. The name that he kept coming back to was that of Dr. Harold W. Smith.

Perhaps that was why Smith had disappeared. He was the mastermind. Having failed, he had gone into hiding. Now, if only there was some way to prove it. . . .

Dr. Harold W. Smith breathed.

That was all. He took his food through a tube that ran into his discolored right forearm. His gray eyes were closed and for the fourth day there was no rapid eye movement to indicate a dream state or even minimal brain activity.

Dr. Martin Kimble checked the progress chart that was clipped to the foot of the hospital bed on which Smith lay. It was a flat horizontal line. There was no rise or fall. They had brought Smith in in this state. It was not a coma, because there were no obvious signs of brain activity. But Smith was not dead. His heart continued to beat—if the slow-motion gulp his vascular organ gave every twenty minutes could be called a beat. Perhaps the lungs worked too. It was impossible to tell. Dr. Kimble had ordered life-support systems hooked up to the man who had been found at his desk, inert, without any sign of trauma or violence or poison.

As Dr. Kimble had explained to Smith's frightened wife, "I don't have a firm prognosis. This could be a long vigil. You'd be better off at home."

What he didn't say was that for all his vital signs, Dr.

Harold W. Smith might have been a block of cheese carved to resemble a human being. He even had the same waxy, yellowish color to his skin.

A rush of ammonia-scented air came from the direction of the doorway, causing Dr. Kimble to turn. An elderly Oriental man in a teal-blue embroidered gown stepped in and, ignoring Dr. Kimble, floated over to Smith's bedside.

"Excuse me, but visiting hours are over," said Dr. Kimble stuffily.

"I am not visiting," said the old Oriental in a squeaky, querulous voice. "I am Smith's personal physician."

"Oh? Mrs. Smith never mentioned you, Dr. . . ."

"Dr. Chiun. I have just returned to this country from my native Korea, where I attended a serious burn patient."

"I assume you have some identification," prompted Dr. Kimble, who knew that there were a lot of foreign medical schools turning out third-rate doctors these days.

"I can vouch for him," said a cool voice from the door.

Dr. Kimble saw a lean man in a white T-shirt and black slacks. "And who are you supposed to be?" he asked.

"I'm Dr. Chiun's personal assistant. Call me Remo."

"I'm going to have to ask you both to come with me. We have procedures at this hospital regarding visiting doctors."

"No time," said Remo, taking Dr. Kimble by the arm. The man merely touched his funny bone, but the pins-and-needles feeling started immediately. It ran up his arm, over his chest, and up his neck. Dr. Kimble knew that it was impossible to feel pins and needles in the brain, but he felt them nonetheless. His vision started to cloud over.

When the man called Remo let go, Dr. Kimble found himself on his knees. He could see again.

"Tell us about Smith," said Remo.

Dr. Kimble started to speak but the little Oriental, who was fussing over the patient, cut him off.

"Forget that quack," said Dr. Chiun. "Look at what he has done to Smith. Jabbed him with needles and hooked him up to machines. Where are the leeches? I am surprised that he has not attached leeches to Smith's arm to suck out the rest of the vitality."

"Leeching hasn't been used in centuries, Little Father."

"Actually, it's coming back," said Dr. Kimble, groping to his feet. He felt woozy and began looking around for an oxygen tank. When he found one, he pushed the clear oxygen mask to his face and breathed deeply. As he inhaled, he watched and listened.

Dr. Chiun strode around the bed, examining Smith critically.

"He's been like that for four days," Dr. Kimble told him.

Dr. Chiun nodded silently.

"There's no sign of injury," Dr. Kimble said.

"Wrong," said Chiun, pointing with an impossibly long fingernail at Smith's forehead. "What is this?"

Still clutching the oxygen mask, Dr. Kimble learned over. In the middle of Smith's forehead was a tiny purplish spot.

"That's a liver spot," said Dr. Kimble. "Probably a birthmark."

"You call yourself a physician and you do not recognize an inflamed third eye when you see it," snapped Chiun. He began probing Smith's temples.

"Third eye? That's New Age mumbo jumbo."

Chiun ignored him. He shifted his massaging fingers to Smith's waxy forehead. He closed his eyes in concentrations.

"What is he doing?" Dr. Kimble asked Remo.

"Search me."

"I thought you were his assistant."

"Mostly I watch and keep people like you from getting in his way."

"I am testing the *kotdi*," said Chiun, opening his eyes. He withdrew his hands from Smith's head.

"What's that?"

"The *kotdi* is like your television on-and-off switch. When it is correctly pressed, a person is shut off. Like Smith."

"Shut off! That's preposterous," sputtered Dr. Kimble.

"Remo will demonstrate for you."

Remo reached up and tapped Dr. Kimble's forehead in its exact geometrical center. Dr. Kimble's eyes rolled up in his head and he collapsed like a sack of kitty litter. Remo caught him under the arms and asked Chiun, "What do I do with him?"

"Turn him back on, if you wish."

Remo felt for his forehead and tapped once. The doctor struggled to his feet and smoothed his doctor's smock.

"Was I out?"

"Actually, you were off," Chiun told him absently.

Dr. Kimble said, "I don't believe it."

Remo shrugged. "Then don't." He joined Chiun. "How is he?"

"This is terrible. His inner harmony is totally gone. I fear permanent damage."

"We can't let Smith die. You've got to do something."

"I am not talking about Smith," said Chiun, pulling an intravenous tube out of Smith's arm and unplugging electrodes from his head. "Smith will be fine. I was referring to the Dutchman. Look at the force he used to press the *kotdi.*"

"Too hard?"

"Not hard enough. He intended a death blow, merciful but final. I saw signs of this in Sinanju. Now I am certain. The blow with which he stole Mah-Li's life was also flawed. Remember the red tear? The Dutchman is losing control and this clumsy blow is the surest sign of it."

"Oh," said Remo. "What about Smith?"

Chiun set one finger so that it covered the purple bruise on Smith's brow and pressed lightly. As if triggered by rubber bands, Smith's eyes snapped open.

"Master of Sinanju?" he said clearly. He tried to sit up.

Chiun pushed him back. "You are well, Emperor. Thanks to your faithful servant."

"The Dutchman!"

"We know, Smitty," Remo put in. "He was behind everything."

"Quiet!" Smith barked, indicating Dr. Kimble with his eyes.

In a corner, Dr. Kimble was feeling his forehead with both hands, pressing different spots experimentally.

"I think I understand," he said. "By disrupting a nerve center hitherto unknown to medical science, you shut off all electrical activity in the brain. The result is suspended animation with no tissue deterioration. But I can't seem to find the nerve."

"I'll help you," said Remo, taking the doctor's hand and making a fist. He straightened the index finger and placed it over the doctor's eyes, which rolled up in a ridiculous effort to watch his own forehead.

"You press there," Remo suggested, stepping back.

The doctor did. And fell onto the floor.

"Works every time." Remo whistled airily.

"So the Dutchman was the mastermind behind the assassination attempts," said Smith, sitting up in bed. Color flooded back to his face like pale wine filling a glass. "Adonis and the ninja master were impostors."

"Had you listened carefully to my story of the thieving ninja," Chiun scolded, "this would not surprise you. Only Sinanju is true."

"He followed us to Sinanju," Remo said grimly. "But he got away. I've got a score to settle with him."

"Where is he now?"

"We don't know."

"What about the presidential candidates? Are they safe?"

"Yes," said Remo.

"No," said Chiun.

"No?" asked Remo.

"No," repeated Chiun in a firm voice. "His reason is fleeing. His purpose in attacking those politicians was to embarrass Remo and me and force us to return to my village in disgrace, where he intended to complete his vengeance. Now that he has failed, he has returned to America to finish the killings he did not complete."

"Why would he do that?" asked Remo. "He doesn't give a hang about the election."

"He is a wounded scorpion who is lashing out in his pain. He has always been driven to kill. He fears you, desires to be my pupil, and thinks that he has killed Smith. He will strike at those we were once hired to protect. It is the only way he can cause us pain without risking another confrontation he knows he cannot win."

"I don't buy it," disagreed Remo.

"But I do," said Smith. "Or at least I can't take the chance that Chiun is wrong. I need your help, both of you."

"I have a personal thing to settle with the Dutchman," Remo assured him. "You can count on us."

"But I do not," said Chiun, surreptitiously kicking Remo in the shin.

"Oww," muttered Remo.

"I may be persuaded to reenter your service, however, Emperor Smith."

"I'm happy to hear that," said Smith. "Of course I'm

prepared to sign a contract on the terms we discussed earlier.''

''I am afraid that cannot be,'' said Chiun.

''Why not?''

''Because you tore up that contract.''

''Can't you prepare another.''

''I could, but it would take several days, for I am old and my memory is slipping. It may be that I would have to reopen negotiations simply to refresh my feeble mind.''

''Then what do we do? We can't wait that long. The Dutchman could strike at any time.''

''It just so happens that, anticipating your desires, I took the liberty of preparing a new contract during my journey to America,'' said Chiun, brandishing a fresh scroll. He untied the blue ribbon and presented it to Smith.

Smith took the scroll. He blinked at it. ''I can't see. Of course, my glasses. Where are they?''

Remembering that he had them, Remo pulled the glasses from his pocket and placed them over Smith's bleary eyes.

''The Dutchman brought them to Sinanju as proof he'd killed you,'' Remo explained.

''This is worse,'' said Smith. ''I can't see a thing.''

''Oh,'' cried Chiun. ''I do not know what to do. We could wait for you to obtain new spectacles, but I fear for the lives of your nominees.''

''What are the terms?''

''Excellent. I am certain you would find them agreeable. Why don't you simply sign now and read later?''

Smith hesitated. ''This is exceedingly irregular.''

''These are irregular times,'' said Chiun.

''Very well,'' said Smith unhappily. ''There's still a chance that CURE will be terminated after the election. It can't hurt to keep operations going another few months.''

''Excellent,'' said Chiun, plucking a goose-quill pen from one sleeve and offering it to Smith. An ink stone came out of the other sleeve. Chiun lifted the tiny lid and Smith dipped into the well. He signed the bottom of the scroll.

''You will never regret this,'' promised Chiun, recovering the quill and the scroll.

''I trust not,'' said Smith, moving his glasses in front of his eyes at different focal lengths. He still could not see. ''Your first task is to protect the presidential candidates.''

"Immediately," declared Chiun.

"Count me out," said Remo. "I'm after the Dutchman, remember?"

"Who perhaps even now is on his way to murder one of them."

"Count me in," said Remo.

"One last thing before you go," said Smith. "I need to contact the President as soon as possible. Could you go to my office and bring my briefcase?"

"It's already here," Remo told him, reaching out into the corridor. He placed Smith's worn leather briefcase on his lap.

"Folcroft was the first place we went," said Remo. "Your secretary told us you were in the hospital. I figured it wouldn't hurt to bring the briefcase, just in case."

"Good thinking."

"Actually it was my idea, Emperor Smith," Chiun pointed out. "Remo merely carried your property."

"Yes," said Smith vaguely, unlocking the briefcase. Inside, a compact computer link gleamed under the weak fluorescent lights. Smith plucked out the handset of a cellular phone. "I must speak with the President. Alone. Could you remove that doctor on your way out?"

"At once," said Chiun, bowing. "Remo," he said, snapping his fingers.

Reluctantly Remo toted the doctor out to the corridor, where Chiun stood before an elevator. Remo shoved Dr. Kimble into a broom closet and joined Chiun.

"I'm worried about Smitty," he told Chiun.

"He will be fine."

"I mean his vision. He acted half-blind."

"I am sure he will recover. Sometimes when the *kotdi* is improperly manipulated, the vision is slow to return."

"The doctor didn't have that problem when I brought him around."

"You are not old and feeble like me."

"I also wasn't carrying a contract I wanted signed, sight unseen," said Remo, stepping into the elevator.

"That too." Chiun beamed as the elevator doors closed on them.

* * *

When the red telephone rang, the President heard it all the way down the hall in the Oval Office.

He raced out of the office past Secret Service guards, who tried to follow him.

"Stay there. I'll be right back. Diarrhea," he yelled. The Secret Service guards stayed put.

In his bedroom, the President snatched up the red telephone.

"Yes?" he said.

"Smith here."

"I've been trying to reach you for two days. Where the heck have you been?"

"I've been indisposed. I'm sorry," apologized Smith. "Without going into details, Mr. President, I can now clear up the matter that is before us."

"I'd like to hear the details," said the President.

"They would take too long, and I doubt that you would believe them."

"Let's hear the broad outlines, then."

"I have identified the force behind the assassination attempts. The man calling himself Tulip is actually an opponent force my operation has dealt with in the past. His motive was revenge against my enforcement arm. He failed, and I have reason to believe that he is back in this country. He may try to complete the assassinations."

"I'll double the security around the nominees."

"No, pull them back. My special person is on the job. I've signed him on for another year."

"And those personal records of his?"

"You mean his scrolls?" Smith's voice lost its sharp edge.

"Yes, I asked that their destruction be part of the new contract."

"Of course. You're right. I had forgotten. I've been quite ill, but strangely, my mind feels quite sharp now. I don't know how I could have forgotten that detail."

"So what are the details of the new contract?"

Smith paused. "As you know, I have full autonomy in undertaking contractual obligations," he said.

"I'm not asking for veto power," the President snapped. "I just want to know what guarantees we have that this won't happen again."

"I'll have to get back to you on that, Mr. President. But rest assured, this situation will not be repeated."

The President grunted unhappily. "Very well. Anything else—or can't you tell me?"

"The two bodyguards, the one called Adonis and the ninja. I have identified them. They are both this Tulip person. And he hired the killers involved in all of the assassination attempts."

"My information is that one was a muscle-bound American and the other a short Japanese man. How could they be the same man?"

"I told you you would not believe it."

The President sighed. "The only thing I can say, Smith, is that you've found out more than all of the other intelligence services combined. On that score I have to go with you."

"Thank you, Mr. President," said Harold W. Smith, and hung up.

"I hate it when he does that," muttered the President as he replaced the receiver. "Sometimes that fellow acts like I work for him instead of the other way around."

34

Remo Williams didn't like it.

He had been following the Vice-President for several hours. The Vice-President was on a final campaign swing through the South. He traveled by limousine motorcade, and because a trailing vehicle would have been an instant tipoff, Remo could not follow in a car.

He had sneaked into the Vice-President's trunk when no one was looking.

Each time they got to a campaign stop, Remo sneaked out and tried to be inconspicuous as he kept an eye on the Vice-President. But no one had attempted to harm the man. Remo didn't think that anyone was going to. Back in Rye, Chiun had insisted that they split up, because, as he had put it, "There is no predicting where the Dutchman will strike first."

"Fine," said Remo. "I'll cover the Vice-President."

"No, I will cover the President of Vice," declared Chiun.

"If there's no predicting where he'll turn up, why do you want the Vice-President?"

"Because you do," said Chiun.

"He's mine," Remo had said firmly.

"Very well. I will not argue. You can have him."

Looking back, Remo decided that Chiun had agreed too readily. But it was still a coin toss where the Dutchman would strike, assuming Chiun was right. But what if he wasn't? What if Chiun was bluffing? Remo wondered if he shouldn't skip the Vice-President and find Governor Princippi.

Then it came time for the motorcade to start again and Remo was too preoccupied trying to get back into the Vice-President's trunk without being seen to give the problem further thought.

* * *

The Master of Sinanju knew it was just a matter of time.

He had figured out that Governor Princippi would be the Dutchman's next target. It was not an equal coin toss as Remo had thought. It was more of a two-in-three chance that the governor would be next. The Master of Sinanju recalled that the Dutchman had ordered two hits on the Vice-President. But only one on Governor Princippi. To the Sinanju-trained mind, symmetry was instinctual. The Dutchman was Sinanju. Mad or not, he would, without thinking, seek equilibrium.

Therefore the governor had to be next. And Chiun would deal with the Dutchman without risking Remo's life.

Governor Princippi was in Los Angeles promising to institute free national earthquake insurance before a group of prominent businessmen. Chiun clung to a window of the high-rise office building where the meeting was taking place.

The music told him that the Dutchman was coming. It was louder than before, more disoriented, as if a musician played from sheet music whose notes were frightened ants.

Chiun hugged the window because he knew the Dutchman would come up the building's side and he did not wish to be seen first. The element of surprise was crucial for what Chiun intended to do.

Jeremiah Purcell paused at the twelfth floor to look in at the lighted windows. It was night and most of the building was dark. The newspaper had mentioned the late-evening meeting between the governor and the Los Angeles business community. One of the lighted windows would be the correct one. But not this one. And so he reached up for the next ledge and the next floor.

At the thirteenth floor he paused. None of the windows were lighted on this side. He made a complete circuit of the floor, walking confidently along on a ledge so narrow a pigeon would have scorned it.

He had just turned the last corner of the ledge when the flutter of settling cloth caused him to swivel suddenly.

Too late. The blow caught him in the right shoulder. With a subcutaneous pop, the bone separated.

He grabbed his shoulder, setting his teeth against the sudden white-hot pain.

"You!" he cried. "Where is your pupil?"

"Look behind you," said the Master of Sinanju coolly.

The Dutchman whirled again. But the kick came, not from the front, but from behind him. It struck behind his left knee, causing the leg to buckle. Too late, he realized the Master of Sinanju had tricked him. They were alone on the ledge.

The Dutchman clung to the ledge. He looked up at the cold face of the Master of Sinanju.

"The four blows?" asked Jeremiah Purcell through teeth that ground against each other.

"You know the tradition?" Chiun asked him.

"A Master of Sinanju shows his contempt for a foe by striking four blows and then walking away, to leave the vanquished one in death or mutilated humiliation. But I do not deserve such treatment. I could be a good pupil to you. Better than Remo. I could be the next Master of Sinanju. I could be the Shiva of the legends."

"The next Master of Sinanju would not harm one such as Mah-Li," spat Chiun. "You deserve my contempt." And he kicked the Dutchman on the right kneecap just hard enough to open a hairline fracture, but not to fragment the bone.

"I could be the Shiva of the legends, the dead night tiger who is white. How do you know it is Remo and not me?"

"Remo is Shiva," said Chiun, zeroing in to strike the fourth and final blow.

"No!" screamed Jeremiah Purcell. "I will not allow you to defeat me! I will throw myself off this ledge first!" His limbs like jelly, he allowed himself to slip off the ledge like an octopus sliding bonelessly over the side of a fishing boat.

The Master of Sinanju snapped him back by his long hair. Just in time. He deposited him on the ledge.

"I do not wish your death, only to see you helpless forever," Chiun said.

"I am never helpless," said the Dutchman. "You forget my mind."

Suddenly the Master of Sinanju stood, not on a ledge, but in the hand of a monster of steel and chrome. The building shook under his feet. The windows on either side of him turned into square eyes and focused cross-eyed upon him.

A hand made of concrete and reinforced steel and larger than an automobile reached up for him.

The Master of Sinanju knew it was an illusion. Buildings do not become monsters of metal. But he could not make his eyes see behind the illusion. He clutched the Dutchman's hair frantically. If Purcell fell, he would die. And so would Remo.

Then the burning began. Blue flame—real flame—erupted at the tips of Chiun's long-nailed fingers on one hand.

Chiun windmilled his burning hand, putting out the fire. He jumped to avoid the huge concrete paw swiping at him, and clung to the building. He could feel that, at least. It was his rock of safety. He could still feel the Dutchman's hair in his other hand. It jerked suddenly. Chiun's fist clenched tighter.

When the illusions stopped, the discordant music died too. Chiun blinked. His hand still clutched the Dutchman's blond hair. But only the hair. It had been shorn off by sharp fingernails.

Chiun was alone on the ledge. He scurried to the next floor, where the governor was holding his meeting. Peering in through the window, Chiun saw that the meeting went on undisturbed.

Climbing down, he searched the street with frightened eyes. But there was no crumpled figure in purple lying in the street.

The Dutchman had slunk off, alone, vanquished, to lick his wounds once again. Good. Perhaps this would truly be the end of it, Chiun hoped.

In Atlanta the Vice-President's motorcade pulled up at a Holiday Inn for the night.

Remo got out of the trunk as soon as the car was left alone. He called Smith from a pay phone.

"Remo, I'm glad you called in," Smith said. "Chiun reports that he thwarted an attempt by the Dutchman to kill Governor Princippi. But Purcell got away. Chiun believes he's going to try for the Vice-President next."

"I'm ready for him."

"Sit tight. Chiun is on the way to join you."

"Tell him to knock three times on the trunk of the Vice-President's limo."

* * *

The Dutchman limped for several blocks, searching. He was in a run-down business district in East Los Angeles. Somewhere there would be a hardware store. When he found one, he broke in through the back. Every hardware store had a vise. There was a big one in the back room, bolted to a workbench. He flopped his right forearm into the vise and closed it painfully with his other elbow. Setting himself, he yanked. The right shoulder strained, bringing sweat to his brow. The ball joint popped back into the socket. The pain was incredible. But he could use the arm now. That made resetting everything else that much easier. . . .

Herm Accord waited in the bar for nearly an hour. He was about to leave when the man walked in, briefcase in hand.

He was a youthful guy with a dissipated face. His hair was like cornsilk, and cut in a punk style that made it look like the blond locks had been sheared by the ruthless swipe of a sickle.

"You Dutch?" he asked.

"Yes," said the blond man, limping to the table. He waved the waitress off.

"What's the job?"

"Tomorrow night the two presidential candidates are going to debate on national television."

"Yeah, so what?"

"I want it to go down in history as the unfinished debate."

"Like the unfinished symphony, huh? It's doable. But it's a little late to do anything with explosives. That's my specialty."

"Your specialty is death. You are ex-CIA. A renegade. And you have a reputation for doing the impossible. I don't care how you do it. Here," Dutch said, lifting the briefcase to the table with tired hands. "There's one million and fifty thousand dollars."

"I said a million over the phone. What's the extra fifty grand for?"

"You own a private plane. I need you to fly me someplace."

"Where?"

"Home," said the Dutchman.

* * *

Remo paced the roof of the Holiday Inn. Two floors below, the Vice-President worked on last-minute preparations for the great debate. There had been no sign of the Dutchman all night, and now morning was brightening the sky.

The Master of Sinanju came up through a fire door.

"Anything?" Remo asked anxiously.

"No," said Chiun. "There are no suspicious persons in the lobby. Here, I brought you a newspaper. Perhaps if you focus your limited attention upon it, you will cease your incessant pacing."

"At a time like this?" asked Remo, taking the paper without thinking.

"We may be in for a long wait."

"What makes you say that?"

"The Dutchman has a long journey to this city. It will not help him that he now limps."

"The four blows."

"Three, actually," corrected Chiun, looking over the edge of the roof to the front entrance below. Remo noticed that Chiun seemed less alert than he should have.

"I guess you figured if the Dutchman was crippled, I'd have a better shot at taking him alive," Remo suggested.

"That possibility might have crossed my mind," Chiun admitted in a distant voice. "But my duty was to protect the governor. I could not kill Purcell, so I did the next best thing."

"I still want him."

"I will let you know the moment he sets foot in this building," said Chiun.

And because he was bored, Remo flipped through the newspaper. On page four, a boxed item caught his eye. Remo tore it out and called to Chiun.

"Forget the entrance," said Remo. "The Dutchman isn't anywhere near here."

Chiun asked, "How did you know that?" Then he caught himself. "I mean, how can you say that, Remo?"

Grimly Remo gave the article to Chiun.

The Master of Sinanju looked at the headline: "PTERO-DACTYLS SIGHTED OVER SAINT MARTIN."

"They've been circling a certain ruined castle since last

night," Remo said. "When people try to photograph them, the developed pictures show only empty air. I don't suppose you'd have any idea what castle that might be?"

"You tell me," said Chiun unhappily. "You are the deductive genius."

"The castle on Devil's Mountain where we first encountered Purcell," Remo said. "His home. And the place where he's gone to hide and heal. The place where you figured he'd go all along. Am I right?"

"A lucky guess," said Chiun, turning the clipping into confetti with fussy motions of his fingernails.

"I'm going to Saint Martin."

"That does not worry me. What worries me is: will you return from Saint Martin?"

35

When the plane banked over Saint Martin, Remo could see Devil's Mountain, a black horn of evil thrusting up from one end of the beautiful French-Dutch island in the Caribbean.

"There it is," Remo said, pointing to a tumble of white stones high on a ledge overlooking the bay.

"I see no purple terrorbirds," sniffed Chiun. He was thinking how much Devil's Mountain reminded him of Mount Paektusan.

But they saw the pterodactyls when the taxi driver brought them as far as he dared to go. The rumor on the island was that the former inhabitant of Devil's Mountain, the feared Dutchman, had returned from the dead to haunt his ruined castle.

Remo paid the driver and they started walking.

The pterodactyls arose from the ruins and made lazy circle over the ledge. They ignored Remo and Chiun, who had begun to scale the sheer side of the volcanic mountain.

"Remember," warned Remo. "You had a shot at him. Now it's my turn."

As they climbed, the music seeped into their consciousness, the subliminal sounds of the Dutchman's disordered mind. The sky turned purple, a deeper purple than the pterodactyls. As if envious of the richer hue, the pterodactyls lifted silent wings and flew into the heavens. They were absorbed by the lowering purple sky.

"I think he's playing," said Remo. "Good. That means he doesn't know we are here."

"He does not know anything," said Chiun worriedly. "Look!"

A gargantuan face broke over the lip of the ledge, like a

whale surfacing. It leered, huge and cruel with slitted hazel cat's eyes and a pocked yellow complexion.

"Nuihc," Remo whispered.

"Listen," Chiun said.

"Father! Father!" The voice was thin and sad, but the vocal violence of the cry carried alarmingly.

"It's Purcell. What's he doing?" Remo wanted to know.

Chiun grasped Remo's wrist with clawlike hands.

"Listen to me, my son. I think we should go from this place."

"No way. The Dutchman is up there. I haven't come this far just so you could talk me out of this."

"He has gone over the edge."

"He did that a long time ago," Remo said, shrugging off Chiun's grasp. Chiun's hands reasserted themselves.

"Over the edge into madness. Observe. Listen to the music."

The face of Nuihc, smiling with silent cruelty, lifted like a hot-air balloon. Hanging beneath it from cables, like a wicker basket, was a tiny human-size body. The Nuihc balloon floated into the purple sky. It popped and was gone.

"Looks to me like he's just playing mind games," Remo said.

"Mark the sky. It is purple, the color of the mad mind."

"Fine. It'll make him easier to handle."

"He has nothing to lose now," Chiun warned.

"You can stay down here if you want to, Chiun. Either way, you stay out of it."

Chiun let go of Remo's arms. "Very well. This is your decision. But I will not wait below. I have already stood at the base of Mount Paektusan. This time I will accompany my son to the summit."

"Fair enough," said Remo, starting up again.

The higher they climbed, the steeper the mountain became. The air was warm, not cooled at all by the freshening sea breeze. Beyond them, the water stretched blue-green toward infinity. But above, the sky hung suffocatingly close, like a velvet hanging.

Remo was the first to reach the ledge. The castle ruins covered it. Once sparkling battlements had lifted to the sky. Now only one turret stood. The rest had fallen into great broken blocks like a city lost for thousands of years.

Down in the ruins, the Dutchman walked, his purple clothes loose against his body, his short blond hair sticking up like a cartoon of a man who has jammed a wet finger into an electrical socket.

Remo climbed onto a block of granite and called down to his enemy.

"Purcell!"

The Dutchman did not react. Something in the sky held his attention.

Remo looked up. High in the early-morning sky, like a diamond in a jeweler's case, the planet Venus shone like a star.

Chiun came up behind Remo. "What is he doing?" he asked.

"Search me. He's just staring at the sky."

"No, at that star."

Down below, the Dutchman pointed an accusing finger at the bright planet. His harsh voice ripped up from the center of the ruins. "Explode! Why don't you explode?"

"You're right," said Remo. "He has gone around the bend."

"We must stop him," declared Chiun.

"That's my idea," Remo said resolutely.

Chiun hurried after him. "No, not for revenge. Remember the Dutchman's other powers. The ones that are not illusions."

"Yeah, he can make things catch fire or explode. All he has to do is think it."

"He is trying to make Venus explode. With his mind."

"Can he do that?" Remo asked, stopping suddenly. The concept shook him out of this grim certainty.

"We do not wish to find out. Because if he can, he will not stop with Venus. He will put out the very stars in the sky, one by one, until only our world lies spinning in the Void. And then he will obliterate this world too. I know madness. He is full of power, Remo. Our lives no longer mean anything against this threat. Come."

And the Master of Sinanju surged ahead. But Remo overtook him.

"Purcell!" Remo yelled. His voice bounced off the ruins like an echo in a deep cave. "Purcell. Forget that crap. I've come for you."

The Dutchman turned his electric-blue eyes toward them. They seemed to take a long time to focus.

"I will be with you in a moment, my old enemy. It seems that putting out a star requires more concentration than I realized."

"You don't have that kind of time," said Remo, jumping into the ruins.

"Inside line," said Chiun. And Remo nodded, taking the inside-line approach. He went at the Dutchman in a straight line while Chiun circled around in back. Distracted, the Dutchman reacted to Chiun's circling attack. But Remo was faster. He gathered the Dutchman up in his arms, taking him under one shoulder and around a thigh. Remo spun him like a baton.

The Dutchman stopped his midair cartwheel with a reaching hand. He took Remo by the throat, bringing Remo into the momentum of his spin and throwing Remo against a shattered turret.

"I am more powerful than you," said the Dutchman, picking himself up. He wobbled on his legs dizzily. "I am the Dutchman. I can extinguish the universe with a thought!"

The Master of Sinanju saw that his pupil lay unmoving. There was no time to see if he lived. Chiun moved in on one of the Dutchman's knees. The fourth blow would no longer be denied.

The Dutchman turned, dropping into a fighting crouch. But Chiun did not put up a matching defense. Let the Dutchman have a free strike. Just as long as the Master of Sinanju had his fourth blow.

Chiun felt his toe connect with the Dutchman's knee at the same time the flat-handed blow struck his temple. Chiun rolled with the impact. Both combatants fell.

"You have thrown in your lot with Shiva," the Dutchman said bitterly, trying to rise to his feet. "You should have known better. You could have been father to a god." And the Dutchman, disdaining Chiun's prone form, turned his attention back to the beckoning gleam of Venus, the morning star.

As Chiun watched, the Dutchman lifted his arms to the purple sky, first imploringly, then with a face shaken by rage and wrath. The sky seemed to vibrate.

But all around them another voice suddenly reverberated, deep and full in strength. A voice the Master of Sinanju had heard before. The only voice he had ever learned to fear.

"I am created Shiva, the Destroyer; Death, the shatterer of worlds. The dead night tiger made whole by the Master of Sinanju."

And the Master of Sinanju smiled grimly. For standing on a ruined turret, a block of granite the size of a small car held over his head, stood Remo Williams.

"Who is this dog meat who challenges me?" Remo said in the voice of Shiva.

The granite block accelerated through the air like a bullet. The Dutchman executed a backflip, landing on top of the block a mere second after it crashed onto the spot where he had been standing.

"Not good enough," crowed the Dutchman. And then it was Remo who was flying through the air.

The two men collided, irresistible force meeting immovable object. They grappled, hand to wrist and toe to toe. They strained against one another like wrestlers, their faces warping and contorting. The sudden wave of sweat-smell coming from the spot where they struggled told the Master of Sinanju of the terrific force being expended. Then, under their quivering feet, the ground cracked and buckled.

The Master of Sinanju crawled to avoid a widening tear in the earth. He found his feet with difficulty and moved to one side of the ruined castle.

This was a battle of gods on earth. There was no place in it for a mere Master of Sinanju. With pained eyes Chiun watched the display of naked power and prayed to the gods of Sinanju that he would not be asked to carry a body down the mountain this day.

Remo Williams struggled mightily. He had one hand around the Dutchman's wrist and the Dutchman had his opposite hand around Remo's other wrist. They pushed and strained against one another, their feet stepping and locking like horses trying to pull a too-heavy load.

The Dutchman suddenly brought one foot down on Remo's instep. Remo responded with a circle kick. The Dutchman jumped with both feet. He let go of Remo's wrist, but Remo did not let go of his. With a swift floating motion

Remo caught the Dutchman's other wrist. He had them both now.

When the Dutchman's feet touched ground, Remo pushed him. The Dutchman's weakened knees started to buckle.

"This is for Mah-Li," Remo said angrily.

"You kill me and you die!" snarled the Dutchman, his face working with fury. His eyes grew wilder still. His legs quivered as they were forced further and further down. One knee touched the earth, sending shooting pains up the Dutchman's injured leg.

"No!" he screamed. Beneath their feet, the earth cracked again. A serpent jumped out of the earth, long as a train and bigger around than a redwood. Its orange-brown translucent body writhed like an earthworm. And out of its massive jaws, yellow flames seared.

"You'll need more than your tricks to beat me now, Purcell," Remo said. "You're finished."

"No!" shouted Jeremiah Purcell. And the voice was the voice of the beast within him, but the cry was tinged with fear. He felt his other knee sink inexorably, humiliatingly to the ground. "I am stronger than you! Greater than you! More Sinanju than you!"

Colors swirled around him and the discordant music swelled. The Master of Sinanju put his hands over his eyes to block out the awful glare. The ground bubbled, as if it had turned to lava. Blocks of granite stood up on caterpillar legs and marched toward the center of the ruins, where the combatants were locked in a death grip.

The Master of Sinanju watched in horror, not knowing what was real and what was not.

It had seemed as if Remo were winning, but now, with the music rising to a manic crescendo, the Dutchman suddenly had Remo in a chokehold. Remo's arms flailed, his mouth gulping air like a beached fish. Chiun watched as, brutally, like a python squeezing its prey, the Dutchman continued his cruel hold until Remo's face darkened with congesting blood.

"Remo! Do not let him defeat you!" Chiun cried. He started for them, but with a callous glance the Dutchman made a line of granite blocks between them explode into a thousand pieces. The Master of Sinanju retreated into the shelter of a fallen castle wall. He remained there while the fragments of stone peppered the ruins around him.

When he emerged, the Dutchman stood triumphantly, holding Remo by the scruff of the neck, shouting at the top of his voice.

"I am invincible. I am the Dutchman. There is no greater Master of Sinanju than Jeremiah Purcell. Do you hear me, Chiun? Can you see me, Nuihc, my father? I am supreme! Supreme!"

In his hands, Remo hung limp and unconscious. And the heart went out of the Master of Sinanju.

"You will not live to drink the nectar of your victory," declared Chiun, drawing himself up.

"Supreme!" cried the Dutchman as he dropped Remo scornfully. He flung his arms out as if to offer his glory to the universe. His uplifted face, almost beatific in its exultation, saw the taunting gleam of the morning star hanging in the purple sky.

"Supreme," he whispered, focusing all his energy on one point of light millions of miles away.

Chiun bounded over fallen blocks, his feet leaping, his blazing hazel eyes focused on the Dutchman's imperious form. But he was too late. The music grew. And high in the sky Venus became a tiny flare of silver that swelled and swelled until it filled the mountaintop with unholy light.

The Dutchman lifted triumphant fists. "Supreme!"

And as the dissonant music grew unbearable, the ground opened up beneath the Dutchman's feet.

"No!" cried Chiun. But it was too late. The Dutchman fell into a widening crater, arms flailing as he screamed his final words. They echoed deep from the earth.

"Supreme! Supreme! Supreme!"

And with his agitated purple figure tumbled the limp body of Remo Williams.

When they were lost from sight, the ground closed up with a finality that silenced everything. Including the mind music of the Dutchman.

Chiun landed on the crack. He threw himself upon it, digging and clawing frantically.

"Remo! My son." His fingers excavated the edge of the crack. But he only succeeded in scratching it. The crack had closed fully.

Head bowed, the Master of Sinanju was silent for long moments. Finally he scratched a symbol in the dirt with a long fingernail. It was a bisected trapezoid, the sign of Sinanju. It would forever mark the resting place of the two white Masters, the last of the line.

Resignedly the Master of Sinanju got to his feet. He wiped the red earth from his kimono, muttering a prayer for the dead under his breath. He turned to walk away from Devil's Mountain, empty-handed, realizing that there was a worse thing than carrying a dead son down a mountain. And that was leaving him there.

A voice stopped him outside the ruins.

"Leaving without me, Little Father?"

Chiun wheeled at the sound. His face widened in such surprise, his wrinkles smoothed out.

"Remo!" he breathed. Then, louder, "Remo, my son. You live?"

"More or less," Remo said nonchalantly. His face was streaked with dirt and sweat. Under one arm he carried a lifeless figure in purple whose wrists were bound by a yellow sash. Jeremiah Purcell.

"I saw you both swallowed by the earth."

"Not us," said Remo. He tried to crack a smile, but Chiun could see that it was an effort. The Master of Sinanju walked to Remo's side and touched first his arm, then his face. "You are real. Not a cruel illusion designed to prolong my grief."

"I'm real," said Remo.

"But I saw this carrion defeat you."

Remo shook his head. "You saw what the Dutchman imagined. What he wanted to believe. You were right, Chiun. He had gone around the bend. Remember when the colors got really bright?"

"Yes."

"I had him then. And he knew it. I think his mind really snapped then. He knew he couldn't win. He couldn't bear to lose, so he created the illusion that he was winning. I saw it too. I had him on his knees. Suddenly he collapsed. Then there was another Dutchman and another one of me and they were fighting. When I realized what was happening, I stepped back and watched just as you did."

"But the pit?"

"An illusion. Maybe you could say the pit was real in a way. It was the pit of madness and the Dutchman finally fell in. All I know is that here I am and here he is."

"Not dead?" wondered Chiun.

"He might as well be," Remo said, laying the Dutchman across a block of broken stone. Jeremiah Purcell lay, breathing shallowly, only the faintest of lights in his eyes. His lips moved.

"He is trying to say something," Chiun said.

Remo placed his ear to the Dutchman's writhing lips.

"I win. Even in defeat."

"Don't count on it," Remo told him. But just before the last light of intelligence fled from his eyes, the Dutchman reared up as if electrified. "You will never save the presidential candidates now!" Then he collapsed.

Chiun examined him carefully.

"He lives. But his eyes tell me that his mind has gone."

"He won't menace us again. I guess I did it, Chiun. I stopped the Dutchman without killing him or myself."

"Do not be so boastful. The Dutchman's last words indicate that he may have the final victory yet."

"If we hurry," Remo said, hefting the Dutchman into his arms, "we might be able to get back in time."

"No." Chiun stopped him. "I will carry him down. I have waited many years for this day of atonement."

And together they descended Devil's Mountain, the clear light of the morning star hanging in an untroubled blue sky above them.

36

Every major network and cable service carried Decision America, the election-eve presidential debate broadcast live from a Manhattan television studio. The candidates had been introduced and the Vice-President had given his opening statement, ending with a reaffirmation of his promise to put an end to all covert operations by American intelligence agencies.

Governor Michael Princippi led off his remarks with a solemn vow to expunge all black-budget projects from the federal books.

In the middle of his statement, television screens all over America went black.

The Secret Service had every entrance to the television studio covered. Heavy, bulletproof limousines were parked bumper to bumper all around the block instead of the usual clumsy concrete barriers. They were prepared for anything.

Except for a skinny white man and a frail Oriental who jumped out of a screeching taxi, bounded over the limousines, and passed the Secret Service without even stopping to say: May I?

The agents yelled, "Halt!" and fired warning shots.

"No time," said the white man as he and the Oriental ducked around a corner a flick ahead of a storm of bullets.

At the door leading into the debate studio, two Secret Service agents reacted to the intrusion with lightning speed. They drew down on the pair and for their pains were put to sleep with chopping hands.

Remo Williams slammed into the studio, where three cameras were dollying back and forth before the presidential candidates. There was a small studio audience of selected media representatives.

"The cameras first," Remo yelled. "We don't want this on nationwide TV."

"Of course," said the Master of Sinanju.

Separating, they yanked out the heavy cables that fed the three television cameras. Consternation broke out in the control booth when the monitor screens all went black.

"You again!" screeched the Vice-President, jumping out of his chair.

"Later," said Remo, pulling him from his chair so fast that his lapel mike came loose.

"What do we look for?" asked Chiun, plucking Governor Principi from his seat.

"I don't know. A bomb. Anything," snapped Remo, ripping the chair from its mooring. "Nothing under this one," he said throwing the chair away.

"Bomb?" said the director. The panic was immediate. People flooded out of the studio. They made a human wave that blocked the Secret Service from coming in.

"Anything?" Remo shouted.

"No!" said Chiun, tearing up the planks of the stage. They flew like toothpicks in a storm.

Desperately, Remo looked around. The heavy spotlights inhibited his vision. He could hear the frightened voices of the studio audience as they tried to get through one door, and the angry orders of the frustrated Secret Service for them to clear a path. The three cameras pointed at him dumbly. Then one of them dollied forward.

Remo had a split-second thought that the stupid cameraman must not realize transmission had been cut off, when the camera clicked and a perforated metal tube jutted out under the big lens.

"Machine gun!" Remo yelled.

The Master of Sinanju threw himself across the huddled presidential candidates and held them down.

Remo twisted in midair, avoiding a rattling stream of .30-caliber bullets, and landed on his feet. The camera shifted toward the three crouching figures on the stage and aimed downward.

Remo leapt. There was no time for anything fancy.

Behind him the curtained studio backdrop shivered into rags as the bullet stream sank lower and lower.

Herm Accord jockeyed the camera, certain he had gotten the skinny guy in the white T-shirt. Now, where were the others? It wasn't easy to sight down a TV camera. The lens was larger than the gun muzzle he had installed into the camera the night before. It gave him too big a field of vision, like trying to center on a mosquito through a drainpipe.

Frustrated, he held fire and stuck his head around the camera.

The face of the skinny guy was an inch from his own. Herm Accord started to say, "What the—" when the soft consonant of the next word raising from his throat encountered his teeth as they careened down his gullet.

He jumped back, grabbing his throat, coughing spasmodically. He didn't know that a bicuspid, traveling faster than a bullet, had already fragmented in his throat. He didn't know and he didn't care. He saw the hand reaching for his face. It became a looming mass of pink, and for Herm Accord, like America, the lights had gone out.

Remo didn't bother to check the assassin's body after it fell. He jumped to Chiun's side. The Master of Sinanju was helping the Vice-President to his feet.

"Thank you," said the Vice-President in a shaken voice.

"For both of us," added Governor Princippi.

"Looks like were just in time," commented Remo.

"Sinanju is always on time," said Chiun.

"We gotta get out of here," said Remo, glancing toward the door where the Secret Service agents were screaming that they were going to shoot everyone blocking the door if the way wasn't cleared immediately. "But we want you to know that this is the end of it. There'll be no more assassinations. We took care of the guy behind it all."

"I think I can speak for the governor when I say we appreciate your help," the Vice-President said sincerely, buttoning his jacket.

"Thank Smith," said Remo. "It's his operation. And just so you know, we're back in the fight."

"Glad to have you," said the Vice-President warmly.

"And you can forget about Adonis. He was part of the plot too."

"I can't understand it," muttered Governor Principi, looking around the studio. "Where's my ninja? He said he'd always be by my side even if I couldn't see him. All I had to do was whistle."

"Did you whistle?" asked Chiun blandly.

"Actually, no. I was too busy ducking."

"It would not have mattered," Chiun said. "Everyone knows that ninjas are tone deaf."

Governor Principi placed his pinky fingers at the edges of his mouth and whistled sharply.

"Nothing," he said disappointedly.

"See?" said Chiun. "Remember, with Sinanju you do not even have to whistle. A phone call will do."

And Remo and Chiun slipped into the knot of struggling people at the door. Even though the door resembled a New York subway car during rush hour, they filtered through the people as if by osmosis, right past the frantic Secret Service agents.

When the Secret Service finally got into the studio, they found the two presidential candidates calmly replacing their lapel mikes.

"You're too late," said the Vice-President cockily. "But why don't you people do something useful like getting rid of this body? We've got a debate to finish."

All over America, blackened TV screens came to life again. News anchormen apologized in uncertain terms for what they called "technical difficulties." And when the debate resumed they had no explanation for why the presidential candidates were standing instead of sitting, or for the bullet holes and tears in the ruined studio backdrop.

Governor Principi picked up his unfinished remarks in a serious, unruffled voice.

"Before we were interrupted, I was saying that we need to curb our intelligence services. But I want to make it plain that there will be a place in my administration for certain necessary intelligence operations. Specifically, counterintelligence. After all, these agencies exist so that our armed forces will not have to be used. And I want to publicly thank the anonymous Americans—the Toms, the Dicks, and the

Harolds—who toil in these agencies. They keep America strong. Don't you agree, Mr. Vice-President?''

''Heartily,'' said the Vice-President. ''We got 'em, and God knows we need 'em. And the Browns and Joneses and Smiths who keep 'em running.''

It was the fastest position switch America had ever witnessed. But few Americans were surprised. The presidential candidates were, after all, politicians.

Dr. Harold W. Smith watched the debate from his hospital bed. Only he could guess what had transpired during the network blackout. Remo and Chiun. They had done it again. CURE would go on. He didn't know whether to laugh or cry.

Remo Williams stopped the car at the rusting wrought-iron entrance to Wildwood Cemetery two days later and slipped through the squeaking gates.

The Master of Sinanju walked at his side. Remo's pace was eager.

''Smith would be upset if he knew you were here,'' Chiun warned.

''It was the only place I could think of to meet.''

''Smith is already upset.''

''How could he be? We saved his bacon. And America's bacon. There's a new President coming into office who thinks CURE should go on forever. And the Dutchman is going to spend the rest of his life in a Folcroft rubber room picking lint out of his navel. He's never going to bother any of us again. Our problems are over. I can't wait to tell Jilda.''

''Smith is upset because when his vision returned, he was able to read the contract.''

''What'd you stick him with? Double the last contract?''

''Double would not be enough to pay for the indignity of bargaining the Master of Sinanju down to a lower fee and tearing up that last contract. I charged triple.''

''I can see why he's upset. That's a big jump.''

''It was necessary. He was paying for the Master of Sinanju, for certain disreputable acts visited upon the Master of Sinanju . . . and for you.''

Remo stopped dead in his tracks. Chiun looked up at him with a placid expression.

"Me? You signed me on for another year?"

"Two years. Consider it a form of job security."

"Don't I have a say in this?"

"No. I am still Master. You are the pupil. Technically, you are an apprentice. And as such, I negotiate for you. As always."

Remo shook his head. He continued walking.

"We'll see what Jilda says," Remo said.

"Yes," said Chiun in a hollow voice. "We will see what Jilda says."

At the grave bearing the name of Remo Williams, there were flowers. Remo stopped.

"Funny. Who would put flowers on my grave?" he said.

He bent over and picked them up. Inside, there was an envelope. It was slightly soggy from the recent rain.

Remo dropped the flowers and opened the paper. He saw that it was addressed to him and signed "Jilda."

Remo read.

"What does she say?" Chiun asked quietly when Remo was done.

"She's not coming," Remo said thickly. "Ever."

"It is not meant to be."

"Not as long as I'm in the business I'm in, she says. And she knows that it's the only business for me. She says that this time, it was me who left her. That's what made up her mind. The way I took off for America with you. She says I belong here."

"You know it too," said Chiun.

"She says that Freya misses me already," Remo went on, looking at the letter with caved-in eyes. "And that when the time comes and I wish it, and Freya wishes it, Jilda will consider allowing her to be trained in Sinanju."

"She is dreaming," Chiun said haughtily. "No woman has ever been a Master of Sinanju. No woman can ever become a Master of Sinanju. It is impossible."

"There's a P.S.," Remo said. "It says that Freya has been working on her breathing when she isn't riding her pony. She sends a present to show you that she's trying to grow up to be big and strong like her daddy, as well as her mommy."

Remo reached into the flower basket and came up with a

small horseshoe that had been bent into the shape of a pret-
zel.

"Look, Chiun."

"A twisted horseshoe," Chiun sniffed. "So?"

"Don't you get it?" Remo said. "Freya did that. With
her own little hands."

"Impossible!" sputtered Chiun. "She is too young, she
is white, and she is a female. I could not do that until I was
twelve!"

"So?" Remo said. "You're not white or female."

Chiun stamped his foot angrily. "I do not believe it."

"But I do," Remo said. "And I'm going to keep this
forever."

Chiun frowned. "Are you not even going to attempt to
pry Jilda's whereabouts from my inviolate lips?" he asked.

Remo thought for a long time before he answered. When
he spoke, he stared at the twisted horseshoe wistfully.

"Nope," he said at last. "Jilda knows what she's doing.
I guess she's right. Besides, she's not living in Wales anymore. The letter said so."

"What!" cried Chiun. "You mean she left no forwarding
address! How will I send my granddaughter presents on her
birthdays? How will I monitor her progress through the early
years of her life?"

"We'll see them again," Remo said. "I just don't know
when."

"Then you will remain in America—with me?"

Remo sighed. "Yeah, I don't have anywhere else to go,
I guess. Back in Sinanju, the villagers think I'm a jerk.
There are too many bad memories back there anyway."

"It is not the ideal situation," Chiun agreed. "Not when
living in the pearl of Asia is preferred, but we will make
the best of it. For two years at least."

"Wait a sec," Remo said. "I thought you wanted to live
in America. And what about that whole wardrobe of Western clothes you bought so you could be more American?"

"I have burned them. Sadly, I discovered they are inad-
equate for climbing purposes. It is a major flaw for those in
our honored profession."

"Okay, but didn't you finally admit that Sinanju was a
dung heap?"

Chiun puffed out his cheeks. "Remo!" he said, shocked.

"I said no such thing. And I will deny any slander to the contrary."

"But you do admit you're happy with the way things have worked out, and there'll be no carping from now on?"

"I am not! I am an old man, with an irresponsible white for a pupil and no worthy heir for either of us. It is my sad fate, but I will bear up. I will not complain about these things. I will not mention to you that because of your inability to sire a male, I am forced to work into my final days instead of entering into the traditional period of retirement. It may be that I will have to work forever. No Master of Sinanju has ever been burdened. But I will not complain. "Not I."

"Pterodactyl dung," replied Remo. And in spite of the pain he felt, he smiled.

COMING IN SEPTEMBER—
The Soviets invade the Saudi oilfields on

GOOD FRIDAY

by Robert Lawrence Holt

It is Good Friday—the darkest day on the Christian calendar. An armada of Russian aircraft, led by wiley Soviet Commander Turpolov, is spotted heading toward the Saudi Arabian oilfields. Marine Commander Tom Hemingway pilots a battle-ready U.S. aircraft carrier through the Persian Gulf to oppose them. Thus the most crucial day the world has ever known blazes toward its high noon of decision . . .

"Robert Lawrence Holt has the Middle East in flames and he takes no prisoners. A cracking fast read . . ."—Stephen Coonts, author of *Flight of the Intruder*

"Fast-paced, breakneck action . . . Rousing and clever!" —*Publishers Weekly*

"Warren Murphy and Molly Cochran have done it again.
With *High Priest* they give their legions of readers a grand
read as they tell the new adventures of the Grandmaster."
—Mary Higgins Clark, author of *Weep No More My Lady*

HIGH PRIEST

A Thriller by
Warren Murphy and Molly Cochran

*The unforgettable characters of the national bestseller
Grandmaster return to the sudden-death game of global
espionage. But the ruthless rivalry between these two
enemies is dwarfed when a third player enters the con-
test—an opponent so powerful he makes murder seem
like child's play. This riveting novel takes you on a com-
pelling and hypnotic tour of the tense corridors of
paranoia in Washington and Moscow and the deadly
cold war forces that grip the world.*

**A riveting thriller of a deadly
and terrifying quest through the streets
of New York—where the toughest knight of all
turns out to be . . . the All-American Girl!**

QUEST

A Novel by
Richard Ben Sapir

Three people are desperately seeking a gold, gem-encrusted saltcellar created for Queen Elizabeth I. But only one of them knows what's really being sought. The Holy Grail is hidden inside and if the others discover the secret, they will have to die!

This suspense-packed search for a priceless gem that is hiding a secret, sweeps you into the intrigue-filled criminal world of international gem dealers—from Cairo to Paris to London to Geneva . . . and holds you breathless to its final page.
